The Runaway Bride

PATRICIA McLINN

SILHOUETTE®
SPECIAL EDITION™

*Silhouette, Silhouette Special Edition and Colophon are
registered trademarks of Harlequin Books S.A., used under licence.*

*First published in Great Britain 2003
Silhouette Books, Eton House, 18-24 Paradise Road,
Richmond, Surrey TW9 1SR*

© Patricia McLaughlin 2002

ISBN 0 373 24469 X

23-0603

*Printed and bound in Spain
by Litografia Rosés S.A., Barcelona*

PATRICIA McLINN

finds great satisfaction in transferring to paper the characters crowded in her head, to be enjoyed by readers. 'Writing,' she says, 'is the hardest work I'd never give up.' Writing has brought her new experiences, places and friends—especially friends. After degrees from North-western University and newspaper jobs that have taken her from Illinois to North Carolina to Washington, DC, Patricia now lives in Virginia, in a house that grows piles of paper, books and dog hair at an alarming rate. The paper and books are her own fault, but the dog hair comes from a charismatic collie who helps put things in perspective when neighbourhood kids refer to Patricia as 'the lady who lives in Riley's house.' She would love to hear from readers at PO Box 7052, Arlington, VA 22207, USA.

9-11-01

We will remember

Prologue

"Call it woman's intuition."

Judi Monroe tilted her head back and looked above for the source of those quiet words. Since she was in a church and the words had echoed the niggling thoughts in her own head, it wasn't an unreasonable suspicion. But if God was talking to her, He was doing it in a vaguely familiar woman's voice.

"Something just doesn't feel right."

And He—or rather *She*—sounded frustrated.

So, who was talking in hushed tones somewhere off to her right in these final moments before Judi was to walk down the aisle to become Mrs. Sterling Carroll? With three exceptions, everyone should be in the main part of the church—sitting as a guest, standing as a member of the wedding party, or, in the case of her matron of honor and sister-in-law Bette, walking slowly down the aisle toward the altar. The exceptions were herself, her father and the wedding planner, who was giving James Monroe final instructions.

Wedding planner? Wedding dictator was more like it. From the moment Judi had said yes to Sterling's stunning proposal after a whirlwind courtship, she had felt as if she'd walked into a tornado, and Marjorie Ward—the best money could buy, as Sterling kept reminding her—was running the wind machine.

In fact, Judi strongly suspected that if she thought back she would find that this was the first time she'd been both awake and alone since that momentous ''yes.''

The hushed voice came again. ''If the bride isn't involved, she could help us, and not warning her is letting her walk into one helluva post-honeymoon mess.''

Judi could no more have ignored those comments than she could have flown.

She eased over to the side of the vestibule where she'd spotted the barely open door to the crying room, an area set aside for vociferous children and their parents to retreat to during services.

''I know, I know,'' said the voice. No one was in sight through the narrow opening, and Judi had to lean close to hear over the swelling music. If those trumpets would pipe down she could have heard a lot better. ''That's right. He's got the shipment scheduled to arrive three weeks and two days after they return from their honeymoon. Which will be a little late for her if she doesn't know what's going on, since he's got it all lined up to be in her name.''

There was a pause, then the voice sighed. When it spoke again it was resigned. ''You're right. We can't risk it. Too much is at stake. Okay… Yes… Yeah, right.'' Sarcasm kicked in with those last two words. ''I'm going to have a great time at this wedding. I just wish I knew if I'm about to watch Bonnie and Clyde getting hitched, or Mary Poppins being tied to Al Capone.''

Judi heard the beep of a cell phone call being ended, and started to step back from the door. Her foot caught on the side hem of her dress, and she stumbled—pushing the door wide open.

Judi couldn't remember the name of the woman who was rising from the chair, set out of the view of the crying room's soundproof window to the main church, but she recognized her. She was the brand-new girlfriend of Sterling's best man, Geoff.

They stared at each other, frozen in mutual horror.

Then Judi saw the other woman's expression change. A flash of sympathy passed across her eyes, followed by determination. She strode forward in a tight skirt, a style that Geoff's former girlfriend had also favored, and wrapped a hand around Judi's upper arm.

"You can't—you can't say a *word,* do you understand? It's vital. There's a lot riding on this—more than you can imagine. A lot riding on it for you, too. If the deal gets blown now, nobody would ever believe you didn't tell him. You'd be implicated up to your neck."

"Implicated in what? I don't—"

"Judith! What on earth!" The stage-whispered shout of Marjorie Ward was the only warning Judi had before her other arm was grabbed in an even stronger grip and she was propelled across the vestibule to where her father stood, a worried frown blooming across his face.

"Judi, is something wrong? Are you—?"

"No time! No time! Your music's started!" Marjorie hissed.

She forcibly wrapped Judi's numb right hand around her father's arm, positioned her left arm at her waist, then curled the fingers of that hand around the base of the bouquet.

Vaguely aware her father was regarding her with growing alarm, Judi's mind raced as she stood immobile through another two bars of music. Then two hands shoved her from behind, and her choices were to start walking fast or fall flat on her face. With her father hurrying to keep pace, the bride started down the aisle.

Sights, words, questions and doubts pinwheeled through Judi's brain.

Sterling's expression when they'd run into each other for the first time since high school just over two months ago. *Calculating* had been her first thought, and she'd been on her guard against him trying to get her into bed right away. But he hadn't. Instead, he'd swept her off her feet with a full-blown hearts-and-flowers courtship, including lavish dates and expensive gestures, never once pressuring her for physical intimacy.

The only blemishes in that unreal time had been her uneasy feeling around his friends and associates, and his dismissing her questions about his importing business by saying how he didn't want to waste time on talking business when they were together.

Well, maybe there was one other blemish, but she'd told herself over and over that she was imagining her family's lack of enthusiasm. After all, they'd known the Carroll family forever, as neighbors in Lake Forest, Illinois. And all anybody ever said was that as long as she was happy, that was all that mattered.

How could she help but be happy? She finally had someone head over heels in love with her. It was what her parents had. It was what she'd watched her older brother Paul find with Bette, their cousin Tris discover with Michael, and even long-time ladies' man Grady achieve with Leslie.

Surely that was what had been behind the undercurrent of urgency when Sterling had proposed to her, wasn't it? A man didn't risk public humiliation by proposing via the scoreboard of a Chicago Bulls game, with the TV cameras zooming in for the answer, unless he was gung-ho, right? And that head over heels love had to be the reason for his rush to get married. What else could it be?

I just wish I knew if I'm about to watch Bonnie and Clyde getting hitched, or Mary Poppins being tied to Al Capone.

She wasn't Bonnie, so that made her Mary Poppins, which made the man awaiting her at the altar Al Capone. She didn't like the sound of that.

You can't say a word.

She, Judith Marie Monroe, who'd never kept a secret in her life, was supposed to not tell what she'd heard to the man she was about to pledge as-long-as-we-both-shall-live to?

If the bride isn't involved, she could help us, and not warning her is letting her walk into one helluva post-honeymoon mess.

What kind of a mess? Something was going to happen three weeks and two days after their scheduled return from a two-week Caribbean honeymoon—but what?

If the deal gets blown now, nobody would ever believe you didn't tell him. You'd be implicated up to your neck.

What on earth had Sterling gotten himself into?

What was *she* about to get herself into by marrying him?

An oasis of warmth seeped into her numbness as her father placed his hand over hers where it rested on his arm.

"Are you sure, baby?"

The familiar, loved voice and the simple words stopped the pinwheel in her head, bringing all the sights and sounds, all the questions and doubts into one, solid picture.

She stopped dead halfway down the aisle.

"No." She faced her father. "No, I'm not sure, Daddy. Thank you. I love you."

She kissed his cheek, gave the church a sweeping glance that imprinted the vision of Sterling's members of the wedding party gaping at her and her members of the wedding party—her brother, sister-in-law and cousin—beginning to grin. She dropped the bouquet, turned around, gathered fistfuls of her full skirt and sprinted out.

Chapter One

Judi Monroe felt remarkably cheerful for someone who'd left her groom at the altar four days ago, who was running low on cash and who'd just missed being caught this morning by a man asking about her at the motel she'd stayed in last night in Torrington, Wyoming.

But for the past five hours, she hadn't seen any sign of the man from the motel or the car he drove with the Illinois license plates.

Maybe he was a private detective, in which case he might have been hired by Sterling, or possibly by her family, although she had left them a message assuring them she was okay. Or maybe he was part of whatever organization Geoff's ''girlfriend'' belonged to.

It was all still jumbled in Judi's mind. But she had decided three things. Sterling was doing something wrong. She wasn't going to marry him. And if whatever ''Girlfriend'' was talking about was half as important as she'd made it sound, and it depended on Judi not letting on, then she had to get far away from everybody who knew her.

One look at her face and anyone who knew her would know she was hiding something, and Sterling had known her since she was two years old. Of course, she'd known him from the same age, and he'd fooled her without much trouble. She sighed. Just once it might be nice to keep a secret successfully.

She checked the rearview mirror again. No sign of her friend from the motel.

After eluding him there, she'd continued west on the highway, still undecided on her final destination other than someplace far from Lake Forest, Illinois. But after a half hour of checking the rearview mirror so often she felt as if she was developing a tic, she'd impulsively turned off.

She chose roads at whim, heading north, then west, then north again, heading vaguely in the direction of Montana. It was a big target, so surely she'd hit it. She had five weeks to kill, and she'd always wanted to spend time in Montana. She could find a waitressing job, and earn at least enough to get her a little farther down the road.

That thought reminded her that the road she was on wasn't marked with any of the route numbers that showed on her map. In fact, it was gravel. But from the minimal traffic she'd seen, maybe they'd figured they didn't need anything more than gravel. It didn't matter. As long as she went northwest long enough, she'd have to encounter Interstate 25. And it shouldn't be much longer, judging by how close the mountains to the west looked. According to her map, those were the Big Horns, so she'd be on the Interstate any moment now, which was just as well, because the aging car she'd picked up cheap was running a little low on gas. Still she'd be okay, because carmakers built a fudge factor into that *"E"* the needle was flirting with.

She checked the rearview mirror again. Nothing.

But this time, *nothing* did not make her feel quite as

reassured, because this time she realized that nothing meant it had been a long, long time since she'd seen *anything*. As in another car, a house, telephone poles—much less a gas station or restaurant.

She must be nearly to the Interstate, though. Once there, even if she ran out of gas, someone would surely help her. Everything would be okay.

A stand of trees off to the right caught her eye. Was that solid color among them a roof? No, several roofs. It had to be. And where there were roofs, there should be people. Maybe gasoline. Certainly directions. A sandwich would be nice. Turkey, with lots of lettuce and tomato…

A hillside blocked her view and cut off her culinary musings. Seeing the roofs was one thing, finding a way to them might be another.

Or…wait…up ahead, was that a road leading off to the right, toward the roofs? Yes! In anticipation of turkey with lots of lettuce and tomato, she dropped her foot lower on the gas pedal as she took the turn.

Everything seemed to happen at once. But the only thought that flashed into her head in a tiny fraction of a second was: *The Lone Ranger*.

It must have been all those reruns she'd watched with her older brother, Paul, and his buddies. Although this man wasn't masked. He wasn't even wearing a white hat. And she couldn't remember the Lone Ranger ever being astride Silver in front of a car that was bearing down on man and horse too fast for them to avoid it.

The rider's face came into focus for another of those infinitesimal slices of time that stretched into seeming never-ending. A strong face, with a bone structure meant to stand the test of time. A jaw that didn't know the meaning of wishy-washy. A mouth wide and firm. Eyes steady and narrowed as they concentrated on the moment. A man determined to do everything he could to avoid disaster— and knowing he couldn't do enough.

But she could.

Time collapsed back to normal as Judi pulled her foot off the gas and urgently yanked on the steering wheel. She turned it all the way to the left, using two hands to keep it from returning to a neutral position. The car jolted off the gravel roadway, throwing her sideways. She kept her hold on the wheel, but her foot's desperate pokes for the brake found only air. The front of the car started down, then pulled up sharply, and in that instant, she saw the tree ahead of her. But there was no time, no room and no brake.

She heard the crash as if from far away, felt herself moving forward and sideways while the car remained still, felt the seat belt grab onto her, but she was still going sideways. And then nothing.

"Omigod, omigod, omigod, she's *dead!*"

For the second time in four days, Judi had the strongest feeling that an unfamiliar and disembodied female voice was talking about her. And once again, it was saying something she would rather not be true.

"She is *not* dead, Becky."

She liked the male voice's certainty, but why did he sound annoyed at delivering that good news? Despite the pounding throughout her head, Judi decided she better open her eyes out of self-preservation.

"In fact, it looks like she's coming around."

Judi blinked once, twice, before she could get her eyes all the way open. She looked up directly into a pair of leaf-green eyes. Around those remarkable eyes was the strong face of the rider she'd glimpsed in that frozen moment before the crash.

"The Lone Ranger," she muttered. "Is Silver okay?"

The frown knitting his brows deepened. "What?"

"She's delirious," proclaimed the female voice she'd heard before. Beyond the rider's shoulder, a blond teenager peered at her from under a straw cowboy hat.

"Cut the drama, Becky. Delirious is from a fever. You

don't get delirious from a blow to the head,'' the rider said, crouching beside Judi's seat in the narrow wedge left by the partly opened driver's door. He must have opened it. She was sure she hadn't. The door's window bore a star-patterned crack. ''Are you okay, Miss?''

''I...I don't know.'' She reached toward the focus of the throbbing in her head.

''Don't. You're bleeding some.'' He caught her left wrist, holding it easily. Either he was strong, or she was a lot weaker than she had been a few minutes ago. Or both.

''There's blood all over,'' inserted the girl.

Judi became aware of the warm flow down the left side of her face. The rider pulled a bandanna from his pocket, twisted it loosely, then tied it expertly around her head.

The rhythm of the pounding shifted, and more voices could be heard approaching.

''Anybody hurt?''

The new pounding wasn't in her head, it was horses arriving.

''Not sure yet,'' the rider said over his shoulder to the newcomers.

''She's not making sense, and her head's bleeding all over.'' This girl he'd called Becky definitely had a ghoulish bent.

''Can she move?''

''What happened?''

''Is Dickens okay?''

''Where'd she come from?''

''I didn't think even you could get out of that one, Thomas. How'd you do it?''

''Better get her out of there. It might blow.''

Her head? They thought her head might blow up? It felt like it, but could somebody survive having their head—

''That's only in movies. Takes a lot to get a vehicle to blow up.''

''Who is she?''

"Car's wrecked to smithereens, ain't it?"

"Anything besides your head hurt, Miss?"

The last question came from the rider, and she focused on his calm voice like a lone buoy in the middle of wind-whipped Lake Michigan.

"I don't think so."

"Better find out before you try moving too much."

She started to nod, thought better of that, and said, "Okay."

He looked back over his shoulder toward the group gathered there. "Steve, go bring round the blue truck, and get a clean blanket to put over the straw that's left in it."

"Will do, Boss," said one of the voices.

The rider busied himself pulling the driver's door open wider, with the bent frame groaning at the exertion.

"She don't sound delirious to me," said one of the newer voices.

"She was asking about silver earlier," said the girl.

"Silver," Judi corrected in a mutter. "But he's the wrong color."

"Maybe she *is* delirious, Thomas," said a man with whiskers, apparently addressing the rider, who now had the door open, and was crouched down facing her.

The rider—Thomas—ignored everyone behind him and met her gaze, and ordered, "You tell me if anything hurts. My name's Thomas—Thomas Vance."

He started at her neck, wrapping his large hands gently around it, and tipping her head slightly forward, then back, left, then right. Then he ran his hands out slowly to her shoulders, watching her face apparently for her reaction. She hoped it didn't show.

The warmth and slow friction of his touch was like sliding into a warm bath after a long day. Despite the throbbing in her head, she could have purred.

She must have made a sound when he moved on, using both hands to skim over the cotton sleeve of her blouse, because his frown dropped lower, and he rapped out, "Something hurt?"

"A little sore."

She gripped her bottom lip with her teeth as he continued to her other arm, then backed up a little to start at midthigh and ease down first one leg than the other. By the time he'd cupped her ankle and rotated her foot to his satisfaction, she felt like a puddle. A flammable puddle.

Yet there'd been nothing in the way he'd treated her other than Good Samaritanism—not a look, not a deep breath, not an overlong touch. Nothing. It was all her. Probably simply a case of her hormones knowing she would have been on her honeymoon at this moment if everything had gone according to plan, and responding accordingly.

"Nothing seems to be broken." He cleared his throat. "I'm going to release the seat belt now, unless you want to…?"

Automatically, she reached across her body for the latch. The pull on her sore neck muscles stopped her in midmotion and a groan escaped.

"Help her, Thomas," ordered Becky.

He slid his hand between the webbing of the tightened belt and her hip. It was the back of his hand against her, but that didn't stop her feeling the warm imprint through her shorts, right into her skin and possibly deeper. When he released the catch, and caught the belt before it could retract, she couldn't stop a sigh. At least it wasn't a moan.

"That hurt?"

"A little."

"Might be ribs broke," suggested Whiskers.

She caught a flicker of green as Thomas glanced at her. Something about that look made her think of his hands roaming over her ribs—*all* of her ribs—the way they had over her arms and legs.

Maybe Becky was right, maybe she was delirious. She sure felt as if she had a sudden fever.

"She's breathing well. I don't think she's got any broken ribs," Thomas said. "Becky, ride back to let Gran know we're coming. Okay, let's get her up to the house."

She saw his intention a split second before he reached down to pick her up. Her battered body was complaining too loudly about pain for her to notice much else. He carried her up the embankment to a parked truck, giving out orders about getting it ready, who would drive, who would ride in back, who would take care of Dickens, who would get her gear out of her car, and who should get back to work—all with an assurance that said he was accustomed to having such orders obeyed.

The straw bed he placed her on in the back of the pickup was both soft and prickly, even through the blanket was spread atop it. At the same time the truck started moving, she sneezed and her muscles knotted in protest. She closed her eyes to concentrate on not passing out. She couldn't have sworn she succeeded. The next thing she knew, Thomas was picking her up again, and issuing more orders.

She opened her eyes to a quick impression of a rambling house with a wooden porch, then they were going through a doorway while Becky held the door open.

"Gran says to bring her into her room."

"Her room? I thought she was napping. That's not—"

"You bring her in here, Thomas." The woman's voice wasn't loud but it had even more of that assurance of command than Thomas's had.

Judi not only heard his sigh, she felt it—as a breath across her face, and in the rise and fall of his chest where she rested against it.

With Becky, the driver from the truck, Whiskers and a few others following, Thomas carried her across a roomy kitchen, down a short hallway and into a large, sunny room. In a quilt-covered double bed with a gleaming wooden headboard and footboard, a white-haired woman was lying flat with her head angled up on bright colored pillows. A lump under the light blanket of buttercup yellow that covered her indicated a pillow of some sort was between her legs. Other than the bedding, the room's colors were subdued blues and greens.

"Set her down on the loveseat there," the woman instructed. "Gently now."

"I'll get blood on it," protested Judi.

"That's what slipcovers are for. That's right, Thomas. Now get back, all of you—you'll smother the poor thing." Immediately an aisle opened, leaving no one blocking the woman's view. "Now, what have we got here?"

"That's what I want to know, Gran." Thomas crossed his arms over a chest that started broad at the shoulders and tapered to the waist of his jeans. All the gentleness from when he'd checked her for injuries was gone. His manner as he turned to her wasn't harsh precisely, but it sure wasn't cuddly, either. "Who are you? What were you—"

"Hold on there, Thomas. You and Becky stay, but the rest of you clear on out." While the onlookers shuffled out, the woman they'd called Gran, clearly never doubting that her orders would be followed, continued, "Becky, get a basin from under the sink, and the cloths from the bottom shelf in the linen closet. And that first-aid kit from under the sink."

"But I don't know how to—"

"You don't have to know how yet, you just have to listen."

"What's your name?" Thomas demanded again.

"Not yet, Thomas," said Gran. "Let's take this one step at a time. Becky'll wipe off that blood so we can see the poor girl. And you, Thomas, tell me what happened."

Judi tried to listen to his explanation, which seemed to feature the inexplicability of Judi arriving where she did when she did. But the pounding was getting more insistent, and as Becky's gently hesitant hands wiped the blood from the side of her face, she let her eyes close and her mind shut down.

"That's much better. Good for you, Becky," said Gran.

Judi blinked back to the present, to find everyone staring at her, including the man with the whiskers she remembered from the crash site. She hadn't even been aware of his return. She smiled at Becky, who'd backed up to perch on the chair beside Gran's bed. "Thanks. I feel almost good as new."

"Can't say the same for that car of yours," said Whiskers. "Not that it's been new any time recent. And it sure isn't any good to anybody now."

"Total loss?" Thomas asked from his seat in a side chair near the door.

"Total. And it's going to be a doozy to get out of there, the way it's angled in. But it probably has parts that'd be worth taking off 'er. I know a couple boys trying to keep old Buicks running."

"Thanks, Gandy," said Gran. "We'll figure what to do with it later. Right now, I'm more concerned about this young lady."

As Gandy departed with a nod, Thomas stood up abruptly, arms crossed once more, seeming to tower over Judi as she half reclined against the loveseat's arm.

"How'd you come to be on our back road—our private back road?"

He gave it enough of an edge to make it clear he expected an answer.

The whole truth was out of the question. She could tell him part of the truth, but she'd never been good at that. She suspected that under the current circumstances, she'd probably be worse than ever. But she had to say something. They were all looking at her, waiting.

"I don't know…" She drew in a breath to finish the rest of the extremely lame answer that was the only thing she could think of—*I don't know what to tell you*—and to send up a little prayer that inspiration would give her something brilliant to say next.

But there was no *next* said, at least not by her.

"Omigod, omigod!" Becky said in an awed whisper. "She has amnesia!"

"Amnesia? That's a bunch of—"

"Thomas."

Gran's warning stopped the word, but not the sentiment. "She's been watching too much TV again."

"It's the only logical explanation." Becky jumped up from her chair, squaring off with Thomas. "We hired an aide to help Gran for these six weeks while she recuperates from the surgery, and *she* shows up. Who else could she be? It's not like we're near the highway where we'd have strangers arriving unexpectedly all the time. Besides, you said just this morning that the agency said Helga should be here any time—obviously she decided to drive here instead of writing or calling first, she got lost, had the accident, hit her head—which she wouldn't have done if she hadn't swerved to miss you and Dickens. And now—" Her voice caught. "Now she doesn't remember who she is. It's all so obvious!"

Thomas's response made it clear he saw nothing obvious in Becky's scenario, but the girl steadfastly stuck to her explanation. As they squabbled, and between the downbeats of throbbing in Judi's head, several phrases wove into a pattern.

Six weeks… Hired… Who else could she be?… Not near the highway…

She had little money, no car and five weeks to pass before she could surface. What could be better? She not only wouldn't be spending money, she'd be *making* it. No car was no problem, because she wouldn't have to go anywhere. Best of all, no one would ever think to look for her here. A ranch might be the perfect place to sit down and think through how she'd gotten into this mess and what she was going to do with her life when it was over.

It wasn't like she'd be cheating these people—she'd do all the work this Helga was supposed to have done. And Helga had stood them up so Judi felt no guilt about taking her job.

As for that job, surely she could handle it. She'd been thinking about waitressing in Montana, and she *knew* she was a lousy waitress. This had to be better.

"It's total nonsense, Becky," Thomas declared, not for the first time.

"Gran hasn't said it's nonsense."

Judi noticed that observation stopped Thomas. He turned toward his grandmother. The woman simply looked back at him. His eyes narrowed to green slits.

"Don't tell me you're crazy enough to believe—"

"I'll tell you what I believe, Thomas," she interrupted calmly. "I believe it makes sense to ask the only one of us here who might have an answer."

A tip of Gran's head indicated Judi, and she felt three sets of eyes zero in on her.

"Well?" Thomas demanded.

Judi's heart sped up like someone had hit its accelerator. Could she? Should she? She was famed for being a lousy liar, but these people didn't know her, so maybe, just maybe she could pull this off.

"I...I can't remember, but I think I must be Helga."

Chapter Two

"You think? You can't remember?"

"Stop badgering, Thomas. Can't you see you're hurting the poor girl's head?"

Thomas had seen the stranger's wince, and it jabbed him with a dose of guilt. But Gran was way off in calling her a girl. The battered, pale and still bloodied stranger sitting on the little couch under the window in what used to be his room was definitely a woman. He still had the tingling in his hands, alertness in his groin and heat in his blood to attest to that.

And, as if that wasn't reason enough to get her on her way—which it was—it was damned sure that there was nothing *poor* about her. Other than the heap she'd been driving, he could practically hear his one-time stepmother *ka-ching-ing* a cash register as she totaled up big figures in everything this stranger wore. All new, too.

How many home aides had money for clothes like that?

How many home aides looked like that with gleaming reddish-brown hair and wide eyes, and a mouth that...

"So, what's your last name?"

She hesitated, then shook her head and drooped. "I don't know."

"What's the name of agency you work for?"

"I don't remember."

"That's convenient."

"I don't remember because I took a blow to the head." Her pointed look reminded him how she'd received that blow. "That can cause amnesia, you know."

"Oh, that's great—you're remembering your medical background!" Becky beamed.

"Oh, yeah, that's damn technical," he said.

"Thomas." Gran made his name a reprimand. It was a skill Iris Swift had honed over several decades of teaching. "Don't swear."

"Medical background?" If the stranger got any paler she could pass for a snowbank in sunlight. If she fainted he was going to have to catch her, pick her up again, have her curled up against his chest again...

"You're a home health aide," Becky said solicitously. "We hired you to come take care of Gran while she recovers from hip replacement surgery."

The woman put a hand to her head. "Uh, I don't seem to remember anything about being a health aide."

Thomas rolled his eyes and turned away. Maybe that way his body would stop rooting for her to faint.

"The agency's in South Dakota? Do you think you're from South Dakota?" Becky asked.

"Car's got Nebraska plates," he muttered.

"I don't know. It doesn't sound familiar."

"That's okay, Helga. Don't let my brother badger you. That's how amnesia works sometimes—you might remember bits and pieces at first and some you might never recover. But the job isn't super technical. Besides, there're pages and pages of instructions. Thomas and I've been doing it, and it's been okay, hasn't it, Gran?''

"You and Thomas have done wonderfully, Becky. And I'm sure Helga will, too, even with amnesia. Thomas can help when there's real strength required.''

Thomas turned toward the woman who'd raised him since he was eight. She couldn't be serious. But she was.

He tried to inject sanity into the discussion again. "If that bump on her head's made her lose her memory, we should get her to a doctor, let him look at it.''

"Any doctor will tell her to rest and her memory will come back in flashes over the next few months,'' Becky said. "That's what the doctors always say for amnesia from bumps on the head. Now with traumatic amnesia—''

"Soap opera doctors! You're quoting medical advice from those slick actors on TV? You've got to be kidding—''

"They do a lot of research for those shows and—''

"Both of you be quiet. I've had a good deal of experience with looking after blows to the head in my day, and I'm satisfied that Helga doesn't need stitches or to see a doctor.'' Before he could say what he was thinking, Gran sent him a cool look and added, "Becky, you could help by taking Helga's things upstairs. I'm sure I heard Gandy bring in her suitcase a while back.''

But that gave him an idea. Without saying anything, he strode out, down the hall to the kitchen, where Gandy had left one rollable suitcase and a tote—both new—a badly crumpled map of Wyoming, and one empty bag from a fast-food restaurant. That was it. No purse, no wallet. No ID. Gandy wouldn't have missed it. Gran had said bring everything, so he had—right down to an empty paper sack.

Thomas returned to the room that had been his until Gran needed it during her recuperation, walked right up to where the stranger sat so she had to tilt her head back to look at him, and talked over Becky's nonsense about what soap operas had taught her about amnesia.

"You don't have a wallet?"

"No, I—I don't remember."

Bull. She'd started to say something else, then she remembered all right—she remembered she wasn't supposed to remember.

"What kind of woman drives around without a purse? You've got to have a driver's license."

She opened her eyes wide and gave a shrug that brought the points of her shoulders up nearly to her ears, and sent her long-fingered hands wide.

"You weren't demanding her license or that she prove she's Helga Helgerson when she drove that car like a stunt woman to avoid smearing you and Dickens all over the road. You're being such a—"

He talked over his sister and demanded of the woman on the sofa. "What the hell do you remember?"

She put her hand to her forehead like she was concentrating. "I remember a motel... Long, painted reddish brown with rounded ends...yes...and a special sign. Oh, it's clear now! It's the Hot Dog Inn. Yes, I definitely remember the Hot Dog Inn."

"What the—"

"That's enough, Thomas. You, too, Becky," Gran added. "Right now what this girl needs is a shower and rest. Becky, take Helga upstairs to the rose room and—"

"What?" The rose room was next to the one he was using, and shared a bathroom. "Why can't she bunk with Becky down here?"

"Because it's senseless to cram Helga and Becky in one room when we have an empty one upstairs."

"Then I'll swap with Becky." But that wouldn't work, either. He slept like a log, and someone downstairs had to respond if Gran called out. "Or put Becky in the rose room and put *her* down here."

"Hey! Just because you moved, which you only did because you had the biggest room in the first place—"

"We're not going to move Becky around for no reason." Gran gave him a look. "Unless you have a reason?"

Not one he was going to expound on in front of his grandmother, his half sister and the cause of the reason. He shrugged.

Gran turned to the woman on the loveseat. "Take a shower, but don't let the water hit your wound. You can dab out the blood with a damp cloth."

"You'd think a medical aide would know that," grumbled Thomas.

Gran paid him no heed. "Becky, get her clothes to use, help her unpack her things, then get her something to eat."

God, she was moving in.

"Gran—"

"I know you have a lot of work to get done this afternoon, Thomas, and Helga needs rest. We'll talk more at supper. Go on now you two."

He kept his silence while Becky escorted the woman out. But when their footsteps could be heard heading up the stairs, he couldn't contain himself.

"You can't be buying that bunk of Becky's about amnesia. Whatever that kid knows about any medical condition is from TV, and I'm not talking *Nova*. And this…this stranger—" the name Helga wouldn't come out of his mouth "—and the things she can't remember, but, gee, she thinks she's the health aide we hired."

"Well, she should know."

"Not according to her," he shot back. "I'm going to contact the agency. They can send a photograph or something. Maybe fingerprints."

"That girl is not a criminal. If you can't tell that, I have no hope for you, Thomas. But what will you do if they say, yes, this is Helga—and you're liable for her medical care."

"That's what insurance is for," he said with a confidence he didn't feel.

"And what will you do if you find out she's not Helga?"

"Throw her out." He'd get her out of here as fast as humanly possible, so she couldn't sink her tentacles in any deeper than they already were. How could a woman do that—turning Becky's head he understood, but Gran's? She had seen firsthand what came of letting an outsider in.

"Oh, that would be a fine thing to do to a woman who wrecked her car and risked her life to save that renegade horse, not to mention your sorry neck."

"She had no reason to be on our road. Unless she was up to no good."

His words sounded certain enough, but they didn't match what he'd seen in her face in that instant their eyes met—that instant he'd known he couldn't wheel Dickens fast enough or far enough to avoid horse and rider colliding with some three thousand pounds of automobile. When he'd seen her slumped and bloody in the crumpled car…then those hazel eyes opened. Dazed, yet somehow clear, as if showing her soul. And when he'd felt the warmth of her body, soft and smooth and—

No. No, dammit. She wasn't going to pull him in. He knew even better than Gran about the dangers of outsiders. Especially outsiders who looked like this.

"Putting aside what you might owe her in the way of gratitude," Gran said, "how long would it take the agency to get somebody else here? We started more than a month ahead to line up Helga. How would you manage if it took that long?"

He wanted to say he would manage. Damn, he wanted to say it. But it wasn't true. And Gran knew it.

With Helga already two days late, there was no getting around that he needed someone to care for Gran. He'd stolen the time from days that needed every second in them, what with running the ranch a couple of hands short, and training Dickens. As for running the house…he'd be satisfied if they didn't starve and it didn't fall down.

Any other time, he'd have looked to Becky to step into Gran's shoes and run the household. But Becky was already doing nearly as much ranch work as a regular hand to help fill that gap, plus tending Gran during the nights. It wouldn't be right to expect her to do more.

Besides, with the way she'd been lately, if she'd been standing with her heels at the edge of a cliff and he told her not to back up, she'd go over the side to spite him.

They just had to hold on a few more weeks.

Forty days—that's what he had left to teach Dickens manners. He'd made progress with the mule-headed horse these first twenty days, but not enough. But he would. Then he'd get that fat training fee and the bonus, and that would put him over the top to make the payment five days later to keep a quarter of the Diamond V from going on the open market. Keeping the ranch intact, that's what mattered.

Forty days.

To get through these forty days, he'd even put up with a stranger telling lies. But that didn't mean he had to like it.

"It's your bones that have to mend," he said. It didn't move Gran. "You've made up your mind that you want her to stay."

"It only makes sense to give her a try."

He clamped his hat on his head and turned to go. "I've already burned too much daylight with this woman and her wrecked car and her supposedly not remembering things. What I should do is call the sheriff—"

"You will do no such thing."

"Only because I don't have time for this nonsense."

"No," his grandmother's voice followed him, "I didn't think you would have time for it."

* * *

"Oh, this is beautiful, too." Becky let the flowered silk of Judi's never-worn robe slide across her palm as she carried it to the closet.

At least someone appreciated it. Sterling would never see it, that was for sure. And by the time she was ready to marry anyone else—if she ever reached that point—the silk would probably be in tatters.

Judi had intended to wear it before revealing a less modest garment for her wedding night. That was the problem with running away from your wedding with barely enough time to grab the bags packed for your Caribbean honeymoon. Your wardrobe was long on sexy and short on practical.

And some of it was just plain short.

"Becky!"

Thomas's shout came clearly up the stairs, but the teenager gave no sign of hearing it.

Becky had hung the robe in the closet and now took out a short silk nightshirt, which was positively Victorian compared to some others.

Judi could imagine Thomas's reaction if he thought she was corrupting his baby sister. How old was Becky? With her makeup-free face and straightforward manner she might be a mature thirteen or a sheltered nineteen. Judi bundled a thigh-skimming red lace nightie into a drawer while Becky had her back turned.

"Isn't that your brother calling?"

"Half brother," Becky said, as if that wiped out anything else.

"Rebecca Jane!"

"What?" Becky bellowed back.

Judi counted her blessings that Becky had been facing into the closet at that moment, or her head might have exploded like a glass hit by too many sound waves.

"Gran needs to get out of bed. Come help her."

Becky glared at the door, and Judi could practically hear the rebellious words trembling on the girl's lips. *Do it yourself. You're not the boss. I don't have to do what you tell me.*

Or maybe those were echoes of her battles with her older brother Paul.

Then Judi saw something else flit across Becky's mobile face, followed closely by a sort of resigned sympathy that Judi guessed was for Gran. But she wondered about that other expression she'd seen so fleetingly. Could it have been guilt? And what on earth could this fresh-faced girl have to be guilty about?

"I gotta go. The bathroom's through there." She nodded to a door across from the bed. "If you need any more help…"

"Thank you, Becky. I'll be fine. I'll take a shower, then rest a bit."

The adrenaline that had surged as she fought the steering wheel to avoid hitting Thomas and his horse had long since ebbed, leaving her achy and weary.

"Okay. If you don't want to unpack everything right away, I could help you more later." She cast a covetous eye toward Judi's open suitcase. Then she grinned. "By the way, I'd already seen the red lace job—you didn't have to hide it. You know, if my underwear had as many holes in it as yours does, Gran would make me throw it out."

"It's not my usual style, either—uh, I mean, I don't think it is. Maybe I had something special to buy all this for."

Becky studied her a moment. "Maybe you did. And you'll remember it eventually."

Without waiting for an answer the teenager sauntered out.

Judi heard her hit the bottom of the steps, then say, "You should see the clothes she has. Wow!"

Thomas made no response she could hear. But clearly Becky didn't need words. In an entirely different tone, she snapped, "You don't have to look like that. Pretty clothes aren't contagious."

The sound of feet stomping away, and a distant door slamming was followed by what might have been a masculine sigh.

She'd had her share of battles with Paul at that age. But there was something in the tension between the brother and sister that she didn't quite understand. Almost as if Becky saw significance in words and looks, while Thomas had not a clue.

She took a pair of lacy underwear out of her suitcase—Becky was right, there were a lot of holes—and headed toward the bathroom. Two closet doors confronted her, but she found towels in the first.

Moist heat on her aching muscles and the satisfaction of washing almost all the blood from her hair by following Gran's instructions left her skin tingling as she dressed in the underwear and a terry beach coverup, then curled up on the bed.

Considering how the day had started, with the potential for being caught by that guy at the motel in Torrington, things hadn't turned out so bad.

Pretty stupid of him, really, to use a car with Illinois plates. She'd done better than that, and she was a rank amateur.

Her first move had been a stroke of genius, if she said so herself. She'd run down the church steps and slid into the driver's seat of the first car parked there, which happened to be the bride and groom's limo with the keys in the ignition. The limo driver had chased her down the driveway, waving the cigarette he'd been indulging in.

The good thing about the limo was that her sister-in-law Bette, with her usual organization, had put Judi's bags for the honeymoon, her purse and the cash and travelers' checks they planned to use on the honeymoon in the trunk.

Judi had taken the limo through the drive-in window at a nearby bank to cash the travelers' checks. Sure the limo was a little conspicuous, especially with a bride complete with white dress and veil driving it, but that couldn't be helped since she didn't want to leave a credit card trail.

She left the limo at the airport, stopping to change clothes, stow the wedding dress in a locker, leave a message on her own answering machine to tell her family she was okay and where to find the limo—the time it would take them to think of checking her machine would give her a head start.

She took a bus from the airport to a downtown hotel, where she rented a car changing her name and birthdate on the form. She almost fainted when the clerk looked at her driver's license, but he never compared it against the rental agreement. She reached Detroit, knowing she should be exhausted, but instead feeling exhilarated. She turned in the car, took three taxis to reach the bus station, then caught an overnighter with a ticket for Louisville.

But she got off in Indianapolis. She found an ancient used car through an ad in the *Star*. The seller was more than happy to take cash in return for the title and no questions. Then she headed West.

The Indiana plates began to feel conspicuous as she crossed Iowa. When she got off the Interstate for a late breakfast just after crossing into Nebraska, she had a stroke of luck. She missed the turn to get back onto the Interstate. That's how she came across the junkyard and the car with Nebraska plates that had three months registration left before they expired.

She removed the plates with her Swiss Army knife screwdriver and went another five miles to find a secluded spot to switch the plates, returning to the Interstate as a Nebraskan, and throwing out the Indiana plates at another rest stop. The brilliance of that move had been proved this morning when she'd heard the man asking about a young woman driving alone in a car with Indiana plates.

She'd considered picking up a hitchhiker to further her disguise, but her mother's horrified voice in her head wouldn't allow that. Now, if her mother had had the foresight to give her advice about passing herself off as another woman, she'd be all set.

Although her performance as Helga the health aide wasn't her biggest concern, a certain member of the audience was.

Judi pulled a coverlet over her bare legs and snuggled deeper.

Gran and Becky seemed perfectly willing to accept her at face value. Even when her face was notoriously easy to read. She would reward their trust—misplaced as it was in this case—by doing her absolute best. She could do the job. She would read the instructions about caring for Gran during her recuperation and do everything they called for—more than everything. She would make life better for them. All of them.

And then she wouldn't feel so bad about telling them she was Helga.

Would that be enough to stop Thomas glowering at her? She could use advice about this guy who made her feel as if a thundercloud formed every time he looked at her… except when he'd touched her and the thunder reverberated through her nerve endings.

Sudden tears pricked her eyes and slid through her lashes. If she'd been home, she'd have called Bette. Or if the whole gang was in town, she and Bette and Tris and Leslie might have thrashed out how to deal with Thomas, and all the rest.

For the first time since she'd run out of the church Judi felt very alone.

Thomas wasn't particularly proud of himself.

Those were tears. Definitely tears. Not bawling out loud, sobbing pathetically tears. Not even streaked down her cheeks. But tears sparkling through lowered eyelashes turned into spikes by the moisture. Tears held in check.

She'd taken a hell of a blow to the head. It had to be

aching something fierce. Red marks on her forearms and cheek promised to blossom into bruises.

He pressed his lips together. Feeling sorry for her didn't do anybody any good. Neither did feeling any qualms.

If she was who she said she was, then there'd be no real harm done.

If she wasn't who she said she was—far more likely— he'd be in a better position to protect the Diamond V. That was all the reason he needed.

It would have helped if Becky had noticed something more than that this woman's clothes were "hot." Hell, it would have helped even more if she and Gran—*Gran* for heaven's sake—hadn't fallen for this malarkey about amnesia.

He wasn't going to feel sorry for her. Wasn't going to try to understand her problems. He was going to protect his ranch from outsiders.

Still, it didn't mean it had to be done right now. She was sleeping.

But it wasn't because he felt sorry for her that he eased back across the threshold, through the bathroom and out the connecting door to his room. Having her wake up and find him at it wouldn't gain anything.

He'd search her room later.

"*This* is what you wear to take care of a woman who's had a hip replacement?"

Judi knew the question was aimed at her but she didn't budge from the counter where she'd found a sandwich with a note that she guessed Becky had written: This is for Helga. No one else eat it on pain of death. P.S. Dinner's at 7:30.

Now—five minutes after Judi came downstairs—the note remained on the counter. The sandwich had been reduced to two crusts, a shred of lettuce and crumbs, and a tall glass had only a white film left in it. It had been a long time since breakfast.

She'd been considering looking into the enticing, smoky smells coming from outdoors when the screen door's squawk warned her of someone's arrival. Since she was still chewing the last bite she didn't turn around. When Thomas's voice came from behind her, she looked over her shoulder with her best queen-talking-to-a-commoner gaze. Maybe she'd play Helga as a long-lost descendent of Scandinavian royalty.

"I wasn't aware there was a uniform requirement for the job."

"Or maybe you just don't remember it."

The quirk of humor that accompanied those words was more than the lifting of his mouth into not-quite-a-grin. More than the deepening of faint lines at the corners of his eyes. It was more like a breeze had pushed away clouds and let out the sun.

Uh-oh.

That was as close as her mind came to spelling out that thought, but that was enough. *Better watch your step, Judi-Helga.*

She started to turn to face him with regal dignity. But as she finished the pivot, her left leg slid between the two layers of material of her sarong, exposing halfway up her thigh. It would have been up to her hip if she hadn't grabbed the material in a fist, ruining the regal effect.

Thomas's face reverted to the more familiar frown. "We expected a health aide to wear something practical."

She'd put on the sarong because it covered a lot and it wasn't something she would wear when she started working. The tie-at-the-midriff blouse went with it.

"We? Gran said nothing about a dress code, and a health aide can like pretty things, you know."

"Like 'em maybe, but not afford 'em. Your clothes must've cost a fortune."

"How would you know that?"

"Because I'm out here in the wilds of Wyoming?"

"No, because you're just like—" She'd almost said *my*

brother. "Like every other man I've met. With no idea and no interest in clothes."

She let her gaze skim down his body, as if to judge— and find lacking—his outfit.

Big mistake. His jeans and faded blue plaid work shirt not only suited him, they fit him. To a *T.* Come to think of it, that was how he was built, with broad shoulders and narrow hips.

To cover her reaction, she hurriedly added, "Besides, I'm not taking care of anyone yet. Gran said to start in the morning. She said to rest and eat, so I'm here for dinner." She looked around, seeing no signs of food preparation.

"Outside. I came in to get the catsup."

"Smells great."

"Enjoy it tonight, because starting tomorrow, you're cooking. The job's not just to help Gran. You agreed to cook dinner six nights a week."

She heard the echo of a gauntlet being thrown down. "Was that really in the agreement, or are you taking advantage of my unfortunate injury?"

"The tragedy of amnesia is that you might never know."

How could she both want to belt him and laugh?

Without succumbing to either temptation, she returned his look. "Six dinners a week, it is."

"And breakfasts."

"But no lunches except for the patient."

"Of course," he said solemnly. "That was the agreement."

She nodded, though she suspected him of yanking her chain. As she headed out the door he held open, she decided that was fair, since what she'd told him so far had not even a nodding acquaintance with the truth.

Outside, Gran was in straight-backed chair set on a square of plywood that connected to the porch steps by way of a wide path of plywood. Her chair sat at the head of a picnic table ungraced by a cloth.

Gandy was tending something on a grill. The table held three oversized bags of chips, four loaves of white bread, a tub of butter, a huge jar of pickles, miscellaneous relishes, a stack of paper plates, another of paper napkins, a jumble of cutlery and three six-packs of soft drinks.

"First ones're about ready," announced Gandy. "Grab a seat."

In addition to the three Vances and Gandy, two more men sat down. By the way the tall, thin one moved, Judi guessed he was fifty, though his weathered face could have been pushing seventy. His companion was probably a few years older than Becky. He had the physical assurance of a man, while his smile was almost bashful.

"Helga, this is Keith." Gran said, indicating the older man. "And Steve. They eat with us most days, though only Gandy lives on the place. Boys this is Helga."

While she said "How do you dos" with her most winning smile, they each gave her a nod. Gran continued. "That accident shook her up, and she can't remember real well, but we figure she's the aide Thomas hired from South Dakota."

Keith nodded acceptance, but Steve said, "Really?"

"Yeah. She has amnesia," Becky said.

Thomas grunted. Any further comment was forestalled by Gandy arriving at the table with a platter piled with hamburger patties. Gran gave a simple blessing then the platter was passed around. Judi was astonished at how fast the stacks diminished. Each of the men took three pieces of meat and twice as many slices of bread. Butter was slathered on the bread, a burger was set between them, then consumed in what seemed to be three or four bites, before the process was repeated. As soon as space appeared on their plates it was covered with chips and a half-dozen pickle slices. And Becky was not far behind.

There was no conversation at all. No one wolfed down the food, but they ate with a concentrated attention that spoke of hunger.

Gandy produced another platter, and it too was emptied, along with the bread wrappers and chip bags.

Gandy finished first, closing the dampers on the grill and saying something about checking on "the wreck" before heading off. He was followed shortly by Keith. Becky said she was going to ride out to check on a foal she'd doctored. Thomas got up and told Gran to give him a holler in the barn when she was ready to go in. Steve ate another burger and polished off the chips, taking a pickle for the road as he headed in the direction Thomas had gone.

The whole thing couldn't have taken more than twenty-five minutes, and Judi felt as if she'd been caught in a culinary whirlwind.

Gran chuckled. "It's something isn't it? It's the old way on ranches—used to be the hands ate as fast as possible because there was always something more to do. I'd had them broke of that, but with this—" she gave an impatient wave toward her hip and leg, made bulky by bandaging "—the meals aren't much, and they've fallen back to the old ways. You'll have to eat a sight faster if you want to get enough to keep body and soul together, Helga. If you're still hungry—"

"Oh, no, no, I'm fine. Becky left me a sandwich, so I wasn't hungry."

"Sandwich and milk." Gran nodded. "You've got milk around your mouth."

"What? Oh—" She dabbed at her mouth. Great. She'd been trying to win over the ranch hands while wearing a milk mustache.

Thomas must have noticed, but hadn't warned her, Judi thought as she washed the platter and the few stainless utensils. Everything else she'd thrown out after helping Gran inside to a straight-backed chair in the kitchen's far corner, watching a tiny TV crowded onto a corner of a paper-strewn desk.

Well, she'd spent a few years in corporate America, and

she'd learned a few things about such warfare. Come to think of it, her boss in the job she'd quit two weeks before her wedding had a few things in common with Thomas Vance. Including making no effort to hide a low opinion of Judi Monroe—or Helga Helgerson as the case might be.

The door screeched open, and before Judi recovered from the assault on her ears, Thomas's voice boomed, "Becky!"

"Becky's not back yet, though she probably heard you holler wherever she is."

Thomas stood in the middle of the kitchen, hands on his hips, frowning, though not apparently at her. It was more disapproval of the world in general.

"Becky didn't help Gran in? Who did?"

"I did."

"You did." He repeated the words, but his mind clearly wasn't on that. "Damn. I sent Steve home."

"I wish I could…" Gran's words trailed off, though her frustration echoed in the silence. "Maybe Helga can help you."

At his grandmother's first words Thomas had turned toward where she sat. Now he turned back to Judi. Judi felt like she was caught in the beam of a spotlight. If she'd been one of those old computer cards, she'd have come out bent, folded, spindled and mutilated from the going-over she received from those green eyes.

"Maybe."

As a vote of confidence it wasn't much.

"Riding? I might not—"

"I'm not putting you on any of my horses." Why did she think he was concerned about the horses and not her? "I need somebody to drive, and at least we know you know how to drive. Unless you've forgotten that, too."

She widened her eyes at him, putting her clasped hands to her chest, and said in a whispery voice, "Oh, dear, I don't know. I suppose the only way to know is to put it to the test. This is all so terrifying.''

He snorted and turned away, heading out the protesting door and toward the barn. At least Gran chuckled.

"If you don't want to help, just ignore him," Gran said. "He'll get the idea eventually."

"I don't mind helping, it's just…"

"My grandson's manners could use polishing, but he's got a good heart."

Judi resisted the temptation to suggest starting that polishing with a power sander, gave Gran what she hoped was a smile and headed outside. She hurried after Thomas, trying to catch up with his ground-gobbling loose-limbed stride.

"So, Becky's sixteen?" She sounded a little breathless as they neared a truck that might have started as silver before streaks of dirt and pockets of rust took over.

"Just turned fifteen. Why?"

"You were going to have her drive."

"Round here kids drive ranch trucks as soon as their feet reach the pedals. It's no big deal. Here's the truck. What you're going to do is—''

"Wait a minute, I need keys."

"They're in the ignition. We don't get many truck-jackings.''

"I wonder why," she murmured, considering the dent in the door and the crack in the windshield.

He ignored that. "Have you ever driven a stick shift?"

"I don't—"

"Remember," he finished for her. He grunted. "Start 'er up, and we'll find out." Judi turned over the ignition and closed her eyes as if trying to dredge up a memory. She'd really closed them to hide that she didn't have to dredge very deep. She'd been taught to drive standard transmission as well as automatic from the start, and her car had a stick shift because it helped to get around in Chicago's snow.

The truck vibrated like one of those massage chairs overdosed on caffeine, but the engine didn't stall.

"When I raise my right hand, drive straight across the open area and stop. Slow and steady. Okay?"

"I think I can handle it. What are you going to be doing?"

"Riding Dickens."

"Near the truck? Desensitizing him because of the accident?"

He gave her a look she couldn't read with the slanting sun and the brim of his hat conspiring to shadow his face. "Guess that would be the fancy term. Drive across there then turn down the road. This side of that turn in the fence—" he pointed "—there's a wide spot to turn around. Come back and do the same route in reverse. Then repeat the whole thing. But don't start any leg until I signal. Got it?"

"Is this where I'm supposed to salute?"

From the angle of his head she suspected he was staring at her from those hat shadows. She stared back at him through the open window.

"You got a smart mouth on you, you know that, Helga?"

Without giving her a chance to respond, he turned on one boot heel and strode toward the pen—a corral?— where Dickens waited already saddled.

"At least he admits I'm smart," she muttered to herself.

It was more than she'd ever gotten out of her previous boss, Christine Welmer. In her family circle—those directly related to her as well as those who knew her so well they were like family—the opinion was that while she had intelligence, the jury was out on the degree of her good sense. Of the group, Judi's sister-in-law Bette had the most faith in her, yet, Bette too, sometimes slipped and treated Judi like a precocious child.

Thomas took his time, moving slowly and deliberately around the horse. Riding lessons had been part of the repertoire where she grew up, along with tennis, skiing and golf. So Judi recognized the control it took for Thomas to swing into the saddle lightly when Dickens minced sideways. From this distance it appeared as if Thomas held absolutely still, yet from the horse's reactions, especially the ears flickering around like radar, there was a lot of communicating going on.

Thomas moved the horse into position, then raised his right hand. Judi eased out the clutch, and nearly stalled the thing. She gunned the engine to keep it from dying. Dickens sidestepped and snorted. Thomas shot her a glare.

She hadn't actually seen the glare because of the hat shadows, but she'd felt it.

"Sorry!" she called out cheerfully as the truck moved across the horse's path.

She went down the road, found the spot he'd mentioned, turned the truck in two awkward stages and waited. When he raised his right hand she retraced the path, then turned around by dint of hard yanking on the recalcitrant steering wheel. Another hand signal from Thomas and she was off on her putt-putt circuit for a second time. And a third. A fourth. A fifth. Each pass a little closer to horse and rider.

On the sixth near-intersection of truck and horse she yawned hugely, and could have sworn she caught a look of empathy in Dickens's eyes. The man never looked at her and never wavered. Patient, steady, inexorable.

Seventh pass, eighth and ninth.

They were close enough now that as she returned to the starting spot for the tenth circuit, even with twilight beginning to lose its grip, she realized Thomas was not holding still at all. When Dickens tried to shy away from the truck, Thomas exerted pressure with his outside leg. As soon as the horse stopped pulling away, the pressure stopped. Time after time, telling Dickens what he was doing wrong, and removing the pressure the instant he started doing right.

Each motion of the powerful horse was met by an equal

motion by the rider, the bunching and shifting of Thomas's muscles illustrated through the faded denim. She'd been right—the jeans did fit him to a *T*. Snug enough to show all his power. There was a certain pattern in the fading denim that called attention to the fact that the area under the zipper was not nearly as flat as the area above his belt. No, not anywhere close to flat. In fact—

She jerked into sudden awareness of something beyond Thomas's…uh, looks. That something happened to be his voice.

"Helga! Hey! Wake up!" He'd ridden Dickens within a couple feet of the idling truck. The horse's eyes and ears scanned for trouble, but he didn't back away.

"What?"

"I said, turn off the truck. Now you know why I have to holler." He emphasized the word, reminding her of her complaint when he'd come in the kitchen looking for his sister. "You and Becky don't listen. Or maybe you forgot your name. Again."

Every darn stair creaked as Judi tiptoed down them. It was after midnight and the house was totally quiet—except for the protest of wood on wood as she stepped on the far right side of the last stair. Left, right, middle—they all creaked.

But she needed a glass of water beside her bed. She rarely drank it, but there'd been a glass with water on her nightstand since she'd been old enough to have her own bed and, at the moment, she needed that tiny piece of continuity. Finding no glass in the bathroom, she'd headed downstairs.

A faint light came from the kitchen. Maybe the Vances left a light on, like her mother did over the stove to guide any nocturnal wanderers.

She peered around the doorframe and saw Thomas at the desk with the goosenecked lamp aimed at papers in front of him. He had his shirt pulled out of his jeans, showing the T-shirt underneath. He had one elbow on the desk, with his cheek supported by his palm and the top of his head propped against the wall. He was asleep.

Not quite snoring, but breathing deeply and steadily.

Judi took one step into the room. Then another. She reached the cabinets on the opposite side of the room from him.

He hadn't budged. How tired would a man have to be to sleep in such an uncomfortable position? Should she wake him up so he could go to bed?

Abruptly, she became aware of what she wore—and didn't wear. She'd pulled the beach coverup over her nightie, but neither reached beyond the middle of her thighs, and she had nothing else on.

She could imagine what he would say about her clothes if he woke up and saw her in this outfit. A flush of heat pulsed through her.

Embarrassment at that vision. Had to be.

She would not wake him. Letting sleeping dogs lie and all that.

Pulling the hem of the coverup down on the side facing Thomas, she reached into the cabinet with her other hand, stealthily withdrawing a cartoon-decorated plastic cup. She eased the door closed and took the deep breath she hadn't wanted to risk with the lower edge of her outfit elevated by her stretch.

Thomas stirred, his head bumping against the wall.

She was out of the room and halfway up the stairs with no concern about their creaking and groaning before she drew another breath. Under the covers, with the light out, and her filled glass on the nightstand, her heart banged away. Had she made a clean escape?

One thing for certain, Thomas would let her know if he'd spotted this outfit.

Chapter Three

Judi woke around seven, feeling nearly as bright as the dazzling blue sky visible whenever the breeze pushed aside the flowered curtains.

She washed up quickly and pulled on linen shorts, a T-shirt and the lone sweater she'd packed—an airy cotton knit cardigan—ignoring the gooseflesh popping up on her arms and legs.

Some of her good mood, she realized, was the feeling she'd had ever since Saturday. Like the weight of the world had lifted off her shoulders. A sensation that had coincided with reversing her course down the aisle. Clearly, when Sterling had asked "Will you marry me?" via the Chicago Bulls scoreboard seven weeks ago, she'd picked the wrong answer.

The stairs announced her descent again, but this time there was no one in the kitchen to hear. Crumbs on the counter and a streak that might have been strawberry jelly haphazardly wiped up attested to breakfasts having been consumed.

She heard voices down the hall—too low to make out words but still identifiable as a duet of Thomas and Gran. She headed that way.

Her first day of work, and she better learn what needed to be done. Thomas wouldn't waste any time throwing her out on her ear—or any other body part that happened to connect with the ground—if she didn't earn her keep.

Strange that he'd been so wonderful to her right after the accident, but had been cool, if not hostile, ever since. It was going to be a long six weeks if he was only cordial when he thought she might be seriously injured.

The first thing that came into sight in Gran's room was a foam wedge on the side chair by the door. It was the right shape to have made the lump in Gran's bedcovers she'd noticed yesterday. Another step revealed Gran lying flat on her back and wearing sweatpants with the left leg slit to accommodate a bulky bandage.

Thomas hooked the looped end of a long elasticized band under Gran's foot, then handed her the opposite end. Holding the band taut, Gran swung her leg over the side of the bed, while Thomas appeared to almost scoop her upper body up and set her on her feet.

They both remained still for a moment, and Judi could hear Gran breathing harder from the exertion. Or was it from pain?

"Okay?" Thomas murmured in a tone Judi had heard only in the moments after her accident.

"Right as rain," Gran replied with what sounded to Judi like forced cheer.

Without releasing his hold around Gran's waist, Thomas grabbed the walker with his free hand to position it in front of her. She turned, and caught sight of Judi.

"Good morning, dear. How's your head?"

"Much better, thank you."

"We'll take a look at that after I get settled. I'll be back in a moment." She hobbled to the bathroom using the walker, closing the door behind her.

"She'll be okay in there alone?"

"Yeah."

Clearly morning didn't stir Thomas's sociability any more than late afternoon or evening had the day before.

He started making up the king-size bed, reaching across the expanse to try to snag the covers. Judi automatically moved so she could flip the covers toward him, and straightened the ones on her side.

"Why make the bed? She'll be getting right back in, won't she?"

"No."

"Why don't you let the poor woman stay in bed?"

"Because staying in bed all day could give the poor woman blood clots. It's a major concern after hip replacement surgery. As you would know if you'd ever had any medical training."

"If I *remembered* my medical training," she shot back, smoothing the covers over the pillows.

He tossed a folder to her side of the bed. "You better read up, and remember what you read, because you're going to give Gran the best care possible."

That smacked of ultimatum rather than confidence.

Since his opinion of her skills obviously couldn't go lower, she figured it didn't hurt to show ignorance. "What were you doing with the band thingy you put under her foot?"

"It helps her swing her leg without bending her hip. She can't bend her hip—ever. That's one of the things you better remember."

"What else?"

"She shouldn't put weight on that foot. If her ankle gets more swollen than it is now, call the doctor—the number's by the phone in the kitchen. She's running a fever, that's normal, and she can have aspirin, but if it spikes, call the doctor. Don't let her sit for more than forty-five minutes at a time. If her leg gets really sore and rock hard, that's a sign of a blood clot—call the doctor immediately. And if any of this stuff happens, call me on the cell phone. No excuses."

"Yes, sir!" She added a mock salute that coincided with Gran opening the bathroom door.

"Ah, I see Helga's caught on to your managerial style, Thomas."

He glowered. "If you think you'll be okay, now, Gran, I'll go. Or I can stay if—"

"What, and have Thundercloud Thomas around ruining an otherwise sunny day? Not a chance. Helga will take good care of me. You get back to your work."

Judi bit her lip to keep from grinning at Thundercloud Thomas.

After a moment of hesitation, he left. The sound of his boot heels on the hall floor brought a vision of his confident stride in those nicely fitting jeans. Judi shook her head to try to clear it.

"Everything all right, dear?"

"Wh— Oh. Yes. Fine. Now, how about if you tell me what I can do to help you."

The older woman needed help getting out of some of her nightclothes. She maneuvered over the shower stall's small threshold, and said she'd be fine with the handheld showerhead. Despite those assurances, Judi wasn't about to leave her alone in the bathroom, so she kept her back to the shower while she straightened, cleaned the sink and gathered towels for the laundry. She noticed a riser attachment on the toilet seat that would help the occupant stand without bending a hip.

Drying off and dressing were further exercises in instant intimacy. Then Gran talked Judi through pulling on the anti-embolism stockings she had to wear all day. The thigh-highs had strong elastic and a tight fit to fight blood clots, which made working them over her foot, heel and calf akin to pulling up a wet swimsuit three sizes too small over wet skin.

By the time she'd finished, Judi was panting, both with the physical exertion and the strain of making sure she didn't hurt Gran.

"I'm not made of spun glass," the older woman said with a snap.

"Hey, it's not you I'm thinking about. I'm worried about what Thomas would do to me if I put the slightest dent in you."

They both chuckled, and Gran headed for the kitchen using her walker, with Judi trailing worriedly behind.

The older woman took a seat in the same uncomfortable-looking straight-backed chair she'd used yesterday evening. Following her directions, Judi positioned a fat, firm cushion about eight inches thick to elevate Gran's foot.

"We'll have a quiet day today. You shouldn't be doing too much with that knot on your head."

Judi wasn't going to argue. She felt as if she'd put in a full day's labor, and it was barely eight o'clock. Gran also appeared worn out.

Judi made them toast, poured coffee and settled down with the folder of instructions to see what she'd gotten herself into.

Gran said she was satisfied. So that had to be good enough.

He'd stuck close to the house yesterday to stop by a half-dozen times. Everything seemed to be going okay. Actually, Gran's exact words had been, "Helga's doing great. Quit worrying."

Right.

She'd said one more thing. "Give the girl a chance."

A chance to what? That's what worried him.

A couple times when he'd gone in she'd been talking with Gran. Another time she'd had everything out of the refrigerator's freezer and was reorganizing. Later, he'd found her scrubbing with white paste stuff where the aging coffeemaker sat.

But what got him today was finding her sitting cross-legged on the floor in front of a cabinet rearranging storage containers under Gran's supervision. Gran viewed her storage containers the way some women viewed diamonds. Letting Helga handle them was a clear signal she'd awarded the stranger the Iris Swift stamp of approval.

He'd been pushing it when he'd told Helga she had to cook. The agreement actually said light housework only in the patient's room. So why was she doing this?

As he hooked up Klute to drag a tree trunk that had obstructed the east fork of Six-Mile Creek, he mentally listed three possibilities.

She was Helga Helgerson and she had amnesia.

No damn way.

She was Helga Helgerson and she'd decided to do extra work from the goodness of her heart.

That ranked as only slightly less unlikely.

She was an unknown quantity pretending to be Helga Helgerson for unknown reasons and she thought cleaning the Diamond V ranch kitchen was going to gain her something somehow.

Bingo.

He had to figure out what she thought it could gain her, her reason for the masquerade and who she really was. That way she couldn't blindside him.

Thomas couldn't see any reasons yet, but they had to be there. She was not a stupid woman. Not by a long shot. And that made her all the more dangerous.

As long as he kept his mind on that, he wouldn't keep having dreams of long, bare legs speeding in front of his bleary eyes fast enough to stir a breeze that brought the scent of clean female.

* * *

The truck slowly towed the twisted corpse of Judi's car to a mechanical cemetery between the big barn and a slope-roofed shed.

Would that make it easier or harder to do what she needed to do? She wouldn't have as far to go to the car, but anyone could stand at this window and see her as clearly as she saw Thomas get out of the passenger door and stride to a gap between a truck skeleton and the unidentifiable bones of other vehicles that had passed on.

He surveyed the open area, then talked to Gandy, who was driving. Against the faded blue of his shirt a darker stripe showed down the center of his back.

He gestured with his arms wide, and that pulled the pale blue material tight across his shoulders. Another twitch, and it looked like the material might rip, and hang in tatters down his back like on a B-movie hero who'd been wandering the desert. Shreds of material that showed off the actor's physique even better than no shirt at all.

"You should get out and see more of the ranch, instead of spending all day inside." Gran's voice came from the other side of the large room.

Judi realized she'd gone up on her toes to better see out the window. She rocked back to flat feet as Thomas directed Gandy to back in the towed car.

"I'd love to see the ranch." As if the ranch had been what she'd been looking at. Her hormones better get over this honeymoon mood pretty quick. "But I don't think it's a good time. I'm still learning—relearning—so I have to go full-tilt all day to have a hope of keeping up."

"It's a great help to have you here."

Tell that to Thomas. Dealing with him was like watching thunderclouds boiling up on the horizon and wondering if they might crash over her. Come to think of it, the atmosphere changed whenever he was around.

Everything would be calm and sunny when she and Gran were alone, with maybe a freshening breeze and a few clouds dotted around when Becky joined them. Then

Thomas would come in, and it was like a front coming
through. The trees tossed uneasily in the wind, the clouds
churned up

Growing up in the Chicago area, she'd learned about
changeable weather. And she knew to pay attention to the
signs. The way the birds chirped, the behavior of dogs,
the bending of trees and her own body's warning signs.
Not her joints—not yet, thank heavens—but headaches
and an odd restlessness. She'd felt it as a kid when she
had been sailing with her brother Paul and his friend
Grady on Lake Michigan. Paul and Grady had tried to josh
her out of her feeling, but she'd insisted they get to shore,
saying she didn't feel right. They'd grumbled, but they'd
brought the boat in at the Monroes' house, intending to
drop her off and go back out. Mom had been waiting for
them. Funnel clouds had been spotted. They'd all spent an
hour in the Monroes' basement.

When they emerged, there'd been storm damage all
around. And a report that a boat that had been sailing near
where they'd been had disappeared with two on board. It
was never found.

"You should get out, though. Get some air, and sun.
After lunch, you could—"

"Thanks, but we can finish organizing those containers
if I stay inside today."

Where she wouldn't get swept into a funnel cloud.

The following day, the beckoning sun was too strong to
resist.

Gran was taking a nap, Becky had left with Steve and
Keith on horseback after breakfast and the kitchen was
passably clean. When she heard voices by the barn, she
didn't hesitate to wander out and see what was going on.

She might have reconsidered if she'd known Thomas
was at the center of it.

He was inside the pen beside the barn, along with
Gandy. Dickens was also there, and the young horse did
not appear eager to be caught and put to work. He trotted

easily away from the men. They split, walking to either side of Dickens. The horse kept his attention on the younger man.

Judi realized why when she got close enough to hear Thomas's low voice talking calmly to the horse.

"Okay, Gandy," Thomas said in the same even voice. "This time."

Thomas moved in almost close enough to reach the horse's head. His outstretched arms showed the rib of muscles at work holding his arms steady, making no move that would give the horse an excuse to spook.

At the last second Dickens started to wheel away from him. Just as he did, Gandy shouted while staying out of Dickens' line of sight. The noise was enough to make Dickens decide that direction wasn't a good idea. He reversed course and turned—right into Thomas's hands.

Thomas's voice deepened and warmed. Judi couldn't hear the words, but the tone was such pure praise that she half expected the young horse to purr. Or maybe that was her reaction. Dickens stayed tense for a long moment then seemed to give a sigh, while Thomas kept talking, stroking him and putting on the halter.

He led Dickens around the pen, still talking. When they passed by her, the horse's eyes and ears flicked toward her, but the man's attention never wavered.

Their circuit complete, Thomas removed the halter, let the horse trot free for a few minutes, then repeated the process two more times. The third time, Dickens still started to wheel away when Thomas neared his head, but when the shout sounded from his off side, he turned back to Thomas with what almost looked like relief, and he relaxed much more quickly.

Judi didn't hear any words exchanged, but Gandy unobtrusively left the pen, easing out of the gate when Thomas had Dickens's back turned.

"Afternoon, Missy. Think we made real progress with that devilish horse today, yes I do." He chuckled at his play on the horse's name as he leaned his crossed arms on the rail beside her.

"It looked that way. But it's a slow process, isn't it?"

"Slow and steady, that's what works with a horse, Missy. Specially one as deep in bad habits as that critter. Takes a real patient man to work out the kinks of another man's mistakes. Best get to work now."

Patience was not a virtue Judi would have identified with Thomas Vance. But the evidence was before her eyes.

He tied Dickens to the rail near where a saddle blanket and a saddle were laid out atop the fence.

With deliberate motions, he saddled up the horse. At one point Dickens started to step into him. But Thomas was obviously on the alert for the game some horses played of trying to step on a saddler's foot, enjoying the comical sight of a human hopping up and down on one foot and swearing. He pushed back at the horse, saving his foot, and informing Dickens in a no-nonsense voice and with a few four-letter words that his behavior was unacceptable. When the horse stood still and quiet, Thomas's voice immediately returned to smooth and low.

Once mounted, he controlled Dickens's edginess with the same ease she'd noted the first night.

On their second circuit, Thomas made eye contact with her for the first time. She interpreted that as permission to speak. "If you were half as patient with Becky as you are with this guy, you'd be getting a lot farther."

"He's only half as irritating."

"That isn't what it sounded like a minute ago."

"I didn't know I had an audience. I usually keep those thoughts to myself—about Becky and about Dickens."

"I'd say you usually keep all your thoughts to yourself." Except about distrusting and disbelieving her, of course. Oh, no, those thoughts he was happy to share with the class. She'd also caught his concern for his grandmother, and his frustration with his sister, and his worry about something else...though she hadn't pinned that down yet. But it had only been a few days. Feeling cheered, she added, "At least you try."

His head jerked around to her. That took him aback, and she loved it.

"Even if you believe the horse is easier to deal with than your sister, surely you're not saying training Dickens is more important than getting along with her."

"Right now, nothing's more important than getting this colt trained."

She waited, but he added no explanation. She made a sound of exasperation that had Dickens pricking his ears as if it was familiar. She wouldn't be the least surprised. Stubborn and ornery creatures often elicited that sort of response.

She turned her back on man and beast and started toward the house.

"Hey, Helga."

For an instant she thought he was going to admit she was right, or tell her why it was so important to train this horse, or maybe say it had been nice to see her. Then she saw his face, intent and puzzled, and knew he would not be admitting or sharing or complimenting.

She had to get a grip on her fantasies.

"Mind opening the gate?"

That was his reason for calling her back? But she complied. She closed it again after he and Dickens had passed through.

"What did you mean, right after you crashed your car, that the horse isn't the right color?" He asked it like he'd just thought of the question, but she would have bet it had been rolling around in his head since that first moment.

She propped her hands on her hips. "You make it sound like I crashed the car for the fun of it. You mean right after I hit the tree to save your neck."

And of course, then, with her feeling justifiably huffy, he grinned and said, "Yeah, that's what I meant to say."

So what could she do? "I said he's the wrong color because he's reddish brown."

"And what color should he be?"

"White."

"I don't know why I'm asking, but—why?" His mouth curved, as if anticipating amusement.

"For the Lone Ranger. The Lone Ranger's horse was called Silver, but he was white."

"Okay, I follow that, but why would you have expected to see the Lone Ranger?"

"I didn't *expect* to see anything. I *did* see you—a lone ranger."

That's how she saw him? A lone ranger?

The questions had echoed throughout the hour-long ride to check heifers in the home pasture, then the return to the corral.

"Why do I think that doesn't mean she sees me as a masked hero?"

Dickens's ears flickered at the question.

"You're right. Better not to ask questions like that."

Thomas unsaddled the horse, and got the bucket with curry combs. Dickens looked around with wary eyes, started to take a step toward Thomas as if to catch his foot, then thought better of it. Thomas gave him a rub and words of praise.

"You won't get this treatment often like some prissy show horse, but you need to get used to this, too."

He brought the comb down in a firm but gentle stroke, giving the animal a predictable rhythm and pressure. A rhythm that also left Thomas's mind free.

The Lone Ranger had roamed from place to place. That sure didn't fit. As for fighting injustice where he found it, it was more like trouble found him, and it sure seemed like he lost more than he won. Some TV series his adventures would make.

But he sure as hell felt like a lone ranger sometimes.

He had for a long time. Maybe since his mother had died and his father had fallen into his grief. Gran had been around, of course, but with her job teaching plus running the house, there hadn't been a lot of time for cozy chats. Besides, that wasn't his way. Maybe he got that from his father.

The only thing that seemed to pull Rick Vance out of his grieving was when an unexpected guest showed up at the ranch one summer. Unexpected, female, attractive and determined.

In short order Thomas had had a stepmother and a baby sister. There'd been a brief period when he hadn't felt so alone—when Becky was big enough to get around, and his father had been okay…then Becky's mother had taken off.

There'd been no choice but to do things himself—if he hadn't done them the ranch would have fallen apart, because Rick Vance sure wasn't paying any heed to the Diamond V. All he did was try to think of ways to get Maureen back.

Right up until the end—and beyond.

Thomas put the combs in the bucket and unhooked Dickens's reins from the fence to lead him to the big pasture where he'd be set loose for the rest of the day.

"If Dad's the example of what happens to a man when he falls for a woman, then I'm damned happy to be a lone ranger."

"…and I'm saying Helga hasn't been outside since—"

"Yesterday." Thomas filled in Gran's sentence, then glanced across the supper table at the object of their conversation.

"That's true," she said. "I watched Thomas and Gandy working with Dickens for a while."

"What? At the corral? Fifteen yards from the kitchen?" Gran scoffed. "That girl—"

"It's farther than that."

"—needs to get away from the home ranch—"

"We could go into town, go shopping?" suggested Becky.

He expected Judi to jump on that suggestion, but she didn't appear disappointed when Gran shook her head.

"Not shopping. What she needs is fresh air. When you're someplace you should take advantage of what it has to offer. And what we have to offer on the Diamond V is wide open spaces. That's the kind of break Helga needs. She looks tired."

"A break? She just got here Wednesday."

"And she hasn't had a moment off since then. She's been working hard."

"I didn't get a day off when I was doing my regular ranch work, along with keeping up with the house and—" He wouldn't say taking care of Gran, because that might sound like he was complaining about her. "All."

"Your idea of 'keeping up with the house' is the reason I'm working so hard," Helga muttered. "But, really, Gran, I'm fine. There's no need to—"

"You need to get out, instead of staying inside all day playing nursemaid to a useless old woman."

"You are not useless or old."

"All I can do is sit in this chair."

Thomas had sensed Gran's frustration, but this was worse than he'd expected.

"How about your knitting?" Helga said.

"If this was World War I, I could knit mufflers for the boys overseas—that would be useful. As it is I'm going to have enough afghans to cover the Rocky Mountains. And that's not anybody's definition of useful." Gran turned to Thomas. "She needs fresh air. When you're checking the herd or gathering or riding fence during the middle of day, take her along."

"Wearing that?"

The blue shorts she had on today would leave her legs bare against the saddle and expose them to brush and brambles. There was a reason people working cattle wore chaps. The ornery critters found the wildest, thorniest spots to get themselves into. Those smooth, pale calves would get scratched and slapped. The long expanse of thigh that finally disappeared under the blue hem in the nick of time would be rubbed raw by the friction of the saddle. Why she'd need salve rubbed all the way—

"Thomas!"

He blinked at Gran. "What?"

"I said just because she's wearing shorts today doesn't mean the girl doesn't have a pair of jeans with her."

Thomas glanced toward Helga, and her expression confirmed what he'd suspected from her silence. "Do you?"

"Uh, no. No jeans."

Skirts slit up to her waist, shirts that didn't come down to her waist, and shorts that seemed to barely cover her waist. But no jeans.

"But you should see what she does have!" Becky said.

Pink rose up from the collar of Helga's sleeveless shirt, climbing her throat and into her cheeks.

What the heck could she have that made Becky crow like that and Helga blush? No, no he didn't want to know. And that sure wasn't why he intended to look through her things. That was solely to find out about her so she couldn't pull any fast ones.

Blanking out any curiosity, he said, "It can't be worse than the outfits we've been seeing."

"Oh, if you only knew!"

He wondered which delighted Becky more—that she knew something he didn't or that she thought he'd be somehow taken down a peg if he did know what she did. He looked at his half sister, trying to remember when she used to be his ally.

"All I need to know is she doesn't have the clothes needed for riding."

"Don't be so quick to give up, Thomas." Gran's admonition had an undertone of sarcasm that said she knew darn right well he wasn't "giving up"—he was escaping.

"She could wear a pair of mine," Becky volunteered.

"I don't think—"

"Wouldn't fit."

His declaration overrode Helga's tentative start and he wanted to kick himself when both his grandmother and his sister turned speculative eyes toward him.

"You've noticed that, have you?" murmured Gran.

After her earlier surge of pink, Helga's skin had nearly returned to normal. Now another tide of pink came in. But she sounded nonchalant as she said, "I'm taller and Becky's so slender, I'm afraid I couldn't get into her jeans."

If he didn't know better he'd have said she was trying to distract Gran and Becky from his comment, which they probably thought had a whole lot more significance than it did. All it meant was he wasn't blind. Any halfway observant human being would have noticed that Helga had more curves than Becky.

"I guess I won't be riding." She sighed and cupped her cheek in her palm.

"Don't you be so quick to give up, either. Next time anyone goes into town, we'll get them to pick you up a pair. Nothing could be simpler."

Thomas made a mental note that Gandy would make the next provision run into town.

Judi heard Thomas coming up the porch steps in a hurry, but she had two more spots on the door hinge to squirt with oil—he could wait an extra few seconds for her to finish and climb down from the chair she was standing on.

She'd applied the last squirt when he yanked the partially opened door the rest of the way open and walked right into the chair.

"Hey! Look out!"

"What the hell?"

The chair, with the back legs in the kitchen and the front legs on the slightly lower porch floor, rocked under the impact and Judi grabbed for something to hold on to, finding only air. Thomas seemed to be fighting for his own equilibrium, stumbling from the impact with the chair into the doorframe.

She was going down. There was no way she wasn't.

The chair had rocked forward, but her attempts at balance and another knock against it from Thomas now sent it the opposite way—it was going to tip over backward and she was going to go splat on the floor.

Great, she'd be in a full-body cast and then how would she take care of Gran?

And then she went splat against something that was definitely not the floor. Warm and hard and a considerable distance above the floor. And she'd found something to hold onto at last.

Thomas's shoulders.

How he'd grabbed her she never knew. He'd been off balance, going down himself. But now he had his arms wrapped around her. One under her bottom, the other at her waist.

The expansion and contraction of Thomas's chest brushed against her as he took deep breaths, while she felt as if she couldn't draw in any oxygen at all.

He'd lost his hat. Sunstreaked strands of his hair were just under her nose. They smelled like sun and heat and man. She wanted to bury her face in them.

She squirmed against the temptation and his hold. Neither budged. But she'd slipped, and could see his face. His jaw was tensed, a vein throbbing in his forehead, his mouth compressed, and his gaze staring straight at her breasts.

The tingling, tightening sensation in her nipples might have been a delayed fear reaction. But she knew otherwise. It wasn't only his gaze, it was also the warm brush of his breath across the tips covered in material meant to keep her cool in tropical sunshine.

She wasn't cool now.

"Thomas…"

His gaze flicked up to her face, then away. His arms loosened slightly. Not enough to drop her to the floor, instead letting her slide down the front of his body. She felt the hardness of his chest, the coolness of his belt buckle, then a solid heat below it. That heat flowed across her skin, into her bloodstream and burrowed into her bones.

Her toes touched the floor and she braced her knees to support herself. Only then did she realize she still had her fingers curled into the muscles of his shoulders.

She snatched her hands away and backed up.

He didn't look at her. He bent with an uncharacteristically awkward motion to pick up his hat. She heard him grunt as if in discomfort. Then he repeated the motion to retrieve the chair, letting the screen door close. He set the chair in front of himself as if presenting a piece of evidence.

"I—"

"What—"

"Sorry, you go ahead," she told him.

"What the hell were you doing on a chair in the middle of a doorway? It's dangerous."

All thoughts of warmly thanking him for catching her disappeared like a single hot stone being dropped into Lake Michigan in February.

"It was perfectly safe until you tried to run me over."

"I didn't see you."

"Maybe if you got sleep at night you'd be able to see straight. I would have thought a rancher would be attuned to the rhythm of nature."

Thomas's forehead creased. "What's that supposed to mean?"

"I thought only city folks were workaholics."

He shrugged. "Just doing what needs doing."

"Baloney. You work too hard."

His eyes met hers. The look lasted a fraction of a second, but her words had caught him off guard. He picked up the chair and returned it to its place at the table.

"That's your professional medical opinion?" He moved the chair two inches to the left then back an inch.

"It's my professional opinion as a human being. Gran needs you."

He released the chair and strode to the desk. He let the moment stretch while he shifted aside an uneven stack of papers, obviously looking for something. When his voice came it had that hard edge again. He picked up a paper, folded it lengthwise, put it in his shirt pocket. Then he fished out an envelope. "That's what we're paying you for."

"Not to be her grandson you're not. And Becky needs you, too."

Thomas snorted, as he crossed the room. "Not likely."

"I've been meaning to talk to you about that. What's going on with you and Becky is—"

"We're not *paying* you to stick your nose into family business." He thumped an envelope on the table beside her, growled, "First week's pay," and started for the door.

"Consider my advice a bonus."

He glanced her way, but his eyes weren't letting her in. "No."

"That's it? Just no? I can help you and your sister—"

"Just no." He pushed out of the door, never pausing.

"Thomas Vance," she told the closing door—which did not squeak, thank-you-very-much! "You are the most unreasonable, pigheaded—"

"Comes by it honestly."

Gran's voice made Judi jump.

She was going to have to put bells on that walker.

"Well, he sure doesn't take after you, so it must be some other aggravating DNA in his gene pool."

"He picked up a double dose of stubborn—his father on the one side and his grandfather on the other. My Hal could make a mule look like the soul of reason when he set his feet."

"Your husband wasn't on the Vance side? So you're—"

"Thomas's mother's mother. My name's Iris Swift—most everyone calls me Gran, though. Yes, and I see that mind of yours putting the next piece together—I'm not kin to Becky. Not blood kin. But she's mine, nonetheless. I raised the girl, even more than I raised Thomas. Because at least he had a mother to start with."

Judi had enough questions to run a quiz show all on her own, but she figured Gran would tell it the way she wanted to tell it, or not at all. In fear of *not at all,* Judi kept her mouth shut.

Gran gave an approving nod as she slowly moved into position in front of her chair. Judi positioned the cushion that raised Gran's foot to the right height.

"But it wasn't his genes I was thinking about when I said he came by his stubbornness honestly. It was his experiences. Come sit down here."

Judi pulled up a chair.

"My Denise died young. She had a heart condition nobody knew anything about until she collapsed, like you hear happening to athletes sometimes. Doctors never had any reason to think there was a problem. When she died, it about ripped Rick Vance, Thomas's father, to shreds. And Thomas was like a lost wraith. Hal had passed on the year before, so I moved out here from town. Things settled in. Rick was working the ranch, I was taking care of the two of them and teaching, and Thomas was growing like a weed. A towhead, he was, and a smart little dickens." She laughed. "He deserves that horse now, come to think of it!"

Judi envisioned a younger, blonder...happier Thomas.

He was adorable. But instead of making her smile, it made her sad that he'd changed so.

"Rick was a lonely man," Gran was saying. "I understood that, and never would've stood in his way. But I suppose it's hard to say you want to start dating when your dead wife's mother is running your house and caring for your son."

She sighed. Then gave her head a shake, as if to dispel the regret.

"Didn't see all that 'til too long after to make any difference. Maureen showed up the summer Thomas was fourteen. Came driving in with that blond hair shining and that smile gleaming. She and her girlfriends from St. Louis said there'd been a mix-up with their arrangements with the Lazy C—that's a dude ranch over the east end of the county—and Laura Carter suggested they try here. Laura tells a different tale, but in the end it's neither here nor there. After a week, the two girlfriends had moved on, and Rick and Maureen were off to Las Vegas to get married."

"A week?" Judi's voice rose in astonishment.

Gran's mouth stayed straight but her eyes crinkled. "Thomas is made of sterner stuff than his father was."

Judi felt heat rising up her throat. Did Gran think she…that they…? Why that was ridiculous. Besides, Maureen sounded like a femme fatale, and no one had ever accused Judi Monroe of being that. Not even Sterling who had supposedly been so head-over-heels in love with her that they had to get married right away.

She stood. "C'mon, Gran, let's get you into the recliner in the family room so you can watch TV in comfort while I clean up."

"There's more story to tell."

"You can tell me another time. You know what the doctor said about moving. Besides, the recliner's more comfortable for you."

"You're getting as bossy as Thomas," Gran grumbled.

But she gave a relieved grunt as Judi helped her into the recliner.

"What're you doing here?"

Judi shook her head. This business of disembodied voices speaking her thoughts had to quit.

She'd been entertaining that very thought—what was she doing here? These past few days she had not felt as carefree as she had earlier in the Great Escape. Probably a result of being around Thundercloud Thomas.

No, in fairness he wasn't alone.

Gran had become increasingly restless. This morning, when Judi had tried to check for signs of blood clots, as Thomas and the instructions had emphasized, Gran had swatted her hand. She'd grumbled about lunch—not the sandwich Judi served, but that she had to be served at all. Judging from the frazzled state Alice displayed when she'd left an hour ago, physical therapy hadn't gone well, either.

When Judi had ventured into Gran's room after Alice left, Gran had been in bed for a nap. And, she'd declared, she didn't want to be awakened by Judi rustling around, so she'd better get herself outside if she knew what was good for her.

Considering Gran's mood, Judi had taken the warning literally. She'd wandered toward the area she was interested in. But first Steve had driven in, calling hello. Next Gandy had come from the shed with something mechanical in a rag and started checking the remains of a truck. At that point, she'd decided she would wait for darkness for this particular chore.

She'd pretended to adjust her shoe, in case anyone was watching, and tucked the items under the porch steps where they were out of sight but easy to retrieve. For lack of anything better, she'd decided to circle the house, planning to widen her exploration after that. Halfway around the house she made a decision, tracked down Gandy and asked for tools and gloves.

Ever since, she'd been unearthing the remnants of a vegetable garden from the weeds and neglect that had nearly choked it. Roses along the house's side also needed tending—she'd get to those later.

As she pulled up thistles and scrub grass, she discovered spindly tomato plants, chewed-to-the-nub lettuce, a possible patch of carrots, sad-looking bean plants, and a vine she thought might be pumpkin.

But her mind had been on other matters.

Gran was not the only one proving testy. Becky tightened up like a guitar string given a good hard yank any time Thomas opened his mouth.

Last night at dinner when he'd asked how the fence was in an area where she'd gone to check mares and their foals, she'd gone sarcastic about how there was a huge gap in it and horses were caught up in the wire, but she'd left them there because she did exactly what she was told and no more than she was told.

Thomas had scowled, but had kept his response remarkably mild, considering.

"Helga? Did you hear me?"

Not a disembodied voice. Definitely Becky. Judi turned her head cautiously.

"Oh, hi, Becky. Were you talking to me?"

Becky looked around. "You see anybody else?" She sounded amused, not hostile.

Judi was tempted to point out that if Becky used that tone with Thomas she'd get a lot further. But she knew it would sound exactly like her mother used to sound to her as a teenager and kept a lid on temptation.

She'd been tempted before to say things to Becky that would have sounded like her mother—her own mother, not Becky's. Although Judi loved her mother dearly, it was a bit depressing to be turning into her at the age of twenty-eight.

Besides, it raised the question—what had happened to Becky's mother? The beautiful Maureen.

"Uh, no, I don't see anyone else. Sorry, I was thinking deep thoughts about zucchini and how it got named," she improvised.

"Oh, God, did Gran plant zucchini this spring?"

"Not that I'm aware of." Judi pondered the pile of vegetation she'd pulled up. "Not that I recognized, anyway."

Becky followed the direction of her gaze and giggled. "No great loss if you did pull it out. I'd be real surprised if Gran planted it. She didn't get in as big a garden as she usually does because her hip was bothering her and with the surgery and everybody working extra, nobody's been taking care of it. I'd forgotten all about it."

"It's pretty sad, but I think it'll come back with TLC and water. Here. Can you tie up this tomato plant while I hold it to this stake?"

"Is that what this is, a tomato plant?"

"Hey, don't let it hear you. You have to talk nice to get tomatoes to grow."

"Sorry, Mr. Tomato. I'd love for you to grow—so I can eat you,"

Judi chuckled. "Better watch out, it'll turn out to be zucchini, and I'll hold you to it about eating it." Except she wouldn't be here when these plants produced.

"Nah. Besides, the more I think about it the more I'm sure Gran wouldn't plant zucchini. She always says there's no need to plant it because Tellie Cushwell grows it and she's always bringing stuff over—zucchini bread, zucchini soup, zucchini muffins, zucchini casserole. I swear, one time she made zucchini ice cream."

"Good Lord! Does the woman have a zucchini fetish?"

"No. A Thomas fetish."

"You'll have to explain that one."

"Tellie's one of the women who's always after Thomas. About five years back we were paired up with the Cushwells for a roundup, and Tellie brought zucchini bread.

Thomas said he liked it—he'd been in the saddle all day without anything to eat, he probably would have liked cardboard. But that's all it took for Tellie.''

''She's not alone, I take it?''

''Nah. Just about every single, divorced or widowed woman in three counties has come through here with food at one time or another. Gandy was pulling for Mary Weed a while back because she makes brownies with chocolate chips and nuts.''

''But nothing came of it?''

''With Thomas? Give me a break. They're all over him and he's totally dense.'' She rolled her eyes. ''So then they start in on me. As if he'd want to hear anything from me these days.''

''Why's that?''

''Who knows. I just know he treats me like I'm about three years old. He won't even let me date.'' Judi knew that was a true grievance in the girl's mind, but the way Becky looked off to the side and wouldn't meet her eyes renewed Judi's belief there was more. ''Just because he's too blind to see that there's more to life than this ranch.''

''So you want to get off the ranch?''

''No!'' That was genuinely horrified, but quickly covered by teen ennui. ''I mean it's great, but it's not like we'd die if we didn't have the ranch. You know? But that's how Thomas acts. Sometimes I think it would do him a lot of good to take up one of these women on what they're offering.''

That surprised a laugh out of Judi, though the image was not particularly amusing to her. ''Becky!''

''Well, I mean it. It might make him lighten up. Besides, it would make one of the women really, really happy, and then maybe the rest would leave me alone. You wouldn't believe how they go on and on about his eyes.''

''They are pretty unusual, and—''

"They're just green," Becky interrupted firmly. "I like blue eyes."

Like Steve's. Ah, and now the he-won't-let-me-date complaint took on more weight. She'd noticed Becky's voice seemed to change when Steve was around. And he looked everywhere but at Becky—unless he thought no one was watching him.

First love could sure explain some of Becky's moodiness.

She'd also been in Becky's position as the younger sister of a hunky brother, which compounded the slings and arrows of a first love by contrast. She remembered all the females who'd figured little sister was both a prime source for information and a conduit for getting into Paul's good graces. And while all these women were trying to win over Paul, were any males paying attention to Judi? Oh, no.

"Green is pretty ordinary," she agreed. "You see it all over. Just look at this tomato plant. Green. Or that cottonwood tree. Green."

"Or grass."

"Or broccoli.

Becky giggled. "Or peas."

"Money."

"Frogs," Becky contributed with relish.

Judi supposed the girl deserved this mild bit of payback to Thomas. Would-be girlfriends weren't the only baggage a younger sister had to carry. Paul had considered himself a parental consultant. Not only did he tell Judi when he thought she was off track but he would tell their mother when he felt she needed more discipline, stricter rules or less freedom. How much worse must it be for Becky, since her older brother was also acting as her parent?

"Seaweed."

"Slimy seaweed."

What had finally helped Paul see her as a grown-up, most of the time, was his falling in love, then marrying Bette. Bette treated Judi as a friend and an equal. Because

Paul respected his wife—in addition to adoring her—he'd followed her lead.

All Becky needed to solve her problems with her over-bearing, overprotective brother was to have Thomas fall in love with someone beautiful and wise. Certainly too wise to get caught in the kind of mess Judi now found herself in. Yeah, Thomas would be real happy with his beautiful, smart wife. She wondered what Tellie Cushwell and Mary Weed looked like.

"Mold," Judi contributed grimly.

"Vom—"

"Oh, no—no more! Don't say it."

Becky giggled, but she complied. And as they moved on to the next pathetic tomato plant, the conversation shifted to horses, clothes, hair and cattle—an interesting mix that came absolutely naturally to Becky.

The teenager had her problems, but she knew where she belonged, knew where she fit, and was comfortable with her life. Judi stifled a sigh.

Good grief, what was she doing envying this girl her place in life? It must be part of the what-am-I-doing-here mood she'd been indulging in earlier.

Come to think of it, her mood probably had nothing to do with the people of the Diamond V ranch. After all, she wasn't destined to be a major part of their lives, so surely she wasn't letting their mood affect hers. More like this came as a natural result of being isolated from her family, uncertain of her future, without wheels and with the rem-nants of an egg on her head that could have been laid by an ostrich.

Sure, that must be the reason.

Chapter Four

Hah! Let Christine Welmer say now that she wasn't capable, didn't deserve responsibility, didn't have leadership qualities. Judi had retrieved the bag from under the steps, and she was zeroing in on her destination, and not even James Bond could have done a better job.

Well, Christine hadn't actually said any of those things. But she'd implied them by the way she'd acted—or not acted. The way she hadn't given Judi vital jobs, the way she hadn't listened to her comments, the way she hadn't acted on her suggestions.

It had started the first month Judi was with the company. When she'd told a prospective employee the truth about advancement possibilities. Christine had not approved. Especially when the employee didn't accept the company's low-ball offer. After that, Christine relegated her to exit interviews. That wasn't so bad at first, because after interviewing disgruntled employees she'd developed ideas about how the company could improve, along with the turnover statistics to prove it. Christine hadn't listened.

She sighed, her exultant mood dissipating with the exhalation.

Judi had wanted to leave. But she didn't know where she wanted to go. Running away without running to something seemed like exactly the sort of thing people expected from the youngest child of a successful lawyer from Lake Forest.

So, instead, she'd jumped into the whirlwind courtship with Sterling…and run away from her wedding to…here.

But what happened after these few weeks? What would she do after Geoff's "girlfriend" caught Sterling, and she could go back to Illinois without risking giving away the little she knew?

She'd be right back where she had been—no, worse, since she didn't have a job. Sterling had said there was no reason for her to work, he would provide for her. No reason for her to worry. Each place they went, he pointed out he was sparing no expense. He'd made a big deal of intending to sign over assets to her when they returned from the honeymoon. She'd figured the need to impress her with money was a foible—wasn't everyone entitled to them? She'd given in and quit her job.

Looking back she realized he hadn't offered to help with the wedding expenses, while she'd used up most of her savings. Her parents had offered to pay, but it didn't seem right for them to pay the premiums charged because Sterling wanted to get married fast.

Thank heavens she hadn't let him talk her into giving up her apartment. The lease ran for another six months and she'd planned to sublet it. At least she had a place to live when she went back.

In the meantime, she would use this time of being Helga Helgerson to figure out things about Judi Monroe. And while she was telling Thomas she couldn't remember her name, maybe she'd find out who she was.

* * *

From the porch, Thomas watched the shadow that was Helga Helgerson slip between the wreck of her car and the skeleton of a ranch pickup.

Now that he was more relaxed about the care she was giving Gran, he'd stayed away from the house the past few days. Not that he was avoiding her.

Even if he had been trying to avoid her it had been impossible. It seemed like any time he walked in the door she was there, in the kitchen. Or he heard her in the den with Gran, or down the hall in Gran's room.

Except late this afternoon when he'd come to the house to get a phone number. He'd found Gran napping in her room. But there was no sign of Helga anywhere.

Then he'd heard her laugh through the open window in the den.

When he looked out, he saw her and Becky amid the remnants of Gran's garden out back. Despite dirt-encrusted hands, Helga held a scrawny plant upright like it was made of spun glass while Becky tied it to a stake.

Without making out their words, he could hear and see the animation in his sister. Becky used to talk to him that way. But not lately.

A kind of bleakness pulsed through him. He pushed it away.

He was doing his damnedest to see to Becky's practical welfare. When he had that nailed down, maybe he'd have time to spare to figure out what was up with his younger sister. Or, if he was really lucky, she'd be past this stage by then.

Too bad females had to go through the teenage years to get from girl to woman. Though even the old lady in his life was giving him trouble these days. And that change he could pinpoint to the day Helga had crashed into their lives.

He'd turned from the window then, heading back out.

Not only had the phone number—his reason for going

to the house—gone completely out of his mind, but not until a few minutes ago did he realize he'd missed an ideal opportunity to search her things this afternoon.

This moment, with her out of the house, might count as another opportunity. But as soon as he'd spotted her he'd been determined to see what she was up to.

He'd sat here, silent and still, watching her work her way across the rutted driveway, along the pasture fence, past the barn, along the fence of the corral they mostly used for saddling horses, and in amongst Gandy's relics. Her pace hadn't varied. She hadn't suddenly looked around, but he still had the feeling her car had been her destination all along.

Maybe that was runaway suspiciousness on his part.

He was certain there was nothing for her to retrieve, because he and Gandy had examined it as thoroughly as they could short of stripping it down to its chassis.

She opened the rear passenger door, and he thought he heard a muffled gasp. The car's overhead light didn't come on—he doubted it had worked any time in the past decade. But she wouldn't have needed much light to get a general idea of the inside of her car.

When Gandy had objected to ripping the upholstery to check for anything hidden in the cushions, Thomas had said they'd tell Helga it must have happened when she hit the tree. Gandy had harrumphed and said he wasn't worried about explaining it to "Missy," he regretted the waste of perfectly good bench seats.

Gandy treated a vehicle that no longer ran the way the Indians used to treat the buffalo they hunted—making use and reuse of every scrap and fiber.

She disappeared from sight. No, that darker shadow was the top of her head, wasn't it? Was she sitting on the threshold of the door? Looking for something?

They'd taken the doors apart, too. And found nothing there or anywhere else,

It didn't ease his suspicions.

He was going to have to search her clothes. Sometime.

The idea was distasteful. Except for a little zing some-where down in the part of him that civilization hadn't reached yet—and that was even more distasteful.

She eased the car door closed with no more noise than a *click*.

She completed her circuit, coming up the porch steps quietly, but with no apparent effort at stealth.

"What were you doing?"

She squawked. "You scared the life out of me, Thomas!"

"Guilty conscience?"

"The good sense to not like people materializing out of the dark," she retorted.

He felt a grin tugging at the corners of his mouth. She didn't take any guff from him or anybody else, that was for sure. And she wasn't one of those women who got all fluttery when they were scared.

"I didn't materialize like something out of *Star Trek.* I was here all along."

"You don't exist in my universe until I see you." She didn't even draw a breath before adding, "All along?"

"All along. That's why I asked what you were doing."

"Out for an evening stroll."

"Odd place to stroll—over by the wrecks, and around the corral gate. Considering the horses go in and out of there, it's not safe for your shoes in daylight. At night—"

"Oh!" She balanced with one hand on the railing to bend her knee to see the bottom of her left shoe. When that sole came up clean, she shot him a triumphant look before shifting to check the other shoe. "Oh…yuck."

A short laugh surprised him before he could hold back. "Yuck? That's not the usual term for what you stepped in."

"My mother disapproves of the more technical terms," she informed him.

"So, you remember your mother."

Accompanied by a prim grimace she untied her shoe and held it by the shoelaces to carry it to where a collection of boots resided beside the door.

He thought she might keep going, heading inside and leaving him and his question to chill in the night air.

"I could say that I was making a general allusion under the presumption that at some point I, like most people—even you—have had a mother who cared about such matters, but I was really—" She peered up at him. "Oh, I'm sorry, I forgot—"

"You trying to get out of finishing what you were saying about remembering your mother when you've got such an all-powered terrible case of amnesia?"

She kept her eyes on his face, making him wish he had a hat on. "No. I was going to say that I do remember my mother very well—from my childhood. As Becky would tell you, it's common with amnesia to remember the distant past quite clearly. It's the more immediate past that gets murky."

She looked away on that last sentence, and her voice dropped.

Well, he shouldn't be surprised. Someone who wasn't sharing something as basic as her identity wasn't going to pour out her history.

"Just tell me this, are you a criminal?" He felt like a fool asking it, because what was she going to say? Yes, you got me, I'm a criminal, and I'll slink off now and leave you all be.

"Wh— No!"

She sounded indignant, but so would an accomplished liar or a con woman. But then she did something he couldn't figure. She chuckled.

"What's so funny?"

"Nothing. Sorry. Maybe it's another symptom of the blow to my head. Truly, Thomas, I'm not a criminal and I won't hurt your family or you."

And damned if she didn't more than half convince him.

"So what were you doing out walking in the, uh, *yuck?*"

"I wanted to get to know the place better. Interesting to see how little was left of that truck—at least I think it used to be a truck. Will my car look like that someday?"

"Probably, unless you tell Gandy hands-off. You know you'd do better in daylight. Not only for avoiding stepping in *yuck,* but because you could see what it is you're trying to get to know better." He'd let the sarcasm loose.

She leaned forward as if to confide in him. "Don't I know it—but I have this mean boss. Works me sunup to sundown. Never have a moment to myself, much less a chance to take a walk."

"I'll make sure Becky helps more. You shouldn't—"

"No, no, I was teasing, Thomas. Becky does help—a lot. And I'm starting to get the hang of it. I was just giving you a hard time because…well, because."

She'd placed her hand on his bare forearm, he felt the warmth and the smoothness against his skin. He looked down, and saw her fingers, pale and slender. He had the strangest urge to lift those fingers and kiss them.

Him! Who'd never kissed a woman's hand in his life. What was the matter with him?

Her. That's what was the matter with him. Helga or not Helga or whatever the hell her name was.

"Thomas, I—"

But he'd walked out from under her touch, and he had no intention of being lured back by her voice.

He let the door wheezing closed behind him be his good-night.

Judi squeezed moisturizer onto her right hand. The white lotion created as great a contrast against her skin as her hand had against Thomas's tanned and hair-dusted arm.

Before he'd walked away from her.

Very smooth, Judi. Yes, very smooth.

She'd made so many mistakes in that conversation. She'd never win Thomas over to neutral at this rate.

Was neutral where she wanted him?

She wasn't going to think about that, wasn't going to think about him. Think about something else. Like, her nails would never be the same, she thought a little desperately. Dishes and housework had wiped out the last vestiges of her prewedding manicure. Not even a wizard like Pammy could do much with what remained.

Oh, well, that's what acrylic was for—if she wanted stylish nails.

The more she thought about it, the more she liked the way her hands looked—utilitarian, capable, used.

Plus, they felt better than they had in the weeks she'd worn Sterling's engagement ring. People had said it was quite a rock and that's what it had felt like on her hand— a huge, heavy rock dragging her hand down. Maybe part of the drag had been the number of times he'd told her how valuable it was.

She smiled, knowing the ring and the rest were safely stowed away now.

The bracelet was the worst of all.

A heavy gold chain with gold and gem-studded mementos hanging off it passed as a gaudy and clunky version of an old-fashioned charm bracelet. Instead of following the sentimental tradition of gradually buying charms to mark special occasions, Sterling had presented it to her as a complete piece, with generic charms representing Chicago along with an elaborate rose and a heart totally out of proportion to the rest.

Hanging on her wrist it had felt like an anchor. Maybe that's why he'd insisted she wear it all the time. She rubbed her forehead.

Geoff's ''girlfriend'' could worry about what Sterling was or was not—but probably was—doing in Chicago. But there was no one other than her to try to straighten out this tension between Thomas and Becky.

As if he wanted to hear anything from me right now.

She rubbed extra moisturizer into her cuticle. Was there something significant about Becky's *right now?* Was there something going on that she, as a newcomer, wasn't aware of that was causing trouble?

If so, it seemed to have eluded Gran, too.

Yet the friction between Thomas and Becky clearly worried Gran at the very time she needed to put all her energy into healing, not mending strained sibling relationships.

So it was up to Judi.

"What smells so good?" Gran asked as Judi helped her out of bed with the leg band after a nap.

She wasn't taking naps every day, but the physical therapist, Alice, had come today, and that wore her out.

"Turkey. The trouble is—"

"Turkey? Good heavens, I didn't know we had any turkey."

"Found it way down in the freezer. Thomas said I could use anything in the freezer...." But judging by the woman's expression, this *anything* was a bad move.

Breakfasts were higher volume than she was used to, but pretty standard fare, with plenty of eggs, ham or bacon, toast and lots of toppings. For lunch, everyone was on his or her own, except Gran. Mostly they relied on sandwiches.

Planning the dinners was the biggest chore. In her pre-Sterling life, the only meals she'd planned were dinner parties she could count on one-and-a-half hands. She went out a good bit—every night with Sterling. When it came to cooking for herself, crackers and cheese qualified as a two-course meal.

Last night, digging into the chest freezer in the utility room, she'd found the turkey. She'd helped her mom with Thanksgiving year after year. She knew the drill on stuffing and basting and covering, then uncovering. And afterward…ah, turkey sandwiches.

Her mouth already watering, she'd hefted the package the size of a bowling ball out of the freezer. A night defrosting in the fridge and it should be ready.

She'd discovered this morning that she'd been overly optimistic. Who knew a bowling ball took this long to defrost? When she helped her mother, the turkey was always ready to go.

And this bird wouldn't fit in the microwave to speed defrosting. Between preparing the rest of the fixings, helping Gran and general housework, she'd soaked it in cool water the way the label said.

Finally, at four forty-three she stepped back from closing the oven door after placing the roasting pan inside.

At four-fifty-seven she put down her third attempt at the math, and realized she had a big problem.

Big, as in Thomas would be coming through that door for dinner at 7:30 p.m.

Big, as in by her calculations, she'd be ready to serve dinner at 10:30 p.m.

Then Gran had rung.

"Oh, Helga, this could be a problem. Turkey, I mean."

"You're telling me! This bird is never going to be done on time."

"That's just as well, because this family's not real fond of turkey."

"It won't be dry—I promise. Or tasteless like some you get in restaurants. And wait until you taste the stuffing. It's an old family recipe and—"

"I'm sure it's wonderful. It's just that we lost our taste for turkey and—"

A pounding of feet prepared them for Becky's exuberant arrival. "Turkey! You're fixing turkey!"

This did not sound like a hater of turkey. Judi looked from Becky to Gran, but the older woman wouldn't meet her eyes.

"Well, I was, but there's a problem…"

"I never bought turkey," Gran interrupted, "so how'd it get in the freezer?"

"I bought it," Becky said. "I don't know what Thomas's trouble is, but I decided that this year we'd have a Thanksgiving turkey. And it was on sale, so I bought it."

"You bought it for Thanksgiving? But it looked like it had been in the freezer for ages."

"Oh, I bought it a few months ago. I put it at the bottom for, uh, safekeeping."

In other words, so her grandmother wouldn't see it.

This was getting curiouser and curiouser. This family clearly had issues with turkey.

"Becky, you know—"

"I don't care. We haven't had turkey at Thanksgiving since I was nine years old—and I'm tired of not having it."

"Well," Judi said, inserting calm into the rising tension, "if you're going to have one this year, you'll have to buy another one because this guy's already cooking. Although he's not cooking fast enough. That's what I've been trying to tell you all. I messed up and didn't leave enough time for him to defrost, so there won't be any turkey tonight. Maybe for breakfast, but not tonight."

In one of her lightning changes of mood, Becky giggled. "Turkey for breakfast?"

"Sure. That solves tomorrow morning's breakfast, but what about tonight?"

"How about scrambled eggs?"

They were all chuckling about that when they filed into the kitchen.

Judi decided on pork chops, based on what could be defrosted in the microwave and cooked on the range, since the oven was occupied. For fruit salad, Gran cut up apples and oranges on a board set across the arms of her chair.

It wasn't the best working surface, but at least being useful boosted Gran's mood.

Still, Judi noticed Gran checking the clock over the sink and glancing out the door much more often than usual. It had to be Thomas's reaction to the turkey that had her concerned. And Becky was talking a mile-a-minute about nothing, which didn't soothe Judi's nerves.

By the time boot heels sounded on the porch and the door swung open, Judi half expected them all to scream like overwrought actresses in a horror movie.

Thomas stopped inside the door and took a deep sniff.

"It's turkey," Becky's defiant declaration was too loud.

But Thomas only looked at his sister with a faintly puzzled frown. When he extended the look to her, Judi discovered an urgent need to find the pot holder she wouldn't need for another five or six minutes. Be prepared, put that pot holder on early—that was her motto. And make sure you watch what you're doing while you pull it on. Wouldn't want to get your fingers caught in the seam and—

"Smells great, doesn't it?" Becky demanded.

Judi looked up through her bangs to see Thomas look toward the stove top.

"Smallest turkey I've ever seen if it fits in that pan," he said mildly.

Surprised laughter spurted out of Judi. "Pork chops in the pan. Turkey's in the oven. I got a late start and it's not going to be done until way past dinnertime. So we're having pork chops for dinner and—"

"Turkey for breakfast."

"Well, I don't know about that. That was a joke. We—"

But Becky was not in a soft-pedaling frame of mind. "I bought the turkey for Thanksgiving, but Helga found it and started cooking it. I'm going to buy another one and we're going to have it for Thanksgiving. No matter what. What do you have to say about that, Thomas?"

If the teenager had been a prize fighter, she would have been inviting a knockout with that chin stuck out that way. As Thomas opened his mouth, Judi closed her eyes. She never had liked boxing.

"Aren't we ever going to have beef?" he asked. "This is a cattle ranch you know. It's how we earn our money. Helga's cooked chicken, shrimp, more chicken, and now turkey and pork chops. How about equal time for beef?"

Her eyes popped open. She hadn't thought about that. Not once.

Becky laughed—it sounded nervous for the first few seconds then turned genuine—and she soon joined in.

"Okay, equal time for beef."

While Becky set the table with the high spirits of someone who has faced down a major challenge, Judi decided she'd let her imagination get away with her.

But then she heard Gran say quietly to Thomas, "You okay with this?"

He raised a brow at her. "As long as it's eatable, why wouldn't I be?"

"Last time anybody made turkey in this house, you ended up throwing the whole meal out in the garbage."

For a split second, he didn't seem to remember. Then he stiffened. "That was a long time ago."

"If you want to talk about it—"

"It's best forgotten."

Gran seemed a little older when she said, "Okay, Thomas."

Thomas wasted no time eating his pork chops and excusing himself.

Judi cleaned up the kitchen, checked on the turkey— yup, right on track to finish at 10:30 p.m.—watched the end of a TV news magazine with Gran, then assisted her through her nightly routine.

Only after Gran was in bed and Judi had drawn the

covers up over the bolster to within Gran's reach did she ask the question that had been clamoring for release.

"So what's the deal with turkey?"

"It's a long story."

Judi pulled up the chair and sat. "I've got till the timer goes off on the oven."

"You doing something with that turkey tonight? You'll be up awfully late."

"Yes, I will. Now, let's talk turkey."

Gran gave a wan smile. "It goes back to what I was telling you about Maureen, Becky's mother. It didn't take but weeks to see ranch life wasn't her cup of tea. She got pregnant right off, and you'd have thought she was the first female in the history of the world to have morning sickness and swollen ankles. Rick asked if I could see my way clear to staying, to help out some." She snorted. "Help out. Like we didn't both know I'd be doing all the work. I had a real soft spot for Rick—he'd made my girl happy—but still, I'd've moved out if it hadn't been for Thomas. He needed a buffer between him and his stepmother."

"He and Maureen didn't get along?"

"More like they saw each other as alien species. She kept saying it was too late for Rick, but she could make a gentleman out of Thomas—as if dressing fancy and using four forks ever made anyone a gentleman. As for Thomas, he made it real clear what he thought of her city ways. It got better when Becky came along. Thomas and Rick pure adored her and Maureen acted like she was a princess."

"But...but she left Becky behind," Judi blurted out. "I'm sorry, I know it's none of my business, and—"

"If folks only paid attention to what was their business this would be a damned silent world. Besides, it's the truth. When Maureen picked up and went, she left her five-year-old daughter behind." She shrugged. "I suppose you'd have to be a psychologist to know why. I suspect Thomas would tell you—''

As if she could get Thomas Vance to tell her anything!

''—that it was because Maureen didn't want a kid to slow her down as she tried the fast lane. Probably some truth to that. But I'd say mostly she got bored. And Becky wasn't the pliable little doll she'd been as a baby. She'd always had a mind of her own and by five she was more than capable of holding her own with her mother.''

''Five? Becky said the last turkey Thanksgiving dinner was when she was nine.''

''Maureen first left when Becky was five, but even after the divorce was final, Maureen would show up out of the blue now and then. Never knew for sure, but I always figured she'd come when she was having trouble out there in the fast lane. She would throw everybody into a tizzy thinking maybe this time she'd stay, then she'd get bored, wheedle money out of Rick and sweep out again. That Thanksgiving dinner was the last time. There was a blowup. Things were said. And Thomas… Well, after that, Maureen got some big job with an advertising firm in Seattle and she didn't come back. Maybe she didn't need Rick's help anymore or maybe she wasn't bored anymore. Maybe something else.''

Clearly Gran wasn't going to say what that something else might be.

''And turkey's associated with all that?''

Gran didn't meet her eyes. ''Yeah. It brings all those memories up again, just like having you around does—at least for Thomas.''

''Me? What do I have to do with this?''

''You're young, pretty, from somewhere else and you show up out of the blue. Doesn't take a diagram to see the possible connection in Thomas's head.''

''So he's viewing me the way he views his stepmother?''

''I wouldn't say precisely that.''

Judi decided to ignore the chuckle that accompanied the words.

It made sense that he was wary of women showing up the way she had, the way Maureen had. It could even explain that sensation of stormy weather brewing whenever she was around Thomas. That had to be it.

On the other hand, the man had to get the idea through his head that the past was the past, and she was not Maureen Vance.

"I'll tell you one thing, Gran, I am not throwing out that turkey—I worked too hard on it. And if Thomas doesn't like it he can go hungry. It's about time he gets over his problems with turkey."

A slow smile spread across Gran's face. "Thatagirl. That might just be what's needed."

Humming, Judi snapped the cover onto the large container where she'd put the stuffing, then put it and two packets of sliced turkey in the refrigerator.

Behind her she heard the rustle of papers as Thomas dug into the pile on the desk, muttering. He didn't sound happy.

To someone listening to her humming and his muttering, it might sound like one of those counterpoint duets in an opera, when one character was upbeat and happy and the other was—

A whoosh of papers sliding off the desk segued into an oath.

Cranky.

Yup, the other singer in this duet was definitely cranky.

He bent over, scooped up the papers and thudded them on the desk, obscuring the one open area he'd created.

She set to work cutting the rest of the turkey to freeze for later meals. Maybe she'd make a casserole. Hah! Thomas wouldn't even know he was being fed turkey.

And soup. Gran had a recipe, and helping with the preparations should help her mood. Which brought to mind something Judi wanted to ask about. "Thomas?"

"What *is* that you keep humming?" He sounded thoroughly exasperated. Possibly with her for humming. Possibly with himself for asking.

"The Chicago Bears fight song: *Bear Down, Chicago Bears.*"

"You're from Chicago?"

She'd answered automatically. Now she opened her mouth, closed it, then turned away from him. "I don't know."

For the first time she wondered if the reason she had always been such a bad liar was because she didn't like the way it made her feel.

He grunted, flipping through the papers that had fallen, extracting one, then looking around as if searching for a place to put it.

His desk needed organizing, but he also had to be tired. He seemed to stay up every night working at the desk, yet rise with the summer dawn. From comments from the others, this had been his routine for the past year. The candle he'd been burning at both ends had to be down to a stub.

"Thomas. You said to come to you about anything about Gran, right?"

"What's wrong?"

"It's not wrong. Just something that could be better."

The line of his shoulders seemed to ease, but he still demanded, "What?"

"Gran could use a desk that rolls. Nothing fancy, just a smoothed board on legs with casters on the bottom would do, as long as she can push it or pull it easily." She took the sketch she'd made to him. "I found a board to put across the chair, but it's not real steady and if she wants to get up…"

Thomas was already nodding. "Keith is pretty good at that sort of thing. I'll talk to him about it."

"I could talk to him."

He looked up, with the slant of his brows announcing his surprise. ''You?''

''Sure, why not? You think I'm not capable of discussing a simple project with one of your employees? I'm not incompetent you know.''

''Who said you were?''

His rhetorical retort stopped her cold. There'd been people who'd acted it without ever quite saying it. The high-school counselor had rolled his eyes when she'd said she didn't know what she wanted to do. The college job-fair recruiter had sniffed at her liberal arts degree and said specialization was the way to get ahead. And of course there had been her boss, Christine Welmer.

But those people were in her past. What had she just told Gran about Thomas needing to get over the past? And Thomas, who was looking at her with curiosity mixing into the surprise in his green eyes, was none of those people.

''Sorry. Guess you hit one of my buttons.''

''Guess I did. So, who said you were incompetent?''

He really wanted to know? That, and the fact that she wanted to tell him, stopped her as completely as when she'd thought it was rhetorical.

She'd never talked to anybody about the first two incidents. They'd seemed fleeting, and her family and friends would have told her she could do anything she set her mind to. That was the problem, she didn't know what she wanted to set her mind to. She'd never had a passion like Paul, with the antique toys he appraised, or her cousin Tris, with her efforts to preserve historic buildings. She liked variety, and challenge.

Neither of which she'd had in her late, unlamented job as Christine's assistant.

Her family and friends had known she wasn't particularly happy in her job, but she'd explained it as a personality clash, and they'd accepted that.

She couldn't very well tell Thomas that. He'd wonder

not only how she remembered her recent boss, but how she'd gone from the assistant to the head of Human Resources for a major medical supply company outside of Chicago to a health aide working for an agency in South Dakota.

"I don't remember anyone saying it." Her frustration came through, which made it sound all the more convincing—and nudged her guilt up another notch. This masquerade had definite down sides.

"Go ahead and talk to Keith. It'll be one less thing that needs doing."

"What are you doing?" she asked, glad to steer the topic in a new direction.

"Paperwork."

"I'd figured that much out on my own. What kind?"

"Paying bills. Keeping track of orders. Filling out forms for the fall sales. Doing the payroll and taxes for Gandy, Keith and Steve."

"I could do that for you when I have a chance."

His head came around sharply. "Why?"

She propped her hands on her hips. "Because maybe if I did that you'd get more sleep and then you wouldn't be such a grouch. I know that's a long shot, but I'm willing to give it a try if you are. At least I could organize that mess so you'd have room to work."

Judi had done that task for Christine, too. She just hoped the woman was suffering mightily now that her organizing genie had left.

He looked at the stacks of paper, as if mentally cataloguing what damage she might do.

"If you're worried about me stealing money or financial information, you could lock that up."

But he didn't respond to her sharp tone at all the way she'd expected. His mouth gave that quirk, and he said, "If you can find anything worth your while to steal, more power to you. And I'd be obliged if you organized this desk. Though I'm making no promises about it changing my mood.''

''That's all right. I wouldn't recognize you if you weren't frowning.''

He smiled then, and Judi almost didn't recognize him.

She turned around and looked for something to keep her occupied at the far end of the kitchen, while a voice in the back of her head started screaming, *Uh-oh, uh-oh.*

''Hey, what are you doing?''

His voice overrode the little voice, and she looked down at her hands. ''Emptying out the last of this pot of coffee.''

''Don't. I'll drink it in the morning.''

''You're kidding, right?'' His face said, no. ''Why would you drink this? There's fresh coffee every morning.'' Not great coffee—she doubted the aged coffeemaker had ever been capable of great coffee and it sure wasn't now—but at least fresh coffee.

''Yeah, because I start it going when I get up. But I need something to get the blood moving while the first pot's brewing.''

She looked down at the sludge in the pot again. ''No wonder you're cranky.''

If she hadn't known better, she'd have thought the sound that came next was a chuckle.

Chapter Five

Thomas arrived at the bottom of the porch steps on his way into the house as Judi reached the top of the steps. She couldn't resist firsthand exposure to the bright blue sky, fluffy clouds and easy breeze of this Thursday.

He looked up, and they both hesitated.

"Something wrong?" he demanded. The man had to get out of the habit of expecting the worst.

"No. Why would something be wrong?"

"Thought you might be looking for me. If something happened with Gran, or—"

"I'd take care of it myself or call 9-1-1. I know you're a busy man. I wouldn't call you away from your work." Now, in her second week at the Diamond V ranch, she had never seen him take a break from his long, hard hours.

"If something happened with Gran, you sure as hell better call me away from my work. That's what the cell phone number's for."

It wasn't the most eloquent speech she'd heard, but the

love and concern he felt for his grandmother came through loud and clear. It did him credit.

Her charitable attitude toward him lasted for somewhat less than fifteen seconds—the time it took him to open his mouth again.

He propped his left foot two steps up from where he was standing and rested his hand on his now horizontal thigh.

"Good Lord, I keep thinking I've seen the least practical outfit possible for a ranch, and you keep proving me wrong."

She wasn't too happy with what she was wearing today either. The cotton skirt was perfect for pulling on over a swimsuit to sit at a poolside bar in the Caribbean. But it was so short that it made doing housework an adventure in exposure. Even with no one else around, she'd felt odd bending down to get the scouring pad.

And the strip of midriff exposed by a halter top designed for sultry breezes felt a little chilly in the Wyoming wind.

Eliminating the three bathing suits, beach coverups and lacy nightwear left about half the items in the suitcase. With the days on the road before she'd reached here... She really had to do laundry.

Aiming for cool dignity, she took two steps down, hoping he would move aside. He didn't budge.

"What are you, the fashion police?"

"It's not fashion I'm wondering about, it's common sense."

"Well, fashion police or otherwise, unless you intend to arrest me, I'd appreciate it if you let me get by and go for my walk."

"I wouldn't dream of adding handcuffs to that getup." He nodded toward her woven sandals. "But if you wear those out it won't be only a shoe covered with, uh, yuck."

Oh, how she wanted to keep going. To ignore him with

high disdain. But he was right. If she stepped in anything, the low, open sandals would provide no protection.

She pivoted and went up the stairs quickly. Being careful of the skirt, she bent at the knees to reach for the canvas shoes she'd worn during her nocturnal survey. She had to sit on the bench to unbuckle the sandals or risk giving him a peep show. If he would just go in the house… No, of course not, he had to make it difficult.

She finished changing shoes, and headed down the stairs. He hadn't moved.

"Satisfied?"

"Makes no difference to me. They're your feet. I was just being neighborly."

"Well, then, you wouldn't mind doing me a neighborly favor, would you?" Before he could answer, she took his unresisting hand from his thigh and hooked the back strap of each sandal over his fingers. "Take these inside for me, will you?"

She didn't look back until she was well down the drive. He still hadn't moved.

Thomas reined Dickens to a stop in the ring and gave him a pat on the neck and the words of praise he'd earned.

Under other circumstances he would have worked a little longer on neck reining. But he didn't want to risk undoing the good they'd achieved by having a bad session now. And that could happen when neither man nor beast had his mind entirely on what they were doing.

It didn't matter that he hadn't looked toward her or spoken to her. He was still aware of Helga standing outside the corral fence, silently watching. Dickens was just as aware of her—well, no, probably not just as aware.

When she'd turned around on the stairs forty minutes ago, and the bottom of that short-short skirt had flared out he'd thought he was going to have a coronary. The flare had given him a glimpse of the top of a smooth thigh curving in to where it would round out to her firm behind.

That glimpse had produced recall of his arm wrapped around her there after he'd knocked her off the chair. Along with recall of the rest of her being pressed against him, her breasts so close he could have put his mouth over a nipple outlined by fabric drawn taut.

When she'd started up the stairs, with a tiny bounce of irritation on each step, he'd known he wasn't in danger from a coronary's loss of blood supply. Hell, no, blood flow was fine. Just in a different region.

He could only be grateful that having his one foot on the step above meant his thigh provided cover. And that no one had come along to ask why he remained on the porch stairs for several minutes after she left.

The memory was going to put him back in the same state if he didn't snap out of it. He dismounted—while he could—and set to work unsaddling Dickens.

The horse shifted his weight as Thomas turned back and he thought he noticed something. He removed the saddle blanket, walked Dickens again to make sure, then looked around. The shed door was locked. The only soul in sight was Helga. He looked at her for the first time.

"Have you seen Gandy?"

"He left for town about twenty minutes ago."

He swallowed down the curse that might have relieved his feelings but would make Dickens edgier. "I could use help. Unless you're afraid of horses or—"

"Nope. You want me in there?" She was already on her way.

She spoke softly to Dickens from behind him, but also skirted his rear end, the way wise people did in case the horse decided to be startled anyway. That confirmed his impression that she'd been around horses before.

"He picked up a stone?"

And she was observant.

"Yeah. Get around to his other side," he instructed while he tied the reins to the fence. "If he starts to shift toward you, hold the pressure on his side. Don't shove him, just hold steady. But if he keeps coming, get out of the way." He pulled his pocketknife out and opened the blade. "Don't take chances."

"That's a good idea, isn't it, Dickens?" Her voice changed when she talked to the horse.

She kept talking as he raised the horse's left front leg and bent the knee across his thigh to get a good angle. Dickens naturally shifted his weight to accommodate having one less leg to support himself. He started to shift even further though, as if to pull away from Thomas's hold, then stopped when he met the pressure of Helga's hands. And maybe when he heard her voice.

It didn't get more gentle exactly, because even when she was being sassy, she didn't get sharp. And no baby talk the way some folks did with animals. Instead, her tone remained conversational, like she was chatting while rocking on the porch swing. But even slower and softer.

He closed his knife and released Dickens's foot. "Done."

"Was it deep?"

"Not bad." He untied the reins.

"Now what?" she asked, like they were a team.

"I'm gonna let him out in the pasture."

"Oh, good. I haven't been there yet." She fell in step on the other side of Dickens's head.

"A lot of ground, a little grass and a few horses."

"I promise to *ooh* and *ah* in admiration." The horse nudged her shoulder. She chuckled and rubbed his head. "Besides, Dickens likes me."

"Horses don't like or dislike people. They respect people who treat them fair, and lead their herd."

"You're jealous because he thinks you're a grump."

"You probably just smell good from being in the kitchen." She did smell good, but not from cooking. He'd noticed that those first moments when he'd pulled her dented car door open and bent down. And then when he'd touched her...

"Here's the pasture." As if she couldn't see that—but he'd had to say something to interrupt his own thoughts. "Like I told you, not much to see."

He opened the gate, unhooked Dickens and let him loose, before rejoining her.

"Oh, look at those beauties," she said softly as two mares and their foals came to the fence that divided this pasture from theirs. They seemed to be checking out Dickens's return and showing curiosity about the humans nearby. "Are you boarding them? Or are those yours?"

"They're ours. We've been breeding for about five years. Starting to show success with them."

She turned to him with a smile that said she understood his pride, even though he'd tried to downplay it.

"Great success, I bet—they're gorgeous. It's a beautiful ranch, Thomas. And Gandy says it's mostly your doing."

She'd promised to *ooh* and *ah,* but she hadn't said she'd sound so darn sincere that it would warm him despite himself.

He bent and plucked the top off a long blade of grass. Rolling it between his fingers as if to test what it was made of, he said, "You haven't seen most of it."

"I still hope to get jeans and see the rest, but I've seen enough to know it's beautiful." She didn't concede an inch.

"Beautiful, huh? Too bad beautiful doesn't pay better."

She scowled at him. "Back to money? Money isn't the most important thing you know, Thomas."

"It's right up there when you don't have enough. We're holding our own. But cut away a quarter of the acreage, and red ink will be our best product."

"Why on earth would you cut away a quarter of the acreage?"

"I wouldn't. I'm doing my damnedest to hold it together."

"Okay, now you've lost me."

"What it boils down to is there's somebody with the

right to sell a quarter of the ranch come July 15. And if I don't have the money to meet the price they've set, they'll sell it to somebody else."

"Oh, Thomas…" He felt that low murmur of his name like a balm through his soul—and a sizzle in his bloodstream. "But wouldn't three-quarters still be okay?"

Grateful to address something he understood, he told her, "We'd be on the razor's edge. Everything's geared to the acreage we've got. If we lose a quarter, we've got too many head. We could sell—probably at a loss after expenses with the way the market is. Or we could lease grazing acreage, but there's the leasing fee and the added cost of moving head, and working them somewhere else. Or we could sell some of the younger horses."

"Oh, Thomas, you don't want to do that!"

"I don't want to do any of it. I won't have a choice unless I get that money. And listen, don't go talking to Becky about this. She knows things are tight—we're down a few hands—but not the details."

He braced for her to make a comment about telling her when Becky didn't know, but instead she looked thoughtful. "That's why the training fee for Dickens is so important?"

Nobody ever said she was stupid. "Yeah."

"How close are you?"

"If I can collect that fee for training Dickens along with the early deadline bonus, I'll make it. It'll be tight for a few years, but we'll be okay."

"Well, then, you'll have to be sure Dickens is trained so well and so early you'll not only get your fee, but a bonus on the bonus!"

"Just like that, huh?" Feeling a lift from her energy, her confidence, he smiled.

"Just like that."

And damned if he didn't almost believe her.

"You're too young to date."

Judi stilled the porch swing when she heard Thomas

wave that red flag in front of Becky's fire-breathing fury.

"I'm fifteen!"

Judi had helped Gran get up and prepare for the day as usual, then left her in privacy to make her final touches, and had taken a seat on the porch swing with a cup of coffee to enjoy the morning peace. A peace shattered by the rising voices from inside the kitchen. These two particular voices seemed to rise with increasing frequency.

"Like I said, too young. We'll talk about it when you're sixteen."

"Then I'll get my license and I'll drive away from here and never look back."

Becky flounced out, swinging the screen door wide so it slapped closed with a jolt that Judi felt through the porch floor. Becky never noticed Judi sitting there, as she ran down the porch stairs and around the house.

Thomas followed more slowly, his widespread hand catching the screen door on one of its echoing rebounds. He looked in the direction his sister had gone.

Was his guard dropping or was she getting better at reading his expression? These battles with Becky pained him. And he didn't have a clue what to do about them.

That's why she kept her voice gentle when she said, "Give it up, Thomas."

After a flicker of hesitation, he turned, showing her a face devoid of emotion, and stepped onto the porch, letting the door close gently behind him. "Give what up?"

"You'll never be her hero again."

His guard dropped for an instant. "I'd just be happy to be her friend again."

"You were never friends before, Thomas. Because you were never close to being equals. Friendship takes level ground, and you were always way up on the hill until now. You're her big brother, and you were her hero. But now she's growing up."

His disbelief had been growing like grains of sand trickling onto one side of a seesaw, and when the "Becky growing up" grain—well, maybe that one was more like a boulder—hit the seat, it dropped down, sending the seesaw's opposite end—the end holding Thomas's irritation—shooting up.

"She's a kid," he snapped. "Not to mention a complete stranger to you up until two weeks ago."

"She's a kid, and she's a woman, both and neither, all at the same time. She's finding her path to being an adult. If you won't let her take steps down that path while she still lives here as part of the family—"

"Becky would never run away."

She huffed out a breath in exasperation. "I wonder how many families have said that before a teenager ran away. But it doesn't have to be that way. There are a thousand other ways to get off the main road than being a runaway."

She stood, setting the swing rocking by the abruptness of her move. "And I know more about her after two weeks than you do after fifteen years because I've been there, being the much younger sister of an accomplished and bossy older brother. And because I pay attention."

She reached the door, then looked back. She didn't want to leave that shot as her final word on the subject. Her final word on the subject today, she mentally amended. She knew herself too well to think she'd let it drop for good.

"I'm telling you that you've never been Becky's friend up 'til now, Thomas. And you won't be while she's working at finding her own way. But if you don't mess it up, you will be friends in the future."

Thomas came in after dark, weary and grimy from a full day of haying.

There was a note on the counter.

2 plates in the fridge. Microwave one covered in plastic for 2 minutes on high. Do NOT microwave the one covered in foil. Coffee still warm.

Bossy little thing.

He found himself almost grinning as he pulled out the plates and followed the instructions. He'd had Gandy bring him food so he wouldn't waste any daylight. But if he was going to get the paperwork that needed doing finished tonight, he'd need more to keep him going.

As if in a trance, he stared at the countdown on the microwave, coming to when it dinged. He poured coffee, grabbed a fork and took both plates and headed toward his desk.

Three feet away, he stopped dead.

He could see the desktop's wooden surface, scars, dings and burn marks and all. To one side was a metal rack with different colored file folders hooked between its sides. And smack-dab in the middle rested another note, this one longer.

I couldn't get this done until Gandy brought the folders and holder back from town yesterday. The labels should be clear. The folders are color-coded—see list on back of this page. Be sure to check the beige folder first—those are things I think should be thrown out, but you said not to throw anything out. The red folder has items that I couldn't categorize.

After you get used to this, we can organize the drawers.

If you can't find something you need, wake me up.

Wake her up. Go into her room and put his hand to her warm sleeping shoulder, maybe on the bare skin around a narrow strap. Smell the sweet spice that surrounded her.

Watch her eyes open, and look up at him. See her
breathing change. Hear her say his name…

And ask her where the folder with the IRS quarterly
payment form was.

His bark of laughter was as much pained as amused.

What the hell was he thinking? If he went into her room
it should be to search her things—and he was going to do
that. First chance he got. He was going to find out who
she really was. And then he'd stop this damned nonsense
of fantasizing about a stranger from nowhere who'd be
going back there as soon as Gran healed up.

He speared a piece of meat loaf and got to work.

Thomas's timing couldn't have been worse from Judi's
perspective.

Keith gave her a pleading look as Thomas stepped into
the kitchen, and she returned her most reassuring smile.

She'd suspected the lanky, taciturn ranchhand wasn't
happy. When she'd asked him about the desk for Gran,
she'd been sure of it. Not because he said no—he said
he'd be happy to do that for Gran—but because of the
way he said yes. The way he asked if Thomas knew about
it, and if Thomas had said it was okay and if Thomas had
approved the plans.

She'd withstood the temptation to tell him to forget
Thomas, and had simply said that the design should be
decided between him, as the builder, and Gran, as the user.
From that point, it had taken days of patiently building up
his confidence in her to get him to start to say what was
bothering him.

It was a lot like doing an exit interview. At first, hardly
anybody wanted to say the real reason they were leaving.
They wanted to shake the dust of a crummy job off their
feet. But if you were patient enough and understanding
enough, you could get to the truth. That was important for
an organization, at least it could have been if the head of
Human Resources had been willing to listen.

But this was even more important with Keith—because it could prevent there ever being an exit interview, and Thomas losing help he needed.

Keith had just opened up as he checked the fit of the desk around Gran's chair when Thomas walked in.

Thomas gave Keith a surprised look, then frowned. Was that the man's reaction to everything?

"Thought you were going to check the herd at Bacon Creek today."

"You told me to finish the desk for Gran."

"Oh, right." Thomas took his hat off and ran his hand through his hair as he asked her, "Have there been any calls from a Harry Totten?"

"No. Want me to take a message if there is?"

"No. Give him my cell phone number. I need to talk to him today." Without waiting for a response, he moved over to peer at Keith's work. "Those braces aren't going to hold much weight. Better replace them with bigger ones, even if it means another day away from work. Don't want this thing collapsing on Gran's lap."

Judi wasn't a violent person. Even as a kid she'd seldom resorted to hitting people. But she would have been willing to make an exception at the moment if it would have gotten through to Thomas without wounding Keith's pride even further.

He had dropped his head and was fiddling with the roller on one leg. He wasn't going to say anything. And then one day he'd decide he was sick of it, and he'd quit. And Thomas would never know why.

"Actually," she started as she wiped her hands and came toward them. "Keith was telling me that he talked the matter over with Gran. Weren't you?"

"Uh, yeah."

He didn't exactly take the ball and run with it, so she shoved it more firmly into his gut. "Go ahead, tell Thomas about that."

"I showed Gran a few designs, asked which one she'd

like—she said she'd rather have it lighter and easier to move. I told her it couldn't hold up to a lot of weight, but she said her knitting and such didn't weigh that much.''

"So if you don't go putting granite blocks on it, everything should be fine."

Thomas shot her a look then focused on Keith. "As long as it's what Gran wants, that's fine. How soon can you be done?"

"Couple hours each of the next two days and that should take care of it."

"Okay." He turned to leave, then stopped. "Hey, Helga."

"What?" If there was a bit of snap to that, she figured she was entitled.

"I've been meaning to thank you for cleaning up the desk. It's a real help."

"You're welcome," she said as he headed out.

If that wasn't just like Thomas—get her all righteously indignant, then be nice. What a rotten trick.

Thomas straightened from the well he'd been checking and watched the old silver truck come bouncing toward him. It had to be Helga behind that wheel. No one else would be going that slowly. And no one else would be winding around like she was trying to avoid running over sagebrush.

To cut the agony of suspense, he started toward her.

"Something wrong?" he shouted when he was close enough. "You should have called me on the cell phone."

"I have been calling on the cell phone—that's what's wrong!"

He pulled it from the case clipped to his belt. Damn! The battery was dead.

He must have said something, because she shouted, "What?"

"Battery! Shut off that truck!" But she already had, and

the end of his shout echoed across the hills. "I said, the battery on the cell phone's out. Is it Gran? Is—"

"Gran's fine. But Harry Totten called. I gave him the cell number. When he couldn't get you he called back. He said you need numbers from him, and he's leaving tonight for two weeks, so I wrote it all down."

He looked over the paper she handed him. Her neat handwriting listed the acreages and leasing prices of places he'd scouted in case he needed them next spring...in case he couldn't keep the Diamond V intact. It was all clear and concise. It wasn't her fault the figures made him feel like he'd been gored in the gut.

"Thank you. You didn't have to do all this. It's not part of your job."

She gave him a rather odd look. "I was happy to do it. It was a small thing I could do that I hoped might contribute to the Diamond V. You know there are other people who would like to contribute more, and who would if you'd let them."

"Let them?" he gave a rueful chuckle. "Just let these people get within a mile of me, and I'll rope 'em in."

"You don't need to go a mile. Keith could do a lot for you, for the ranch."

He felt like he'd been transported from one conversation to another without ever moving an inch.

"What are you talking about?"

"I'm talking about Keith wanting respect. He wants the work he does to be appreciated, and respected. And if it were, then he'd do so much more."

"Keith knows I respect his work."

"How would he know that? By the way you assumed he hadn't thought through the building of that rolling desk? The way you made it sound like building it for Gran was his way of getting out of work?"

"I didn't say that."

"'Those braces aren't going to hold. Use bigger ones so it doesn't fall apart and crush Gran. Even if it means another day you're not working.' Sound familiar? And that was an extra chore he did to help out Gran. You really think he knows how much you appreciate his doing that? Much less that you appreciate the regular work he does? Tell me again, how does he know you appreciate his work?''

''Because I keep him hired on here.''

''Oh, right, that's plenty enough praise for anyone. What was I thinking?''

''I'm not in a position to be handing out raises or bonuses or stock options.''

''There you go again, thinking it has to do with money. Money's not the solution. Talk to the man. Let him know you appreciate what he does. *And* show him. Give him responsibility for something. Let him be in charge of something, and don't meddle with it.''

''Like what? You going to tell me that, too?''

''No,'' she said with great dignity. ''I'm going to trust you to come up with the specifics. I have every confidence that you'll pick the right solution.''

''Gee, thanks.''

''You're welcome.''

Then the woman grinned at him. And darned if he didn't grin back.

''Hi, Gandy. Gran said to come out here and bring you and Thomas lunch.''

Apparently Gran figured since Judi had found Thomas the day before, she was now certified to roam the ranch in the truck. Either that or Gran wanted her out of her hair.

''I'll be real pleased to have mine, Missy.'' He gave her a smile and a nod as he took the container from her and peeled back the top with a long sniff of appreciation. ''But this is no time to be interrupting Thomas.''

After handing Gandy a napkin, she looked to where Thomas sat astride Dickens, neither one of them moving.

''What's he doing?''

Gandy finished a large bite then said, "You know the old saying about you can lead a horse to water but you can't make him drink?"

"Sure."

"You don't know for sure until you get him near the water, so first you've gotta lead him to water. But Dickens decided he wasn't going to follow the rest down that trail. Now, you just wait."

"Wait for what?"

"You'll see if you wait long enough."

"You sound like Gran," she grumbled.

He chuckled. "I'd be pleased to think I sound like Iris Swift. Held this place together near single-handed she did."

"Gran did? But she said she's never been involved with the ranch work. She said Thomas is the one who knows the ranch."

"Oh that's for certain. Thomas's as good as the best top hand I ever saw. Knows animals like nobody else. Thomas held the ranch part of the Diamond V together. But Iris held the heart of it together."

"Oh, look! Dickens is going down the path."

"Yup. Never doubted he would." Gandy didn't even look up, his attention devoted to finishing the last few bites of his lunch.

He snapped the top on the container, closing off his commentary at the same time. "You going to stay here?"

"If I can't interrupt him, I guess I'll wait. Shouldn't be much longer, now that he's gotten Dickens down that trail."

"Don't count on it. Thomas don't count a job done until it's done thoroughly." He gave her a sly smile. "Afraid critters will get his lunch?"

"Afraid Gran won't get her container back—and I'll get blamed."

Gandy chuckled. "Best make yourself comfortable in that case."

"You think this could take a while, huh?"

"Depends on Dickens. One thing's for certain, Thomas will last longer than that devil horse. His pa used to say the whole secret to training horses was to insist one time more than the horse did. That's what Thomas does. He's got the patience."

"Too bad he doesn't have that kind of patience with people."

"He can."

"Not with Becky, he doesn't. Or—" she'd gone so far now, what was the sense of not saying what he surely knew she was thinking "—with me. He'd sooner snap my head off as look at me."

He rubbed his hand over his mouth at the same time he said, "I wouldn't say that."

He lowered his hand. His mouth amid the whiskers was straight, but the creases at the corners of his eyes gave the impression he'd been grinning.

"Way I figure it is a man who's been kicked by two, three gray horses in his time is gonna keep his distance from gray horses. Now if he can't keep his distance entirely, say a gray horse is in his brood, or—" the creases deepened "—one shows up unexpected like and he needs the horseflesh, well then a reasonable man could be expected to treat that gray horse cautious like."

"Uh-huh. But a reasonable man would know that not only is one gray horse not responsible for the past actions of another gray horse, but that the next gray horse is no more likely to kick him than a black horse or a white horse. The statistics show that every time."

"Hard for a man to be reasonable or pay attention to statistics when he feels the ache where he got kicked the last time most every day because something's rubbing at the spot real hard. Especially hard when gray horses can tie him up better'n a champion—" he pronounced it *champeen* "—calf roper with a slow-goer. And then, say, he's got a suspicioning that one particular gray horse, say a mare, could deliver a crippling blow if he's not real careful to keep her from getting too close. Why that man's bound to get nervy 'round that gray mare.''

She hadn't followed all the details—What could a woman have done to Thomas that was rubbing against the scar of that hurt?—But she got the gist. She just didn't buy it being applied to her.

Not only had Thomas Vance made clear how he viewed her—not with anything like the warmth Gandy indicated for his hypothetical man—but she wasn't interested, either. She needed to get things straight about how she'd made such a botch of falling for Sterling before she considered getting involved with another man. And when—if!—she got that far, the man wouldn't be a prickly curmudgeon like Thomas Vance.

She squinted up at Gandy, who'd stood and was adjusting the waistband of his jeans around his ample middle. Thomas and Dickens had reappeared at the top of the trail, and they were turning to head down it again.

"Of course," she said, "if the man is real good at staying clear of gray horses, and the newcomer gray horse is more than happy to mind her own business far away from the man, then there shouldn't be any problem at all.''

Chuckles trailed after Gandy like bubbles as he headed to where he'd tied his horse to a branch.

"Mind her own business? That's a good one. This gray mare's right in the middle of the brood taking care of this one, talking sense to that one. Mind her own business...''

All right, so she wasn't entirely minding her own business. But that was because she was sure she could help. And God knew Thomas Vance needed help in getting along with his sister and probably a good portion of the rest of humanity. Sure his hands respected him. And his grandmother loved him dearly. Even his sister would probably admit to that emotion if burning coals were held to her feet.

But in day-to-day dealings he was like the grinding

gears in that old truck she'd driven out here. The man could definitely use more oil in his crankcase.

That's all she was trying to do—add a little oil so people didn't rub up against each other so hard that permanent damage could be done.

Dickens appeared again, but this time his rider didn't start the horse back down the slope. Instead Thomas rode to the same tree Gandy had used, dismounted, looped the reins, then attached a hobble between Dickens's front feet. That would keep the horse from getting far even if he pulled the reins loose.

Ah yes, a cautious man was Thomas Vance.

"What're you doing here?"

And a less than welcoming one.

"Brought you lunch." She held it out to him.

"Thanks. No need for you to wait."

"Gran's container."

He grunted understanding, sank down in the same spot Gandy had occupied, and opened the container. Only when his rate of consumption slowed after three-quarters of the sandwich, all the apple and half the chips did she pose a question.

"Get Dickens to drink?"

"Didn't care if he drank or not. Just needed him to go down that trail."

"Wasn't that so he could drink at the stream?"

"Nope. It was so he knew he had to go down that trail, or any trail, when I told him to. Next time it won't be so bad. And the time after that it'll be sorta fun for him. And then we'll start going across water, which is another thing he's got it in his head he doesn't want to do."

"Poor Dickens," she murmured.

He'd heard her, but he obviously chose to ignore it. "What were you and Gandy talking about that had him in stitches?"

"Gray mares."

"What?"

"You know, the old gray mare she ain't what she used to be… And the new gray mare ain't what the old gray mare was, either. You should remember that the next time you look at a new gray mare."

He shook his head. "I don't have a clue what you're talking about. If Becky were here she'd probably say it was a symptom of amnesia. But I've got a feeling it's more a symptom of you."

She blinked up at him. He was right. She'd often been told that her lines of thought resembled a plate of spaghetti to many listeners. The first time she'd confused Sterling with her conversational leaps and oblique connections, he'd become so peeved that she'd curbed her habit of saying what was on her mind.

Censoring herself, she realized now.

Another reason she'd been wise to get out of that church. How could she have survived a lifetime of self-censorship?

Which she didn't do around Thomas. And he appeared to be perfectly all right with that—confused, but still all right.

Uh-oh. That little phrase echoed in her head again.

"Or maybe it's not just you," he said, sounding grim. "Maybe it's females."

"Someone in particular in mind?"

"Used to be Becky made sense. She was a kid, but she had a good head on her shoulders. There was never a time I worried about her even with the toughest ride. She can still handle horses, but—"

"Maybe she's dealing with something other than horses these days."

The look he slanted at her was as loud as a shout: *There, that's exactly what I'm talking about.*

"But," he picked up, "I never know when she's going to get some wild idea."

She suspected she knew what he was thinking about,

but Thomas needed to get in the habit of saying things instead of letting people around him guess. "Like?"

He slanted a look toward her, and his disdainful *Amnesia?* reaction to Becky's theory rang in her ears.

If he said it now, brought it out in the open, demanded to know if she really had amnesia, what would she say? Sitting here beside him under the open blue sky, with the breeze tickling her neck and no other human being within hearing distance, could she look him in the eyes and lie to him? Did she want to?

No. Heaven help her, she wanted to tell Thomas the truth, the whole truth and nothing but the truth.

A memory of the heat she'd felt when he caught her when she'd been oiling the hinges surfaced. Maybe not the *whole* truth. But at least not lies about who she was and why she was here.

But if she told him about that, she'd be drawing him into a mess. *One helluva post-honeymoon mess.* That's what the woman at the church had said.

But to lie to him now, if he came out and asked her...

"You name it, my sister has a wild idea about it."

Streams of relief and disappointment rushed into her.

She shook her head at herself. Quit mooning over what can't be helped. Telling him the truth would not be any favor to the Vance family. Better to repay their unknowing generosity in providing her a haven by doing the work they thought they'd hired her for...as well as straightening out a few bumps in their interpersonal relationships.

"What are you shaking your head at? You can't be arguing that Becky has wild ideas."

"I'm shaking my head at you. If you listen to her wild ideas you might learn something."

"Like what?"

She didn't know precisely. But she had a *feeling*... And wouldn't Thomas just eat that explanation up with a spoon? Okay, so she couldn't give him specifics. The big picture, however, was completely obvious.

"She wants attention."

"Attention! What for?"

Judi rolled her eyes. "Because you're her big brother, of course. Along with being a sort of parent."

"It's more like she wants to drive me crazy."

"That'll do."

"Yeah, well, I don't have time to spare right now for a teenager's need for attention. I've got other things I've gotta do."

She tipped her head to study him better. "Dickens."

The ground Thomas was sitting on suddenly felt harder. He shifted to find a more comfortable position. That also happened to tip the brim of his hat down, breaking their eye contact.

"Yeah. Dickens," he said.

"So it's not even a little bit about how you work with Dickens, and get him to respond? It's all for the money?"

"Sure." He might get a kick out of the moments when the young horse suddenly understood what was expected, and the even better moments when it felt like a thousand pounds of horseflesh was connected to his mind. "The owner got fed up with Dickens's tricks. Was going to sell him, even though he'd take a big hit. I said I could train him to be a good ride. Warren Upton has more money than patience, so he offered a fifty percent bonus on the fee if Dickens is ready July 15.

"I get that money and the Diamond V can continue to provide for Becky and—"

"Provide? You might think that's what's most important, but you're wrong. Efficiency and the bottom line are not more important than people."

"What does efficiency—?"

"But that would explain why you're still a lone ranger. No woman—no person likes to feel like you're totaling up how much she's cost you every step of the way. It doesn't matter what fancy things you do for them, if you keep going on and on about it, and even though there's no sex, they still end up feeling like a…a…tart!''

''What the hell are you—?''

But she'd already left, her exit punctuated by the rev of the truck engine.

Fine.

Served him right for backing off earlier anyway. She'd given him the perfect opening to dismantle this absurd amnesia story, and he'd let it go by. And look what it had gotten him—a lecture! Not even one that made sense. Efficiency and bottom line? Fancy things and toting up the costs? She must have had someone else in mind, because none of what she'd said applied to him.

Why you're still a lone ranger.

Okay, maybe some of it applied to him. But he didn't owe her any explanation.

Besides, she was wrong. He'd been involved with a few women. There was a widow in Casper with no interest in getting married who he saw now and then.

He'd find the right woman. He just wasn't going to rush into anything. He'd seen where that led.

When the time came, he would pick a wife with care and caution. And it would stick. He'd find a wife who would help on the ranch and be good with the kids they'd have and know how to stretch a dollar and not care that they need stretching.

Helga hadn't complained about stretching the food budget. She'd done okay with Dickens, too. And she was good with Becky.

Helga? What was he doing fitting Helga into this scenario? She was the last kind of woman he wanted.

He took his hat off and slapped it against his thigh to shake off a persistent bee.

If she was who she said she was, she'd be leaving in a few weeks for her next assignment. Although, when she smiled— No. He wasn't going to think that way.

She'd be leaving. She was an agitating kind of person. *And* she didn't know how to dress for a ranch.

Nodding satisfaction at that clincher, he got back to work and didn't think of her more than a dozen times.

He'd almost made a clean exit.

But Becky caught him as he entered the kitchen, immediately identifying the reason he'd taken a shower and changed in the middle of the day.

Then Helga came in from outside, carrying two sorry looking roses.

"We're going to town," Becky announced, in one of her in-the-treetops moods.

She looked from Becky to him and smiled. "Would you pick me up some jeans?"

Buy her clothes? Hell, no, he wasn't going to buy her clothes. "No."

"You can take it out of my wages."

"Money's not the prob—" He bit that off when he realized she would just ask what the problem was. "I don't have time to be running all over looking for your clothes."

"They've got ladies jeans at the WalMart, and you're already going there to pick me up more knitting yarn," contributed Gran.

He glared at his grandmother. "It'll still take time I don't have. If you want clothes, you'll have to come with or go another time."

"I can't leave here."

"Why not?"

She returned his look. All that marred the perfection of its innocence were a dash of deviltry and an ounce of triumph. "Someone has to stay with Gran, and since you promised Becky she could go to town…"

"Becky can st—"

His sister's howl stopped that thought in its tracks. "Oh, no you don't Thomas. I haven't been off this ranch except to the hospital since before Gran's surgery. You promised—and I'm going to town.''

''Fine, then you can pick out jeans for Helga while I'm getting groceries.''

''No, because you're dropping me off at Yvonne's while you do the grocery shopping so I can find out what's been happening.''

''How could there be anything you don't know. You're on the phone with her every time I turn around.''

''That's baloney. I—''

''Both of you, get out of here.'' Thomas instinctively turned at the warm, solid presence of Helga's hand on his back.

She was pushing both him and Becky toward the outside door. ''It's time for Gran to rest. Besides, you're both being pains in the you-know-what. Go argue on the way to town and stop giving your grandmother and me a headache.''

Becky's gaze met his in a flash of shared sheepishness, before she stomped out of the kitchen. But it didn't rattle the floor, so her heart couldn't have been in it.

That hopeful sign carried over, and they returned to the ranch without a single blowup or even sullen silence. That had to be a record for the past year.

Would that continue when they displayed their purchases?

Chapter Six

"Now we'll see who's right," Becky announced as she banged in the kitchen door carrying shopping bags.

Thomas followed with his head tilted to accommodate the large open-topped box balanced on one broad shoulder. "I don't care who's—"

"Shh. Gran's resting. The therapist just left, and she's wiped out," Judi said.

"Of course you care," Becky said to her brother in a much lower voice. "Or you would have let me buy the ones I said would fit, and been done with it."

Judi looked toward Thomas for an explanation. Swinging the large box of nonperishable food supplies down to the counter, he didn't meet her look.

"I gotta get the cooler," he mumbled as he headed out.

"So you didn't get me any jeans?" Judi asked Becky.

"Oh, we got you two pair." Becky dropped her bags on the table and started rooting through them. "My bone-headed brother refused to consider I might actually know better than he did what size you would wear. So we each bought you a pair.''

She triumphantly pulled out a stack of folded denim, and started ripping off tags. ''And now we're going to find out which pair fits.''

''You won't be able to return the pair that doesn't fit without the tags.''

''It has to be a blind test,'' Becky said decisively, handing her a pair of jeans still folded. ''Here—try these on first.''

Thomas thumped at the back door with the cooler, and Becky went to open it, shooing Judi toward the stairs. ''Hurry up. We'll put the food away. Go on.''

Judi changed in record time. It was easy because the jeans Becky had given her skimmed up her body...then threatened to skim back down, even after she zipped and buttoned them. She was a long way from supermodel status, but she also wasn't a sumo wrestler.

She fought the giggles as she descended the stairs, then schooled her face before entering the kitchen. She didn't want to hurt Becky's feelings.

Becky plunked a can of applesauce on a shelf. Pivoting for another item, she caught sight of Judi. ''I knew it!'' Triumph vibrated in her voice and eyes.

Judi's amusement soured. Becky hadn't selected these jeans for her. That meant—

''I told you you were way off, Thomas. Didn't I say that? Didn't I?''

Thomas straightened from stowing lettuce in the refrigerator, glanced Judi's direction for a millisecond and turned to the cooler, taking out a plastic milk jug. ''Yeah, you said it.''

Thomas had picked out these jeans. Thomas, who had glided his talented hands over her after the accident, then had held her so close the day she oiled the hinges, had translated what he'd felt into a body that would wear these jeans.

"You thought these would fit me?" Oh, lord, she hoped that hadn't sounded as plaintive as it felt.

"Comfort's more important than style on a ranch." He sounded strange. For a second she thought he was laughing, but no. "Besides, denim shrinks."

"Not this much," Judi muttered.

"Now go try on these," Becky ordered. "These are the ones I bought."

Having handed over the other jeans, Becky gave her a little shove to get her started, and Judi nearly tripped over the drooping hem. Come to think of it, everything drooped. She grabbed the sliding waistband with her free hand.

A sound came from behind her, but when she turned around, Thomas had his head back in the refrigerator.

Putting the next pair on took significantly longer. Pulling them up her legs was like acquiring a second skin. Gran could have used them as anti-embolism stockings. She struggled to close them, finally flopping back on the bed to zip them up. God, she hadn't done that in ages. The legs were so tight and the material so stiff she could barely bend her knees.

"I feel like Goldilocks and the Three Bears," she said as she crossed the kitchen threshold. "One's too big, one's too small. Wasn't there a size in between that would have been *juuust* right?"

"What do you mean? These aren't too small. They're perfect."

"Becky, honey, I can't move."

"Sure you can. You got down the stairs, didn't you? Break 'em in a little and you'll love them. Besides, they look great on you. Don't they, Thomas?"

Judi had been aware he was standing without moving. Now she realized he had the freezer door open and his hand inside it, while cold fog swirled around his head. He didn't seem to notice. He looked as frozen as the items stored there. Except for the slow glide down, then up of his Adam's apple.

In that instant, Judi knew Becky was right—the jeans looked great on her. A curling warmth pulsed low in her stomach and the tips of her breasts tightened against the inside of her bra.

"C'mon, Thomas, admit it. I was right and you were wrong. She looks really hot in these jeans, just like I told you. I said—"

"I heard you." He jerked his hand out of the freezer as if it had been burned. "It's up to Helga which pair she wants."

"Oh, yeah, like she'd wear *yours*. Who'd want to wear a sack?"

She was a little shaken—at the intensity of his look, even more at her reaction. "If these jeans shrink any they'll crush me like a boa constrictor."

Becky chuckled, but protested, "Just break them in, you'll see."

Upstairs, wriggling out of the tight fabric, Judi wondered just what it was she'd see if she did wear those jeans long enough to break them in. Would she see that look on Thomas's face again? All the time?

She folded the jeans and put them on the dresser. Or would he learn to hide it the way he tried to hide everything else?

Picking the large pair of jeans off the bed, she folded them, too.

She stopped in midmotion. Could it be that Thomas knew her figure perfectly well—knew it and was trying to hide it so he wouldn't be tempted into the kind of reaction he'd shown when she'd worn the pair Becky selected?

She was smiling when she went downstairs.

Thomas gave Keith his instructions, slammed the truck's passenger door and sprinted to avoid a drenching. Jumping an instant puddle, he took the steps two at a time.

When he slowed he saw Helga sitting on the porch swing. Even that far under the overhang she was getting misted.

"What are you doing?"

"Watching the storm. I've become surprisingly partial to storms."

It made no sense. But there was something in the look she gave him that drove the blood from his head, sending it south in a rush of heat. He should have been giving off steam. He had to get a grip on this. Or stay the hell away from her.

"You might want to get soaked, but I'm going to get washed up to go to the bank, so—"

"You're going to lose Keith."

He turned to her. "I've paid attention and he's just like always. I even asked, and he said everything's fine."

"Big surprise, since you're so approachable and open to new ideas and people. You practically accused me of stealing when I offered to do something extra for you."

"I never said that. If you took it that way, that's your problem. And I've always told the hands to talk to me if they have a problem."

"Telling them isn't enough. God, you're just like—" She bit it off.

"Your brother?"

"No. Paul's very approachable—for people he likes. The ones he doesn't like?" She shrugged, dismissing them as Paul would. "Not to mention he has a great sense of humor. He's the one who showed me the Hot Dog Inn off I-90 when we… Well, that's beside the point. The point is you're like a former, unlamented boss of mine."

"A boss." He studied her. "Has to be fairly recent, since you couldn't have been working more than five, six years. So your memory must be getting better."

Seven. But she wasn't going to confuse the issue with that fact. "Sorry, my memory hasn't advanced past childhood—she was my boss at a lemonade stand. She said her door was always open, but she only wanted the people she supervised to do exactly what she said and leave her alone. Keith loves working with the horses, but with so few hands, he has to do a lot of stuff he doesn't like. He understands, but give him something to look forward to. Maybe let him train a few horses or—''

"I thought you were going to leave this up to me."

"I am leaving the specifics up to you." Her dignified restraint collapsed. "Besides, you're taking too long. This can't wait forever, you know."

Because her time here was running out and she wanted to see what he did? There were three weeks left on the contract with the agency. But he'd always thought she had her own timetable. High time he figured out what it was.

He headed for the door.

"Thomas—"

Without slowing he said, "I'll think about it."

She watched him walk away, her heart beating faster.

Maybe it was the intriguing toughness added to his look by a two-day beard. Maybe it was that his *I'll think about it* was the literal truth. Nothing like being listened to to get a girl's heart pounding.

Sure, it didn't have anything to do with a fascination with the lightning she'd discovered was part of the particular weather system named Thomas.

But even someone becoming partial to thunderstorms had to come in out of the rain eventually. She dried off in the utility room, discovered a batch of Gran's clothes were done, and loaded a basket.

"Are those my things?" Gran asked. She was writing to friends at the roll-away desk Keith had built. Judi nodded. "I'll fold them, just leave them on the dresser."

Gran had graduated from the walker to crutches last week, and figured out that by using the crutches and keeping weight off her one leg, she could stand for short periods to fold her clothes and put most of them away. Each week—each day—Gran took back more of her duties.

Pretty soon Judi would be out of a job and she would go back to Illinois and return to her old life.

Oh, no, I won't.

Judi set down the laundry basket on Gran's dresser.

She'd go back, since she wouldn't be needed here, but she would *not* return to her old life. She would not go back to a job where she wasn't appreciated and that didn't use her skills. She would not get stuck in something she hated just because she hadn't found something she loved. Like she'd almost done in marrying Sterling.

She had fallen into the engagement and wedding because she'd thought she might never find someone to love.

Green eyes, sandy hair and a stormy personality flashed into her head.

Oh, no, she wasn't going to fall for him, not after less than a month… Talk about out of the frying pan and into the fire! If she ever fell for anybody again it would be after a long, slow get-acquainted period, followed by several years of dating and then maybe a two- or three-year engagement. All told, a decade ought to be safe. And that was if she ever fell again.

The word *fell* was punctuated by a heavy tread directly over her head.

Judi tipped her head back and looked up. Another footstep. In her room.

It had to be Thomas. Gran couldn't get up the stairs, and those sure weren't Becky's footsteps. Besides, neither Gran nor Becky had any reason to be in her room.

But Thomas did.

He didn't trust her. She knew that. She'd even made provisions for his distrust. So why were her eyes stupidly tearing up?

How long had she been hearing footsteps while she'd been too lost in thought for their significance to penetrate?

The footsteps moved again. Getting dimmer. He was leaving.

She went up the stairs as quietly as they would let her.

The door to her room was open, the way she'd left it since nothing she had to hide was in here.

She checked the closet, the bedside table, the dresser. Nothing appeared to be missing or out of order. She closed the underwear drawer—the last one she'd looked at. He must have been in her room a long time to be so neat about it. A shiver ran down her back and brought goose bumps.

At the idea of her privacy being violated. Only that. In fact, it left her with an urge to wash her hands. Maybe sprinkle cold water on the back of her neck.

She swung open her bathroom door, and nearly crashed into Thomas.

"Hey, watch it! I've got a razor here."

He stepped back, holding that implement aloft.

He had no shirt on. And from the tan bronzing the muscles that laced his chest and back, it wasn't the first time. His jeans were partially unzipped and rode low on his hips, showing a ribbon of hair disappearing into a sliver of white briefs. She snapped her gaze to his face. Shaving cream covered his jawline, his chin and encircled his lips like a white beacon.

She opened her mouth. Nothing came out. She wet her lips and tried again.

"What are you doing in my bathroom?"

He faced the mirror again.

"What I'm doing is shaving—in my bathroom."

He jabbed the end of his razor toward the second closet door. Except it was open and she saw beyond it a bed with a shirt laid out. His shirt. His bedroom.

"But I've taken a shower here every morning, and you were never using it." She'd known his room was upstairs, but if she'd given it any thought, she'd assumed he had his own bathroom.

"I'm up and at work before you get up. I shower at night, before supper." He hitched his shoulders, as if to say *no big deal.* "It's worked out."

Not anymore. Every time she came in here she'd be wondering... Her dreams were going to slide from R-rated straight to X-rated. And then another aspect hit her.

"You can just waltz right from your room through here and into mine. How many times have you searched it before today?"

His hand stopped in midstroke, and his eyes shifted from his reflection to meet her gaze in the mirror. He didn't answer.

"Didn't find anything, did you?" She didn't bother to hide her triumph.

"What makes you think that?"

"Because there's nothing to find!"

"No ID? No wallet? No credit cards? Only way you could know I didn't find any of those is if you hid them. Now, why would you do that?"

"Because I don't like nosy men poking through my underwear drawer." She turned, but his voice caught her.

"If you don't want men seeing your underwear don't leave it hanging around."

She spun back. "I don't—"

He pointed to the handle on the bathroom side of her bedroom door.

Her champagne lace bra hung there by one strap. She snatched it up and stalked out.

Thomas heard the giggling from the three females behind him as he poured a mug of coffee before supper, but giggling wasn't as rare as it used to be before Helga arrived, so he ignored it. He picked up his mug and started toward his desk to check forecasts for winter hay. If he could hay enough to have some to sell this fall—

Belatedly the image recorded by his eyes registered in his brain. He turned back and looked at the appliance he'd just used. A gleaming white gadget with buttons and dials he didn't recognize.

"What the hell is this?"

"A programmable coffeemaker. Program it to start brewing at a certain time and you'll have fresh morning coffee when you get up—no more sludge."

He could swear his mouth watered at the prospect of fresh coffee in the morning. But a man couldn't let himself get distracted.

"You went to town to get this?" If she went to town that would put a dent in his theory that she was hiding out from something. Would she also have bought jeans while she was in town? Would that mean...

"No. We had it delivered."

"How—?"

She raised her brows. "You mean since I don't have a credit card? I gave Keith the cash, and he was kind enough to order it on his card. He helped pick it out, too—he's got one at home. And he liked being included in the decision-making process."

Subtle it wasn't. But he had other issues to cover. "I'll pay you back."

"You will not. You bought me jeans and wouldn't take payment for them."

"You can't wear those jeans—either pair."

"It's the thought that counts. Besides, this is self-protection. I drink the coffee here, too."

Out the window over the kitchen sink, where she was peeling carrots, Judi caught sight of Thomas and Becky. Becky hurried to keep up with his long strides, talking fast and her hands moving in short, angry stabs. Thomas's mouth was thin and flat. The screen door swung open, and Becky's aggrieved voice filled the room.

"I'm fifteen—"

"That's right—and I'm your guardian until you're eighteen. And I said no."

"Every other teenager in the world gets to date and go to dances. You want me to be a drudge. I suppose you'd be happy if I got fat and had zits all over my face. Then nobody would ask me and you wouldn't have to worry about it.''

''I don't care about the zits, but getting fat would be hard on the horses.''

''You care more about the horses than your own flesh-and-blood sister!''

''They might not be relatives but they're not teenagers—thank God.''

''You're keeping me imprisoned here until I'm old and dried up!''

''You'll have the money to go to college, and that's not old and dried up.''

Becky paled then flushed bright red. She sucked in a breath, and Judi thought for sure it was to release another torrent—of words or tears or both. Instead, the girl turned and fled down the hall toward her room.

Judi had braced herself, so she didn't flinch when the slam of Becky's door reverberated through the house. She dried her hands and turned.

Thomas stood by the end of the table. His jaw tight, his mouth still firm. He held his hat in one hand and ran the other through his hair.

''What's that all about?'' Gran asked.

''She wants to go to some dance.''

''You've let her go to dances.''

''With a group. This is different. Steve's asked her— on a date. She's too young,'' he added, as if someone had argued with him.

''Because you worked so much that you didn't date until you were seventeen?''

''I'm not saying she can't do things because I didn't. And I know she's working hard. But, damn it, this teenage rebellion is getting out of hand. I was responsible—''

''Mostly responsible,'' his grandmother amended. ''I remember a certain teenager who would get on the meanest, wildest horse—no matter what his Dad said—and ride and ride and ride. Stay out all night sometimes.''

"That wasn't rebellion. That was…I had to…" His hand holding his hat gave an aborted wave. "Get away."

"Uh-huh. And you don't think Becky feels that?"

"It's not the same. And even if it was, going to a dance wouldn't cure it."

He walked out, but his boot heels didn't clomp down the porch steps.

Judi and Gran looked at each other across the room. Judi tipped her head toward the door to the hallway— Becky's path. Gran shook her head, then tipped it toward the outside door—Thomas's exit.

Judi hesitated. Gran tipped her head toward the outside door again.

Judi gave an I-don't-know-what-good-it'll-do grimace, sighed, and headed out.

Thomas heard the door open and close, but didn't move from the railing.

The go-rounds with Becky were getting worse. What she said didn't change but the emotion climbed. Like a balloon filling and filling. What if it popped?

"I think you should let her go to the dance."

"No." Belatedly, he added, "I didn't ask your opinion."

Helga ignored that. Big surprise. "You can't keep her cooped up on the ranch."

"She's not cooped up. This isn't prison—no matter what she says."

"I didn't mean it as an insult, Thomas." Her voice had shifted to that soft, slow tone she used with Dickens. Her gaze slid to his jaw, and he became aware of a muscle ticking there. "This is a wonderful place. Becky loves it— almost as much as you do. But if you try to tie her too close, eventually, she'll break out and bolt."

"She's a kid."

"Fifteen, going into her sophomore year in high school.

It's not a bad time to be socializing more with the opposite sex. And Steve seems like a responsible guy.''

"He's eighteen—''

"Seventeen. I checked. He skipped a grade.''

"Either way, he'll leaving for college at the end of summer on a rodeo scholarship. He wants to go pro. You know what kind of life that is? A few make it big, but too many end up broken and broke. And their wives and families have to make do with what they get. I want better than that for Becky. She deserves better.''

His outburst sank into silence before she spoke.

"Okay, putting aside that you already have Steve pursuing a rodeo career until he's decrepit—he might succeed, you know—'' She put up a hand to stop his response. "Putting that aside, you also think that going on her first date to a dance with a boy she's known all her life will lead Becky directly to marriage and kids? If that were true, I would be the wife of Alec Tresser, with a passel of little Tressers at my apron strings. Which would surprise the heck out of Alec and his roommate Ron.''

A rush of something had surged up in Thomas at the image of her dancing with the unknown Alec Tresser, never mind her being the guy's wife and having his kids… But what had taken a split second to build to a surprising level crashed into laughter at her finish.

She put her palm lengthwise along his upper arm. It felt cool and clean, yet it made his skin hotter. Or maybe that was his blood heating up.

"Becky's got to start somewhere, Thomas. She needs to take this step toward being an adult. And she wants to dance—didn't you ever want to dance?''

A slow dance. With this woman snug against his body. Her silky hair brushing his mouth. His hands molded to her back. Her arms a warm presence around his neck. His legs moving against hers in the motion of the dance. A motion that promised a dance of a different kind. The best dance. The most intimate dance.

He swallowed hard. "Yeah, I've wanted to dance."

"Well, then, you should understand."

That was just it—he was afraid he did understand. If Steve had the same sort of thoughts about little Becky—

"Thomas? Did you hear what I said? Promise me you'll think about letting her go Saturday. Whatever you do, don't tell Becky you're thinking about it because she'll hound the life out of you, but make the promise to me."

"I'll think about it."

And try not to think about the rest.

"Here." Folded denim landed in front of her on the table.

"What's this?"

"Jeans. And a jacket."

Judi looked up and raised her brows at Thomas, demanding an explanation.

"Alice picked 'em and brought 'em out when she came for Gran's physical therapy session today."

"Alice did. How'd she know to do that?"

Predictably, he frowned at being backed into that corner. "I asked her to."

She checked the label. These should fit. "How'd she know the size?"

"I split the difference between Becky and me."

"Too bad you don't do that more often."

The frown crashed down harder. "You want them or not?"

"Yes, thank you. I'll pay you—"

He'd turned away on her first prim word. "No need."

"Hey, Thomas, now that I've got jeans, when are you going to give me a tour?"

He didn't slow down, and he didn't turn around, but he said loud enough for her to hear, "Tomorrow morning. And you're welcome."

* * *

Judi watched Thomas's face as he looked over the land.

They'd ridden for more than an hour, while he named the creeks, ranges of hills and distant mountains. He explained how they decided where to grow soybeans and hay. He described how they rotated the grazing. And once or twice he slipped, and let his dreams for the future peek through.

Now they'd dismounted to let the horses drink and rest. The stream dropped from a taller hill behind them, but they were high enough to have a panoramic view.

There was something about this man and this land that gave her that heart-swelling, can't-catch-my-breath combination of awe and happiness she felt when she watched a particularly compelling athlete being honored with a gold medal and his or her national anthem at the Olympics. It didn't matter which country or which event, it was the sense of a great endeavor suitably rewarded that always got to her.

"You love ranching, don't you?"

"It's something different every day. You've gotta be good at a lot of things and able to get by at the rest. You can't afford to say there's something you'll never do, and you can't get to thinking there's just one thing you do best."

But she was shaking her head. "Stubborn's what you do best."

"Takes a stubborn man to ranch."

"Or woman," she added. "When do you first remember loving this ranch?"

He stared at the hilled horizon ahead of them. The rises slipped down to troughs before gathering into yet another green and tan rise until it looked like a magician had waved a wand to transform the rolling waves of an ocean into still and solid form. His attention seemed to snag on one particular section of this ocean of grazing.

"Maybe riding with my mom. She would put me in front of her on the saddle when I was still too little to ride on my own. And she'd talk. Tell stories about the land and horses and cattle—I didn't even know she was teaching me stuff then.''

''What else do you remember about her?''

''Sometimes Gran'll use an expression, or make a gesture… It's like seeing an old movie come to life. But Mom's voice was different, lighter. She could always make my dad laugh. He used to say she was worth any two hands. She worked hard, and having her around lit up his day, so he worked even harder.''

''She sounds like a wonderful woman. And your parents obviously loved each other a great deal.''

''Dad said they thought the same things were important. That's why I never understood…'' His laugh was harsh. ''Not that a blind man couldn't see what he saw in Maureen. Becky looks like her. Only Maureen took what Becky has natural, and polished and primped and perfumed it like a ta—'' He bit off the word along with a stem of grass.

''Is that why you won't let Becky go to the dance Saturday with Steve? You think she's just like her mother?''

''What? No! Becky's not like her. Nothing like her.''

''Then give her a chance to prove that. You don't want to open the door and let her loose when she goes to college do you? You need to be treating her more like an adult, so she'll become one. It's like driving the ranch trucks— you didn't put her in a truck and say *Hit the highway, kid.* No, I bet you showed her how first. Then let her try a little, with you right beside her. Gradually let her do more, until she'd learned enough to drive on her own. Dating's not so different. Wouldn't it be better to let her take test drives under your…''

He narrowed his eyes, and she discarded *thumb* as her word choice. No sense riling the fish when you were trying to reel him it.

''Your, uh, watchful eye.''

''And you think this dance would be a good first driving lesson?''

"Sure. There'll be responsible adults chaperoning. It's with kids she knows. She'll be with a boy *you* know. Heck, the kid knows you can fire him if he misbehaves. Besides," she shot him a grin, "it's a fifties theme party. Worst they'll probably do is share a first kiss, and everybody knows those are pretty dull. Now, if it was a sixties party, you might have to worry."

He smiled, but it faded quickly. His attention had settled again in that one direction. The land was as beautiful as the rest of the Diamond V. Why would he be more interested in it than... And then she had it.

"That's the section that would be sold off if you can't raise the money, isn't it?"

He didn't confirm it directly. He didn't need to. "When I told you somebody holds the right to sell a quarter of the ranch, what I didn't tell you is it's Becky's mother, and the person who gave her that power was our father."

Her eyes widened, but she said nothing.

"He left it to her in his will. He thought that somehow after he died she'd care about the ranch, even though she'd never cared about it during all the years he spent trying to get her to come back. It was like meeting her and falling for her was a dose of middle-aged crazy and he never got over it. A terminal case."

"And now she's the reason the ranch could be broken up. That's got to be hard on Becky."

"She doesn't know—not about the sale, and especially not about Maureen. I've never told her, and Gran agreed not to. There's no reason for her to worry about what might happen to the ranch or why."

"And you think that's it—a news blackout? Boy, you don't know teenage girls, do you? But even if she doesn't know what Maureen's doing now, it must have been hard for Becky when she left like that. And for your father. And you."

"Me?"

"To have lost your own mother, and then to have your surrogate mother leave."

His bark of laughter held no humor. "She was no mother to me. As far as I was concerned, her leaving was a relief. Sure cut the whining and moaning around here. Only way it affected me was Dad fell apart, so I took on more of running the place."

She was doing quick figuring in her head. "At twenty."

He lifted one shoulder. "I'd been doing ranch work since I could walk. After Dad married Maureen he spent more and more time—and money—trying to keep her happy, so I'd picked up more. But her leaving was real hard on Becky. I guess she looked to me then. Dad was mooning after Maureen and Gran was running the house plus teaching. Becky used to trail me around like a little shadow."

A smile lit his green eyes like sunshine on grass, then faded to nothing. And that lack of expression was bleaker than any of his frowns.

"That's why it's been…strange these past months." He shrugged, seeming to try to shake off the mood. "Teenagers, huh?"

"I suppose."

"Or maybe it's getting half her genes from Maureen. When I marry and have kids, I'm going to find somebody with deep roots in ranching. Somebody who knows this life and loves it. Not somebody out here on a lark. Someone who knows where she's going in life. Practical, levelheaded, who's never impulsive or gets in scrapes."

"Sounds like a plan," Judi said brightly. "Oh, look at the time! I better get back. No need for you to come—"

But he insisted on accompanying her. At least on the trail they didn't talk.

Could he have been any more obvious? Not that she had any expectations or hopes in that direction. But all he'd had to do was make his ideal mate five-foot-two, blond and blue-eyed and he'd have had her total opposite.

"Thank you for showing me around, Thomas. If you have other things you need to do..."

When didn't he have other things that needed doing? But she'd been trying to get rid of him, and the more she did, the less he felt like being gotten rid off.

"I'm heading to the house, too."

"Uh, I thought I'd check on the garden."

"I don't mind looking in on the garden."

"I might stay a while, do some weeding."

"I could help, since you've been helping me out today."

The growing annoyance on her face gave way to curiosity. "I have?"

"Yeah. With so few hands, our horses aren't getting as much work as they should. They need to keep in training like any other athlete. Was going to ask if you could help out again."

"Sure—if Gran can spare me, of course."

"We'll all be out moving cattle up higher Sunday. Won't expect you to do any cowpunching. But riding along will get Xena some work."

"I'd have to check with Gran, and— Oh, look!" She didn't wait for him to look. She took off into the garden, and dropped to her knees. "Do you see it?"

"What?"

"The first tomato from the garden."

"That's a tomato? Looks like a green bump to me."

She frowned fiercely, but her eyes sparkled with humor and pride. "It's a baby tomato. Give it time. A green bump today, a juicy layer in a sandwich tomorrow."

"*Tomorrow's* a little optimistic. And there's early frost to worry about."

"It wouldn't dare. It's a lovely tomato and— Oh! There're more." She jumped up. "Look at this one! It even looks like a tomato. We're going to have a crop, a real crop of tomatoes. I wonder if Gran has canning supplies."

While she happily contemplated putting up gallons of tomatoes based on a couple of fledgling bumps, he didn't tell her that Iris Swift had never put tomatoes in a can in her life. She took them out of the cans she got at the grocery store.

He didn't have the heart to inject reality into Helga's glory. Her joy.

Reality would set in soon enough. Then she'd see there was no reason to glow over a tomato. That she didn't like the sweep of empty hills and wide blue sky as much as her face said she did. That she got bored with a retired teacher, a teenager and a small-time rancher. That she wanted more. That she wanted different.

He might not know who she was, but he knew the kind of woman she was. The kind with expensive clothes, perfectly cut hair, pampered hands.

For now, all this was fun for her because it was different. She'd probably never tended a garden before. It qualified as a lark, a vacation. She would tire of this triumph, as she would tire of the work, of the life, of the ranch, of him.

So he couldn't let himself think it was real. That she was real.

"Do you smell it, Thomas?"

"Smell what?"

"Summer."

When she breathed in deeply, his sense of sight, not smell went into overdrive.

"The smell of the sun on the earth and the plants. The smell of heat. I love that smell. I store it up during the summer and pull it out in the winter to get warm."

She looked up at him and laughed.

"I know, I know, you think I'm crazy."

No, he didn't. Because he was storing up the sound and sight of her. On her knees in the dirt. Sunlight burning red into her hair, her eyes bright and her smile quick. He would take the memory out when he was cold inside, and it would make him warm. But he would not be like his father. He would not drive himself crazy and threaten the Diamond V by trying to hold on to her. He'd be satisfied with a memory.

He shrugged at her comment. "Whatever works for you."

Judi had steered clear of Thomas since Becky and Steve left for the dance.

Thomas had restrained himself at supper when Becky, swathed in Judi's silk robe after her shower, had chattered about the band, whether they would dance current style or fifties dances, and her outfit—sweater twin set, fake pearls, a wide skirt with a petticoat and matching scarf to tie around her ponytail.

He'd done no more than wince at the door slamming as Becky rushed from her bedroom to the hall bath and back a dozen times before Steve's arrival.

He had rolled his eyes at Becky's excitement when Judi gave her the clunky gold charm bracelet as an added accessory, especially at Becky's squeal when Judi said she could keep it.

Judi even had to give Thomas high marks for limiting his comments to the teenage pair to curfew and expected driving behavior.

But as soon as door closed behind Steve and Becky, he'd gotten such a pained, haunted expression, she'd decided it was a good time for the let-them-go girl to read in her bedroom. But now Gran was in bed, asleep, and the curfew was nearing, and she felt an obligation to be on hand.

Whether that was to make sure Thomas didn't intrude on the end of Becky's date, or to ease his last quarter hour of anxious waiting, she didn't know.

She tracked him down on the darkened porch, sitting on the swing, arms crossed over his chest, legs stretched out and crossed at the ankles. She stepped over his feet and sat beside him, looking up at stars bursting into the sky like kernels of popcorn.

"If you laugh, you'll regret it," he grumbled.

"Who's laughing?"

She felt more than saw his look as he studied her profile. Then he faced straight ahead and sighed his resignation. "You might as well laugh—this is worse."

"No, no, I'm restraining myself now in recognition of how restrained you were when Steve picked Becky up."

A small grin eased his mouth. "I've known him all his life and I still wanted to grill the kid, then scare the be-jeezus out him."

She nodded. "That's what my older brother used to do."

As soon as she said it, she tensed for him to pounce on the fact that she'd remembered something. Surely he wouldn't let a comment like that go by.

"What did your brother do?"

She hid her surprise—no sense giving him ideas.

"Even after he was living on his own, he'd somehow find out when I was going out with a new guy, and he'd show up at the house. He'd answer the door if I didn't tackle him first—" She closed her eyes in mock horror, but felt a grin tug at her mouth. "Once I wasn't quick enough and we got there at the same time, and the sight that greeted the poor guy was Paul and me trying to bump each other out of the way with our hips. Surprisingly, that was the shortest date I ever had. And he never called back."

"Guy was a wimp if that scared him off."

Thomas wouldn't scare off. Not if he really wanted something—someone.

"The door routine was just the start. Paul would fire questions at the poor boy like he expected the kid to admit he had the Lindbergh baby in his back seat."

"Back seat, hum? Did back seats figure prominently in the questioning?"

"You're beginning to catch on. Another time, Paul arranged to have his two great buddies, Grady and Michael, there, too. When my date brought me home, the three of them had their chairs pulled up in a row in front of the door, eating popcorn, like we were the floor show."

"Were you?"

"Not a chance. And I'd had such hopes for that evening. Robby Socere was a hunk. Never had a second date with him, either. You know, it's a wonder I didn't murder all three of them a long time ago—at least Paul and Grady."

"Not Michael?" He was paying close attention. Should she be flattered, or worried that he was hoping she'd trip up?

"Nah. Michael was always the nicest. Sweet really. Use to let me flirt with him like mad when I was a kid—younger than Becky," she added with significance. "And great-looking. 'Course if that had been the reason, I would have spared Grady, too. No, it was Michael's niceness. Which my cousin Tris finally recognized." She smiled. "With a little nudge from me when she was being dense."

"So Michael and your cousin got together?"

"Yup. It started at my brother's wedding to Bette, the best sister-in-law in the world. And the mother of the most adorable nieces and nephew in the world. Tris and Michael's three are pretty cute, too."

"So Grady's the holdout."

"Wrong. He was the last of the three, but he married Leslie, and they've adopted Sandy and Jake, along with bringing up Leslie's cousin, April Gareaux."

"So, you remember all those details of your teen years, and your brother and his friends and their wives and children? Not to mention—what was it?—the Hot Dog Inn?"

She sighed. "I knew you wouldn't be able to resist forever."

"How much do you remember?"

"Right up to when I started taking science courses to become a health aide," she answered promptly.

He laughed. And he didn't ask any more questions.

Instead, he took her hand.

Just like that, he reached over and slid his hand over hers, and curled his fingers around her palm.

For the first second she couldn't breathe.

It wasn't like the touches to see if she'd been hurt in the accident. It wasn't catching her to keep her from falling to the floor off a chair. It couldn't be construed as polite or comforting or accidental or practical or anything other than what it was.

A man holding a woman's hand.

It felt good. Warm, and rather sweet. At least on the surface. Beneath that was a charge of something hot and definitely not sweet. Or was that her imagination?

"Thomas—"

"Let it be."

"Let what be?"

"This moment. Just for now."

And she did. She didn't know the source of his need, but she knew he needed this moment. She owed him that.

Be honest. This had nothing to do with what she owed Thomas or his family for the truth she couldn't tell them. This had to do only with him.

He did so much. Physical work that gave him the broad, muscled shoulders now so close she could feel the warmth.

He carried so much. Worries, hopes, fears for his ranch and his family that weighed down those shoulders.

He needed someone to soothe the aches of both what he did and what he carried. To make him forget for a while. She could do that.

Oh, not permanently, she had no delusions there, even before he'd spelled out his requirements. But for now. For this solitary moment.

She leaned over and kissed him.

She'd aimed for his cheek. He turned as her lips made

contact, and the kiss slid toward his mouth. The center of her mouth met the corner of his.

Flames. In her belly, across her skin. High and hot enough to block her withdrawal for an extra two beats.

She pulled back and clamped her mouth shut to keep from gasping. She'd intended a soothing caress. This had nothing to do with soothing.

"What was that for?"

"You…" Oh, lord, the flames had turned her voice into a raw, smoky whisper. She cleared her throat, looking straight ahead. "You're a good man. That's all."

"Thanks."

"You're welcome."

Neither of them moved more than the slight flex of their ankles that kept the swing's gentle rhythm going. They didn't look at each other. And the heat building between them could have left a vapor trail across the sky.

His hand tightened around hers and she knew, even before he turned to her.

She shouldn't. She was here under false pretenses. She'd leave in a few weeks. She'd made a total mess of it the only other time she'd become involved so quickly.

She turned toward him.

He lowered his head, angling it. She closed her eyes and held her breath, waiting for that first real touch of his mouth on hers.

It didn't come.

Her breath came out in a huff of disappointment as she opened her eyes. But he hadn't pulled back. He was just as close, and now he moved closer. Almost…

Another stilling. Was he giving her time to back out? She wasn't going to. Or was he arguing with himself? If his internal argument was anything like hers… But what if his conclusion was different? What if she was the loser in his argument?

She shifted to match the tilt of his head.

He moved in even closer, and she recognized it was

neither hesitancy nor chivalry. It was anticipation. It was stretching the moment until it hummed. It was finding their way to each other in these tiny feints so that when their lips met, there would be no fumbling, no adjusting, just...

Fireworks.

Their mouths met full, hard and immediate.

The flames had lit the fuse and now the fireworks exploded. A series of bursts down through her body, percussion blasts under her rib cage, sparklers delighting the tips of her breasts and explosions of color behind her eyes.

And she wanted more. She reached out for it with greedy hands, touching his face, following the curve of his ear, sliding her fingers into his thick hair.

What had she said about first kisses? Dull? She was the-earth-is-flat wrong on that one. This first kiss—their first kiss—was what had kept the species going for eons.

His tongue met the seam of her lips, but no resistance. She opened immediately, because the taste of him seemed at this moment like the one nutrient her body had lacked forever. Their tongues touched, slid along each other, and the friction stretched a ribbon of heat down into her chest and to her core, where it coiled in a clutch of pleasure.

The touch of his tongue became an infinite exploration of pleasure. With slow, searching glides, and demanding strokes. She embarked on a return journey. Sliding her tongue into his mouth, lining the strong teeth, finding the taste of heat and strength, and stroking with an urgency that matched his.

He released her mouth to kiss the bridge of her nose, her eyelids, then trail sensation to her temple and along her hairline.

He murmured something in her ear. It didn't matter what. It was the sound not the sense she craved. Then he darted his tongue in, and she arched at the reality of this touch and the anticipation of the ultimate act it hinted at.

His arm curved across her back, supporting her, as he followed the flow of her arching motion by kissing down the side of her throat, and around its base, to lick and suck at the hollow there.

The ribbon inside her turned to a streamer of fire.

His hands stroked under the neckline of her shirt and across her skin. It was almost the same motion he'd made when he'd checked for injuries after her accident. And nothing like it at all. That relaxing warmth had made her want to purr. *This* call-the-troops-to-attention sizzle made her want to howl.

When his fingers snagged against the strap of her bra, she knew she'd really howl if she didn't do something to close her lips. She could have bit them, but why when there was a much better alternative. She raised her head and pressed her mouth to his.

She had his immediate and complete cooperation. Oh, he didn't dampen the howling danger, in fact he upped it, by continuing the caress across her collarbone, and sliding the strap right off the point of her shoulder. The surge of heat and hardness against her hip was another howl-index inflation factor. And the blatant movement of his tongue into her mouth had that ribbon through the center of her body shimmering and clutching.

Ah…and then his hand slid lower, edging ever so slowly under the loosened top edge of her bra.

A blaze of light caught Judi's peripheral attention. Then the earth lurched. Good heavens, what—?

No, not the earth. Them. Her and Thomas. And the swing.

"Ooof," she protested into the base of his throat when something hit her across the back. She became distracted when she opened her mouth against his skin and found his taste there.

The something hit her in the back again. The edge of

the porch swing, she realized. Thomas had wrapped both arms around her and pulled her to the floor in front of the swing.

The light—headlights—came from a car turning into the driveway and had them pinned, like a prison bar of light over their heads. If Becky got out and came up the steps, she'd practically trip over them. While Judi buttoned her blouse, she sent up a small prayer that Steve would manage at least a good-night kiss.

"C'mon, Steve," Thomas muttered. He was pulling for the same thing.

Then blackness and silence.

Thomas tugged her toward the door almost before she realized Steve had turned off the lights and the car engine.

"Gotta move before their eyes adjust," he whispered.

Staying low, they slipped inside the screen door. Thomas closed it without a sound, then pushed the inside door partly closed. His hand on her back guided her past the light from the stove and into the dim hallway.

He turned her, a hand on each of her upper arms.

"You okay? Did I hurt you when I pulled you down—"

"No. I'm fine. Just a little…"

"Undone." His mouth lifted in a faint smile, but his eyes glowed as his hands came to the buttons of her blouse. She tried to take over the task, but his hands were bigger and there first and there was nothing left for her hands to do. He undid two mismatched buttons. Just when she thought he was going to put them in their proper holes, though, his hand smoothed across the skin below her collarbone, where one side of her bra was still displaced because the strap remained down her arm.

She stepped back, pulling the strap up and holding the blouse with her hand.

Her smile was shaky. "How's that for a switch—the

teenagers almost catching the adults, uh…necking on the porch?''

"Helga—''

She winced and backed away. "Good night, Thomas.'' Then she fled.

She was out of her mind.

What else could account for a reasonably intelligent woman—she had the diplomas to prove the first half and the birth certificate to qualify for the second half—letting herself get carried away?

Letting herself. Right. Like she hadn't been a full participant

But he'd thought it was Helga Helgerson responding to him that way.

And look at her experience with rushing into a relationship. Aided by the comments of Geoff's "girlfriend,'' her hindsight was clear. Sterling's latching onto marrying her had something to do with that shipment he expected in mid-July. Smuggling was most likely. It could be drugs, although that was a dangerous world, and he didn't care for danger. All he cared about was Sterling. She'd been too caught up in the excitement of his courtship, in the attention he lavished on her, in the compliments he gave her to see that before her wedding day.

She had no worries about being blinded by such flattery from Thomas. He'd need a vocabulary-expanding course to become acquainted with *courtship, attention* and *compliments.* But he didn't need any lessons on kissing. Oh, my, no.

But that didn't alter that she was in no position to get involved with him.

On the other hand, they needed her here, even more than she needed a place to spend these weeks of waiting. She could always get that waitressing job in Montana. But who would look after Gran? Who would straighten out Becky? Who would kiss Thomas? Well, okay, that last one wasn't a good reason.

So she had her role straight. She looked after Gran, straightened out Becky and as for Thomas, she made him laugh, she helped his relationship with his sister and she provided an outlet for his worries.

But no kissing. Absolutely no more kissing. Or anything else.

"Fifteen minutes late and I can't go out for two weekends—it's not fair!"

Judi had recognized Becky was boiling with injustice since she and Gran had come into the kitchen this morning to find Becky and Thomas exchanging glares across the table. But there had been no opportunity for the girl to talk to her.

Judi had made sure there was no opportunity for Thomas to talk to her either. Not that he'd tried. There'd been one sharp look when she came in the kitchen. She'd avoided meeting it, and he hadn't come near her since.

Becky, Thomas, Keith and Gandy had moved cattle while she stayed out of the way. Now, with the stragglers funneling by a gate, Becky had her chance.

"You agreed to the time, and you were late," Judi said. "If you want privileges, you have to earn them by taking responsibility." Good Lord, she'd just channeled her mother.

"That's not why. He hates me."

"He doesn't hate you. In his odd, big-brotherly way, he loves you very much."

Becky slanted a look at her, clearly connecting with the "odd" comment, but not buying the rest. Time to surround the kid with logic.

"Did he always hate you?"

"No. We used to get along okay."

"When did it change?"

"A year ago or so." Her shoulders tensed and her jaw tightened, making her look more like her brother.

Since she was braced for *What changed a year ago?* Judi took a different route. "What's your definition of getting along okay?"

Becky glared at her, barely relaxing. "He didn't yell at me. He didn't think every single thing I did was wrong. He didn't act like I was this horrible person."

"Those are all the things he didn't do when you got along. I want to know what he did do. Say, when you were four. Did he read to you?"

"I suppose. Gran read more. He'd get me books from the library. About horses."

"You were already interested in horses. Who taught you about them?"

"Thomas." She said it reflexively, then frowned as it sank in. "He put me on my first pony. And showed me how to care for her. Later on he showed me how to rope, and work cattle."

"Doesn't sound like someone who hated you."

But she'd closed down. "It doesn't matter. I'll be out of here for college. Who knows, maybe I'll get of out before then." She sounded miserable at the prospect.

"What on earth—"

Judi paused on her way to put Thursday's breakfast leftovers away. A two-toned bell she'd never heard before sounded somewhere above her head.

Becky and Gran were at the table. Steve, Keith and Gandy had come and gone, bringing word that Thomas had gone to the bank again, an announcement that left everyone subdued. Although, that was an improvement over the one-sided cold war Becky had waged since Sunday. Judi sure couldn't fault his patience this time.

In the next instant Judi recognized the sounds as a doorbell. It took her longer to realize it must be coming from the front door.

Becky's eyes widened almost comically. "I have a bad feeling about this…"

The bell rang a second time. "Don't be dramatic, Becky. I'll go see who it is."

Through the window, she saw a middle-aged woman with short brown hair.

"Is this the Vance residence?"

"Yes, it is."

"Then you should be expecting me. My name is Helga."

Chapter Seven

Becky's gasp from behind Judi sucked in enough air that she felt as if she'd been pulled into a vacuum. Or maybe not being able to move her feet—or fire up the synapses in her brain—came from the knowledge that the jig was most definitely up.

If Becky hadn't heard the woman's announcement, maybe she would have tried to tough this out. But she wasn't going to entangle Becky in her lies.

"Helga Helgerson," the woman said tentatively. "From the Rural Health Aide agency."

A stream of air she hadn't been aware of holding came out of Judi, deflating her lungs, her spirits and hopes.

"You'd better come in."

By the time Judi let the woman in, closed the door, and directed her toward the kitchen, Becky had disappeared. Judi wouldn't blame the teenager if she'd gone to find rotten vegetables to heave at the false Helga. She deserved it. And she'd much prefer absorbing a few soggy tomatoes in the face to the possibility that Becky had gone to find Thomas.

If she got away from the Diamond V before she had to watch Thomas's face as all his distrust of her was confirmed, she would count herself a lucky woman for the rest of her life.

"How is the patient faring?"

Judi blinked back to the present. "Gran's doing great. She's a remarkable woman."

"Older patients need livening up to keep them from sinking into lethargy."

"Not Gran."

She stepped into the kitchen to find Becky urgently talking to her grandmother, her hands going nearly as fast as her lips. When Gran saw Judi and the woman behind her, she placed one hand on Becky's arm. Becky spun around, her mouth still forming a word, and stared at them like they were the Headless Horseman and Medusa come to call.

"Hello! I am so glad to be here after such a long delay," Helga said in the overly bright voice of an insecure kindergarten teacher. "I just know we will all get along wonderfully. Ah, the patient!"

"This is Gran," Judi said with emphasis, not liking the way Helga had labeled the older woman.

"Mrs. Swift, to you," Gran added.

Judi's heart sank before she realized that Gran had aimed her fierce frown and words at Helga, not her.

Helga blinked, then revved up her smile, advancing to twitch at the afghan to cover both Gran's legs and rearrange the crossword puzzle book and the water on her table. "Such a shame I was unavoidably detained on my previous assignment—the patient didn't rally the way we had hoped."

"Probably annoyed to death," Gran muttered, pushing back the afghan to cover only the nonbandaged side the way she liked it.

Helga showed no sign of hearing that, or of recognizing that her manner was not winning over her audience. "I am certain you have found the temporary aide satisfactory, but now I—"

"More than satisfactory," Gran interrupted with a warm look toward Judi.

"Oh. You're from the agency? But I thought you were a member of the family. You—you called the patient Gran." She made it sound like Judi had been caught spitting in the patient's medicine.

"Near enough to being a member of the family," Gran said. "And as for the temporary aide, we told the agency I already had all the care I needed, and not to send one. As a matter—"

"You did?" Judi spluttered.

Could Gran have possibly talked to the agency without finding out that she wasn't Helga? Whatever Gran knew, Becky was clearly in on it, too, or she would have been demanding answers in her usual Spanish Inquisition style. But if Gran and Becky knew… Judi's head pulsed with a beat of combined panic and hope so strong that she expected it to burst right here—what did Thomas know?

"Why would you do that?" Helga asked.

"As a matter of fact," Gran resumed, ignoring both interruptions, "we told them not to send you, either. So you have no reason to be here, and you might as well leave."

"Well, really, this is most extraordinary. I don't know what to say—"

"How about goodbye," Becky suggested in a low voice.

Judi fought a grin, and Gran couldn't hide all her amusement even as she said, "Manners, Becky."

"Yes'm."

But Helga was shaking her head. "The last word I had from the agency was to report here as soon as possible. I won't have it be said that Helga Helgerson did not do her duty.''

"Call the agency, but you have no duty here."

Gran's certainty seemed to shake Helga's. "Maybe I should call. If—''

"Becky will show you the phone in the family room."

"Right this way." Becky hooked Helga's arm and propelled her out of the room.

That left silence and a lot of questions. Not to mention guilt.

"Gran...why?" That was all she could get out.

"We'll talk about that later. First, let's get rid of this other Helga."

"Helga's not my name. My real name—''

"No, don't tell me. And whatever you do, don't tell Becky. If one of us slips in front of Thomas, there could be hell to pay. And she'd never forgive herself.''

Judi's hope sank like the mercury in a Chicago thermometer in January.

"Thomas doesn't know I'm not the health aide?"

If she'd needed any more answer than the expression in Gran's eyes, it came from Becky's squawk behind her.

"Thomas just drove up!"

Becky was staring out the window over the kitchen sink that looked toward the outbuildings.

"Oh, God, if he sees the other Helga—''

"Don't swear," Gran said automatically. "Becky, you go stall that woman. Keep her in the family room until I call you. You—'' she said to Judi, "go get Thomas away from the house. Do whatever you have to.''

"But— He never listens to me. How will I—''

"It's not his listening skills you need to appeal to— now, git! Both of you.''

"Hi!''

Thomas turned from the open truck door at the sound of that bright greeting.

He closed the door before answering with a cautious "Hi."

"What're you doing?"

"Looking for Gandy to give me a hand."

"He's not here. Can I help you?"

She said it so fast it almost came out as one word. Thomas tipped his head to study her better. He hadn't been sure what was going on when she'd run off Saturday night. But he'd gotten the message loud and clear Sunday when she sidled around him like he was a coiled rattler.

He'd run it through his head more times than he cared to admit since then. She had been as involved in the kissing as he had; he hadn't misread that. It was after they were in the kitchen that things had changed. If he'd said something that had triggered the change he sure didn't know what it was. If he'd done something…well, he'd done what he'd felt. Deciding she didn't like it was her right.

And he would live with that for two more weeks if it killed him.

"You don't even know what I need help with."

"I'm pretty handy. What is it?"

She wanted to be in the same square mile with him? That was a change since Saturday night. Something was going on. It was clear as day, as clear as the expression on her face. He could try to get it out of her, which hadn't worked so far. Or he could try to figure it out—but how much time did a man have in one day?

"Working Dickens around water and another horse. He gets hepped up about that."

"Oh, good!" She sounded more relieved than excited. But that was another clue he would have to let go in the interest of sanity and getting work done. "I've got jeans on and I'm all set—let's go!"

She had her hand tucked into his elbow and was tugging toward the corral where Dickens and Xena waited.

"All right, all right, I'm comin'. Awfully eager aren't you?"

"I've got a free afternoon, and I want to ride the ranch."

He spotted an unfamiliar vehicle parked at the front of the house.

"Whose car is that?"

"Alice is here."

"That's not Alice's car."

"She borrowed her sister's."

"Nita's in town?"

She shrugged. "All I know is what they tell me. Are we going or not?"

He seriously doubted the statement, but he satisfied himself with answering the question: "We're going."

"So, you not only led the horse to water, you got him to drink. Pretty impressive, Thomas."

He stretched his legs out on the tarp he'd laid on the ground for them to sit on while they let the horses rest. It covered a flat area up a sharp grade from creek level. It was big, about the size of a double bed. She swore at herself. Now why did she have to think of that? It wasn't like anything was going to happen. If this slick tarp he'd had rolled up behind his saddle had really been a bed they'd be about ready to fall off opposite edges, that's how careful they were being not to touch.

"I'd say I had mixed results along those lines lately."

First, they'd ridden nearly an hour, taking the edge off Dickens, he'd called it. She wished it had taken an edge off what she was feeling.

He'd taken Dickens across the water alone, with Xena following, with Xena ahead, with the horses side by side, then repeated the variations several times and in different order. Dickens had passed with flying colors. The reward for both horses was the freedom to drink, and a chance to wander as far as the combination of a tied lead-line and hobbles let them.

Her reward was sitting on a tarp, trying to pretend she didn't want to make full use of this time alone with Thomas.

"Mixed results in getting a horse to drink, I mean," he added, leaning back on his elbows, and looking at her. When she met his eyes, she had her suspicions confirmed—he wasn't talking about horses, or drinking water.

His green gaze dropped to her lips, and she felt a pulse through the center of her body, as strong from that look as she'd felt from his touch.

A second pulse followed immediately on the first—this one stronger and hotter. It was the knowledge that if she let there be a *this time,* he would not show the restraint he had on the porch swing.

And she didn't want him to.

"Sometimes you think a horse is going to drink, might even start on it, but then he changes his mind and stops. But that's okay. Drinking water's not something a horse should be forced into."

She turned away, facing the creek. She'd worked this out, and knew all the reasons she couldn't do this. But desire was rushing up against her resolutions like flood water overtaking a raft.

"Oh, look at the flower." She stood and started for the bright yellow bloom at the edge of the creek embankment.

"You shouldn't pick wildflowers."

From his voice, he'd sat up, but she didn't look around.

"I'm not going to pick it. I just want a closer look."

"Don't go too far out, because—"

It was the strangest sensation she'd ever felt. Like the earth under her feet had become one of those moving walkways in an airport—only downhill and *fast.*

A band of human steel wrapped around her middle, and swung her away from the edge. She and Thomas stumbled a few feet more, to the edge of the tarp, and looked back to see that a two-foot section of earth had slid into the creek.

They straightened, his arm wrapped around her midriff, his hand spread wide against her side, his thumb brushing the underside of her breast. She leaned back against him.

"Thank you. If you hadn't—"

"Are you okay?" Thomas still had the vision of the earth sliding out from under her in his head.

"I'm fine. I'm…"

Only when her voice trailed away did the details of their contact hit home to him. He was stroking her, letting his hand flirt with the curve of her breast, while her hip snuggled against his fast-hardening groin.

He dropped his hand, and she immediately sank to the tarp, sitting cross-legged with her head down. If she was crying…

"It's okay. Don't worry. Nothing's going to…" Nothing was going to happen? How could he tell her that when it was already happening. But there was one thing he could swear to her. "I won't—"

She interrupted with something close to wail. "Don't be nice to me."

Her hair covered her face. Slowly, he sat beside her, careful not to touch. "Don't be nice to you?"

"Don't any of you be nice to me. I don't deserve it."

This woman who'd never once backed down, who'd coped with everything thrown her way with humor and pleasure was on the edge. Enough of a push, and she'd be over. All he had to do was ask the right question, or maybe ask the wrong questions enough times, and he'd have his answers. One push, and she'd crack like Humpty-Dumpty, revealing the truth at last.

Automatically, she tucked her hair behind her ear, revealing moisture sparkling in her lower lashes.

Splinter like Humpty-Dumpty…and never be put back together again?

Moving slowly he reached out and wiped at the tears

with the pad of his thumb. It left a tiny trail of mud on her cheek.

He bent his head for a better angle as he wiped it again. Her eyes opened and pulled him in like a straw in a twister. "Thomas…"

"Damn. I won't, unless… But if you…?"

"Yes."

He made himself wait. Gave her a chance to reconsider. Just not much of a chance. His hands on her face turned her to him, and then their mouths met. She gasped, and he swallowed it like he'd craved nothing more in life.

She was holding onto him, too. Her hands urging his head closer to hers.

Heat, pleasure, need. They cycled through him fast enough to make him dizzy. So dizzy the world seemed to have tilted so he was looking down at her.

No, he really *was* looking down at her. She was lying on the tarp and he was half on top of her. His shirt gone, hers opened, his hands at the open waist of her jeans, and he didn't remember the steps that had gotten them here.

"Hel—"

She covered his mouth with her hand. "Shh. No more talking."

He shook his head. This had to be said. "If you don't want this to go farther, you better say it now."

"I didn't want it to not go farther last time."

Before he'd untangled that, she'd brought his mouth back down to hers, and gave him an answer he understood fully.

"The ground's too hard. Here…" He rolled, pulling her on top of him, cushioning her body with his.

She breathed a soft kiss at the center of his chest. Enough heat surged through him to mold a horseshoe.

Under her shirt, he stroked his palms down her silken back, dipping to her waist, under the loosened jeans and the top of her panties, and over the soft, rounded flesh below. His movement drew her panties and jeans lower and lower. Pressing down brought her in full contact with his erection straining against the material separating them. She made a small sound and rocked her hips.

He wanted to have her naked and under him, so he could plunge into her heat and softness. But the ground was no welcoming mattress, the tarp no satin coverlet.

"We should have a bed—"

"Now, Thomas. We should have now."

She slid down so her thighs bracketed his, and set to undoing his belt buckle. He sat up to interrupt her, one arm at a time, as he pushed aside her shirt and bra, revealing the delight of her rounded, perfect breasts. She shivered and arched when he drew his thumb across one tip. But she pushed him down with a hand to his chest.

"I can't concentrate."

She fumbled with the button at the top of the jeans zipper, the flesh of his belly clenching and shivering with pleasure at each misguided brush of her fingers. If she didn't get that button, soon…

Ah, the button slipped through, and the zipper started down. He covered her hands with his, to keep the motion slow and nonlethal. But as soon as it was down, he released his hold.

She slid her hands under his briefs and cupped him, and he was this close to making *now* literal.

He jerked up, swinging her off him. For an instant she looked startled, dismayed, then as he tugged at the denim and lace still covering her, she smiled and lifted her hips to let him pull it free. He yanked off his jeans and briefs. And thanked providence that a faint crackle reminded him to take a packet out of his pocket.

"I could—" she started to offer.

"No, you couldn't." Or they'd be back to that *now* problem.

How, he didn't know, but he did it, and then took her mouth as he wrapped his arms around her and leaned back, encouraging her to stretch atop him again. He stroked into her mouth, and she picked up the motion, brushing the tips of her breasts against his chest. It was eternity and less time than a clock could measure before she sat up to position herself over him. His hands guided her hips as he raised his own, pushing into her.

A sound came through her parted lips and she closed her eyes, as she sank down to take him fully.

Then she opened her eyes, and the driving, pulsing force between them rushed into full throat. A shout refusing to be stilled.

He saw it catch her, saw the flush rise up her body. He touched the rosiness on her, traced it up her abdomen, and absorbed the hardened pebbles of her nipples under his fingers. He felt her shudder with it, then clench and squeeze and pulse around him. And then it had him, too. Lifting, pressing, driving… Soaring.

And coming back to earth with her collapsed atop him. His oxygen-greedy lungs raising and lowering her, creating a fine, delicious friction of her nipples against his flesh.

When he had the strength and the breath, he shifted her enough to deal with necessities, then dropped back with her still half sprawled across him. He pulled his shirt across her back, and drifted, beyond content with the sensation and satisfaction.

A shudder of her shoulders pulled him back.

"Cold?" He placed one leg over hers to give her more of his heat.

"It's the crickets."

"They bother you?"

"Not usually. But they sound…sad."

He listened. His mouth nuzzled against her temple. "They sound sad to you?"

"Uh-huh. Or desperate."

"Desperate crickets, huh? Maybe they know it's getting toward the end of the summer and their days are numbered."

Their days are numbered. His own phrase sent a chill through him as surely as a January wind.

It shouldn't. Their days were numbered, too. He knew that, so why the chill? Had hopes of a future been lying somewhere underneath his conscious mind? He wasn't going to fall into that trap. Dammit, he wasn't.

"Do they always call *hur-ry, hur-ry* when it's not even August yet?"

"Summer ends fast around here." Long before summer ended, she'd be gone. "We better get going now."

He reached for his clothes.

She sat up, still naked. He looked away.

"But you still have the memories. The memories you can pull out to make yourself warm."

Was she trying to convince herself or him? He didn't turn around.

"Right, you have memories. All you have are memories."

She wouldn't cry. She would absolutely not cry. What did she expect? He'd spelled it out. She knew, and she'd still made love with him—practically begged him.

Someone practical and levelheaded, who's never impulsive and never gets in scrapes.

Practical and levelheaded—she'd made love with him here on the ground.

Impulsive—it should have been her middle name.

Never gets in scrapes—if he knew that she'd run away from her own wedding, knew why she'd run and how she was lying to him…

She was nothing Thomas Vance was looking for in a woman, and everything he didn't want, including a liar. No wonder he'd pulled back. No wonder when his brain resumed operations, he'd realized this could never work.

But she couldn't regret it. The aftermath maybe, but not making love with him.

If he'd run into the real Helga earlier today, she never

would have had the chance to make love with him. Now she might not have another chance. No, she couldn't regret it.

Becky popped out of the barn when Judi rode up.

"I thought you'd want to know it's all clear. Gran and I—"

"No, wait. Let's wait until we can talk with Gran, too."

She didn't want to have to say these things twice. Actually she didn't want to say them at all. She wanted to go up to her room—the guest room—pull the covers up and cry. But she wouldn't.

Gran was on the porch sitting on a straight-backed chair they'd placed there for her as she continued to gain strength and mobility.

"Sit, both of you," Judi instructed. She perched on the edge of the swing. "I owe you an explanation—and I *want* to tell you—but I've thought about this and I keep coming back to it being better if you don't know right now. When it's over, I'll tell you everything—everything I know, anyhow. But until then…I can tell you I haven't done anything wrong."

"Are you in danger?" Becky asked.

"No, no, it's nothing like that. It's…" She raised her hands then let them drop. "Impossible to explain without explaining. I thought you should know I still can't tell you before you decide what to do."

"We've already decided, and it's done. She's gone, and you're staying." Gran made it sound as simple as choosing mayo or butter on a sandwich.

"When did you— I mean, how long have you—?"

"We knew you weren't Helga Helgerson, and we knew you weren't a health aide. The agency called the week after you arrived, and Becky took the call. We talked it over, and decided you should stay."

"We figured you were running from something awful

and needed our help.'' Becky's whispery voice would have done credit to a secret agent.

"We needed you,'' Gran amended. "You were doing a good job helping me. You got along with Becky, and even made a dent or two in Thomas. Besides, other than a couple insignificant facts, we already knew you are who you've told us you are. In here.'' She tapped her own chest.

Judi's eyes filled.

"But Thomas... If he knew I've been lying...''

"He'll blow a gasket when he finds out. But you can handle that. That's why you're good for him. You don't let him close up. You go right at him. Guess I've seen him sad too much. Maybe I've been too gentle with him.''

She was good for Thomas? Judi had hoped that once. But now...? Not only had she lied to him, she was the absolute last kind of woman he wanted. More important, could she stay knowing he felt that way when she felt...well, something different?

"I really appreciate everything you both did today, and before. I'm so grateful...'' Tears clogged the words. "But it would be best for me to move on now, and—''

"You can't!''

"We need you.''

"Please.'' Gran took her granddaughter's hand in hers as she spoke, uniting them against potential disappointment.

The solitary word and the simple gesture echoed with the departure of another woman from the Diamond V.

Gran had said Thomas saw a connection between her and Maureen. She wasn't about to strengthen that connection in his mind.

As soon as she could, she'd sit him down and tell him the truth—tell them all the truth. She would leave no lies behind her. And maybe, just maybe Thomas would see that his version of the ideal woman was not the only solution for a lone ranger.

In the meantime…

"If I'm going to stay, I have to feel I've earned my way."

And try not to feel too much more.

Chapter Eight

When Thomas came in for a supper of turkey casserole, green beans and baked apples the next day, he discovered she'd started organizing the desk drawers.

Work had kept him away from supper last night. In fact, kept him out until the house went dark. He was out of the house this morning before she stirred. But it wasn't like he was trying to avoid her. She would leave, but not for weeks yet. No big deal. As long as he kept some distance.

"I did as much as I could without consulting you, but we'll need to go over some things before I can finish."

She looked at him across the table there in front of his grandmother and sister, and gave him a bright smile. Like he hadn't held her naked the day before. Like she hadn't closed around him like—

"Thomas?"

He jerked back to now at Gran's voice.

"Did you hear Helga?"

"Yeah, I heard. Do whatever you want." He dug his

spoon into the softened baked apple, sending juice slopping over the edge of the dish and into the saucer below it. Of course Helga had saucers under the dishes. She thought of everything.

"The bills and the business papers I could organize because I'm familiar with those. But the information on the breeding and training business—that you need to decide how to divide up so when—"

"When you leave," he interrupted, deliberate and cold.

Her smile sank like a rock. But she pulled in a breath and said, "It'll be easier to remember if you make up the system."

"After I finish the night's paperwork. If you're still around."

Bad move, he told himself four hours later.

She'd stayed up after Gran and Becky went to bed, which meant it was the two of them, alone, in a pool of light from the desk lamp talking about color-coded file systems, for God's sake, and answering her thousand and one questions about horse breeding and training.

At least she hadn't sat next to him. She'd pulled Gran's chair to the side of the desk, with the open drawers between them. The problem was, he had a clear view of her face this way. Her face, and the line of her throat down into the vee opening of her top to the hollow that had a pulse so strong and skin almost as soft as the satin cream that covered the rounded curve of her—

"Okay? The red folders for potential training clients— red for hot prospects. Does that work for you?"

"Yeah. Sure."

"What color for follow-ups on training clients?"

"Orange."

"You don't think that will be confusing? They're awfully close in color."

"That's why it works. They'll bring those horses back—unless they sell because they decide the problem's with the animal or go to another trainer because they decide the problem's with me."

"Bring them back? For advanced training?"

"Remedial training. Retraining, because the horse has been screwed up again. Nine times out of ten a horse with bad habits has learned them from a bad rider. The tenth time the rider hasn't given the horse enough time and patience to wipe out the bad habits."

"But once you train a horse like Dickens and have him working well..."

"He'll last a while, until Warren Upton or somebody else who doesn't know how to handle horses gets him right back into those bad habits. What ought to be done is training the riders."

"Then why don't you?"

"Folks want fancy places to teach horsemanship, with jodhpurs and jackets. Nobody wants to come to a plain working ranch for that."

"I don't see why not, especially when they're riding on a working ranch like Warren Upton does. He doesn't want jumping or hunter classes or dressage, he wants to know how to ride a horse to cut cattle or rope."

"How do you know about hunter classes and dressage?"

He waited for the familiar *I don't remember.*

She met his eyes for a split second, then looked at the folders in her hands. She put them on the desk.

"You're right, it's time for me to go to bed," she said, as. if he'd just said that instead of it being a good hour ago, "Good night, Thomas."

She got up and walked out of the kitchen without ever looking his way, and he made no move to stop her.

She couldn't say *I don't remember* to him anymore. Well, he supposed that was something. Just not nearly enough.

* * *

Thomas sipped from his first cup of coffee two mornings later.

Good coffee was about all that had kept him going the past two days.

The kitchen was silent except for the low hum of the new coffeemaker. The day's first light spread across the east-facing windows. That was another change Helga had made, leaving those curtains open at night so he had morning light when he came down.

The daylight caught something on the table he hadn't noticed when he'd come in last night—a newspaper folded into quarters, showing the classified section. As he took it to the window to see it better, water came on in the upstairs bathroom.

He took another swallow of coffee as he noted comments in Helga's handwriting in the margin near four ads that had been circled. The ads were for low-priced used cars.

She was leaving.

She could use a ranch truck for any other transportation need. Only reason she'd need her own car was to leave.

She was leaving.

Of course she was. The six weeks were nearly up. She didn't have any other reason to stay.

Did she?

So there was chemistry between them. Powerful, atomic-bomb chemistry. He wasn't stupid enough to start thinking that meant anything you could count on. Thinking any other way was a prescription for disaster. Hadn't he seen that? Wasn't he living with the consequences of it right now?

Being a reasonable human being, he couldn't expect her to do anything but leave. Because the alternative was that she would stay.

So she was looking up used-car ads. Made sense.

She was leaving.

The hell she was.

* * *

Having let the water run long enough to warm up, Judi adjusted the faucets and stepped into the shower.

She shouldn't have been so depressed last night. By the light of day things looked considerably better.

Once the date of Sterling's shipment passed she wouldn't have to keep the secret any longer. So there would no longer be any reason for her not to tell Thomas, tell them all, why she'd hid her identity. She'd tell him the truth, and he'd understand.

She'd have to go back to Illinois for a while—to let her family and friends know she was fine, and she supposed that undercover girlfriend of Geoff's might want to see her. But she'd explain all that to Thomas, and then she'd come back, and they could...

Well, she didn't know what they would do. She put the soap in the dish and turned to rinse.

It wasn't like Thomas had said anything that hinted he'd thought of a future with her.

A vision flashed into her head—Thomas waiting at the front of a church, and her walking down an aisle. "Are you sure?" her father asked, looking at her with concern. "Yes!" she shouted.

Judi waited for the vision to pop like a soap bubble. Nope, still there. Maybe motion would pop it. She turned and let the water cascade down her back. Still there.

She was in love with Thomas. Totally and completely in love with him.

The shower curtain opened and Thomas stepped in.

She covered her own mouth to stop a scream.

"Thomas! What are you doing? Get out of here! You can't do this."

"I already have." He slid his hands around her back and pulled her close to his naked and aroused body then shut the shower curtain. "We have to talk."

"Talk?" she squeaked.

"There's no reason for you to get a car."

"Car? I...oh. But—"

"Gran's not ready to do without help yet. Nowhere near ready." He kissed the spot where her neck met her shoulder, then at the base of her throat, tonguing the hollow there. "We need you for another six weeks."

At the moment she didn't care if he thought Gran would need help for that long or if it was an excuse to keep her around. Either way, it bought her time.

Time to see if Thomas could fall in love with her.

"I'll let the agency know. But it'll be okay, because we can contract on our own after the initial contact," she ad-libbed.

"Consider yourself contracted for another six weeks then."

"Okay." She sucked in a breath as his hand stroked down her back to the curve of her derriere, pulling her tight against his hardened body. "But I still need a car, and I'll need a week or so to go, uh, see if there're ways to get my memory back."

"Where?"

"Uh, I thought maybe the agency could help me."

"South Dakota? I'll take you."

"There's no need—"

"Right after—" He dropped his head and took her nipple into his mouth, sucking and licking. She arched her back, giving him greater access and fitting more tightly against his lower body. He licked at the hollow between her breasts. "I pay off Maureen."

"No need..."

But he'd taken her other nipple, and there was need...just not the same kind. The smooth heat of him pressed against her, seeking entrance.

He muttered against her flesh, then held absolutely still for a half dozen heartbeats. Then he went into motion. He pivoted her around, backing her into the corner of the enclosure.

"Stay there," he ordered. Like she might go wandering off.

He opened the shower curtain, letting water spray across the floor. "Thomas!"

But he was yanking open the medicine cabinet door. "It'll dry."

Before she'd budged the curtain he was back, the curtain closed and he was tearing open a packet.

Hot, wet flesh, stubborn latex and two sets of eager hands turned the next few minutes into a symphony of groans, curses, pleas and laughter.

"We would never make it on a how-to video," she said with another giggle, stroking the back of his neck.

He slid his hand to the inside of her thigh, exerting pressure to draw it up and up, until her leg naturally curled around him. He traced a path down the back of her raised leg, then around, slipping a slow finger into her entrance with a murmur of appreciation. Rocked from the inside out, she grabbed onto his shoulders with one hand and the towel bar with the other for balance.

"This—" he cupped her, opened her wider, then positioned himself "—is the how-to where we shine."

He thrust home, and balance was gone for good.

All that mattered was holding him, welcoming him. Judi had time now. Time to show him, time to build trust at a level deeper and more enduring than words. She took him into her body, and wrapped herself around him, and surely he would understand this for the most honest, most trusting exchange possible between a man and a woman. So this spiral of stroke and thrust where each motion, each touch elaborated on the one that had gone before—and more important what they felt that brought them to this— would endure when the paper walls of words spoken and not spoken tumbled down.

"Thomas…"

He kissed her, his mouth covering hers, his tongue

matching their rhythm. Faster now. Their mouths separated as they gasped for oxygen to fuel the race.

She had wrapped both legs around him, no longer bound by such necessities as standing. The spiral tightened, cycling, reaching for a point she could almost touch, almost…yes…almost…

She pressed her mouth to his shoulder, muffling the cries that wanted to be shouted. He dropped his head back, while his arms crushed her to him, and she felt the power of his response inside and around her.

They collapsed into each other, and simply occupied this slice of time and space until reality returned.

She was held up between the wall and him—she surely couldn't have held herself up even if her feet had been on the ground. Had she ever kept her feet on the ground when Thomas touched her? Still inside her, he was slumped against her, pulling in air.

She moved one hand—that was all she could manage—to stroke his back. Goose bumps.

"Thomas! You're cold."

He raised his head from her shoulder, but it took another second for his eyes to clear. "Hot water must've run out."

"How long ago?"

"Don't know."

And he didn't sound like he cared, but she felt the chill in him now. She nudged him. "Thomas, we have to get out of here. Turn the water off."

He kissed her once, quick and sweet on her closed mouth, then pulled away, turned off the water and held back the shower curtain for her.

He wrapped her in a towel, disposed of the condom and grabbed another towel for himself.

The bath mat had slid to the far side of the bathroom, she pulled it back with her toes and discovered they'd created a puddle on the floor—probably when Thomas had hopped out. She started to sop it up with another towel, but he pulled her up against him, and the only puddle on her mind then was the one where her backbone should have been.

"I want you in my bed."

The puddle turned to steam. "We can't."

He stroked down her arm.

"Really, Thomas. We can't." She retreated a step. "You know how I knew you were in my room that day I came in here and you were shaving?"

He looked at her. And that look said he didn't care how she'd known, because he didn't care what her reasons were for saying they couldn't. And if she looked at him much longer she'd be drawn right along with his not caring.

"I heard your footsteps."

He kissed the side of her neck. The heat there melted her muscles, maybe the bone, too. "Thomas. They'll hear us. My room's right over Gran's."

He raised his head from where her shoulder met her neck. "My room…"

"Is right over Becky's. And if you don't think she would figure it out, you don't know your sister."

He stared at her another beat. Muttered an oath, then tucked her up against him, with his chin on her wet hair.

"Okay, here's what we'll do. Slip out of the house tonight after Gran and Becky are asleep, and meet me down the back road. I'll have the new truck there."

"But where—"

"Will you meet me?"

"Yes, bu—"

"All I want is the yes."

"What took you so long?"

She could hear the grin in Thomas's voice as she climbed into the truck. He leaned across her to shut the passenger door then drew her up against him.

"Those wretched noisy stairs. I thought the whole county could hear me."

"I'll have to fix those." He started the engine but left the lights out as they bumped along the dark road.

"Where are we going?"

"You'll see."

He wouldn't tell her any more, even when they'd parked atop a high hill that seemed to have nothing but sky around it.

"Where are we?"

"Someplace where I can make love to you, and keep on making love to you until you scream."

"What if I'm not a screamer?"

"I'm a patient man."

She made a sound of disbelief. Then turned thoughtful. "You know, that's an incentive for a girl to not scream no matter what. So you'll keep trying and trying."

He smiled. "True. But there are other incentives. Stronger incentives. Wait right there."

He got out and went around the back. She heard him open the tailgate, but before she'd turned to see what he was doing, he was at the passenger door.

"What's going on?"

"Have a little patience."

He scooped her up, leaving her no option but to put her arms around his neck. In a half-dozen strides he was setting her into the bed of the pickup—truly a bed.

Sheets covered an air-mattress, surrounded by bolsters and pillows that cushioned the walls of the enclosed space.

"Scoot on up."

She did, and he followed her, pulling the tailgate up behind him, then shifting two bolsters in front of it. With his back to her, he yanked off his boots, setting them in a corner, followed by his hat.

Then he faced her.

She drew in a quick deep breath, then another, as he advanced on her, his intent clear and carnal.

"Oh, Thomas, this is wonderful. I thought when you said to meet you—"

He kissed her. Wrapping his arms around her like he couldn't wait another second. And neither could she. She opened her mouth and her arms to him. Reveling in the firm, hungry stroke of his tongue into her mouth.

The feel of him was so right and true that she thought she could explode just from this solitary second. But time kept adding seconds and each one had its pleasures. She drew his strength and weight with her as she lay back against the cushions. He unbuttoned the four buttons below the waist of her sarong, but when he tried to push aside the material he met a resistance he clearly hadn't expected.

"How the hell do you—?"

"Wait. Let me…"

"Wait?" he repeated.

She wanted him to *wait?* Waiting was the last thing his body had in mind.

She slid away from him and adjusted the skirt to let her come to her knees beside him. With his full attention on her, and never taking her gaze from his face, she untied the knot at her waist, opened the fabric and let it fall to pool around her. A pair of lacy panties rode low on her hips, a scant triangle of coverage with fragile bands connecting front and back.

The fullness in his groin took a quantum leap.

He reached for her, wanting to feel her body stretched out along his.

"Wait," she said again.

Waiting was still not a concept he was eager to embrace. On the other hand, if she rewarded him again like she just had…

Her hands went behind her neck. In another second the two sides of her top dropped from her shoulders, the descent stopped only by the fullness of her breasts and the tight points of her nipples. She reached lower behind her back this time, and fabric belled loose at her sides.

She drew in a strong, slow breath, and released it. The fabric slid slowly at first, then fell away in an instant.

He came up on his knees before her, bending to touch his mouth to one rose-pointed nipple before straightening.

She didn't have to tell him to wait this time. He wanted this slow, so slow it never ended.

"Take your clothes off, Thomas." The huskiness of her voice was another sensation of pleasure.

"Yes'm."

With the slightest pressure on the top of her shoulders, he urged her to sit back on her heels. He traced the ridge of her collarbone with his thumbs, and kissed the corner of her mouth, his own lifting into a smile as he straightened.

Then, with her watching him as he had watched her, and echoing her deliberateness, he unbuttoned his shirt, pulled it from the waist of his jeans, then shrugged it off. He opened the belt buckle and slid down the zipper of his jeans. Then hooked the waist of briefs and jeans to pull them over his hips, and saw a flush of desire flow across her moon-pale breasts.

He sat to pull his clothes the rest of the way off, then returned to his knees. She came up to meet him. Kneeling there before each other, they feathered touches across each other's skin, stroked and traced. Until they both trembled.

He laid her back among the cushions. Found the first of the packets he'd brought and sheathed himself.

He knelt again, between her legs, bending to press his mouth to her heated wetness through the thin fabric. Her hips came up to meet his caress, and there was no more waiting. He started to draw her panties down, but she made a noise of impatience and it fired him like nothing else could. The fabric bands over her hips ripped free with the first tug.

"Open for me."

She did, her hips elevated. He cupped her rounded buttocks in his hands, and stroked into her.

Thomas had a vague memory of changing an irrigation pipe, but other than that the past two days were foggy at best. But the nights…ah the nights were as clear and warm and changeable as her eyes.

And here he stood again, waiting for her to slip out of the house to join him for the ride into the hills in their portable bed. He'd done fancy talking to keep Gandy from fixing the "broken" truck. He couldn't let anybody else use it or they'd discover the bedding under the tarp. So far so good, but he didn't know how long it could last.

How long *they* could last.

She'd taken the second six weeks, but there was something…

A figure showed under the porch light, carefully closing the door, then coming down the stairs, and slipping into the shadows.

But he could still see the one particular shadow he was interested in. His shadow, he thought with a surge of possessiveness. She was coming to him.

And right now he didn't give a damn that she was lying.

"You know why you want to hold the ranch together?"

Her head was tucked in the crook of his shoulder. Their sweat-slick bodies were cooling fast enough that she was grateful for the blanket he'd pulled up. They'd been lying like this earlier, and he'd started talking about his dreams for the ranch, and there'd been such hope and pride in his voice and his plans that she'd had to kiss him…and then they were lying like this again.

"Because it could be a financial disaster if I don't."

"That's your rational reason. But there's a more important one—the one from the gut." She stroked his bare belly. "The one that's making you work so hard. The one that makes you not just worried about the idea of losing a quarter of the ranch, but crazy at the thought."

"I'm not craz—"

"It's the people."

That stopped him. "What?"

"It's because this ranch to you is not just land, it's people. It's your mother and your father. It's Gran and Becky. It's Gandy and Keith and Steve and all the rest. It's the landscape of your family and all the people you love."

"That's—"

"Shut up and listen for once. When you talk about the ranch, you don't tell me how much it's worth per square foot or what the production is per acre or what kind of grass grows where. Sure you're worried about money now, because of Maureen and everything. But when you talk about the ranch, you talk about your family, and the hands and your dreams for breeding horses. You could give up this land—"

"This land is—"

"Oh, I know, it's important. But it's important because it's what ties together all the people you've cared about in your life. Your mother. Your father. Gran. Becky."

Her. Hope slipped that into her thoughts before she could shut it out.

"The ranch is not just for me," he said. "It's what Becky will have. To know where she belongs, to know she's loved and was wanted."

"Why would she ever doubt those things?"

His expression went blank—almost blank, because she read a bleakness that triggered a memory of his words.

"'If Becky knew about her mother, it could be even tougher on her.' That's what you said. Is there more than that Maureen wants to sell off her share of the ranch? It has to do with that Thanksgiving, doesn't it? Listen to me, Thomas, if you and Becky are going to be close again, you have to bring whatever this is out in the open. It can only help—"

"Not this."

She waited. Waited to see if he was done being the lone

ranger. Waited to see if he would share this burden with her. Waited to see if he would trust her.

"Maureen came back that Thanksgiving. Cooked this turkey dinner, made it seem like she was going to stick around forever. Before dinner, she took Dad aside. Came out after an hour, and she's all smiles as she sets the table and starts putting food out. Dad had given her a wad of money again, and she was leaving in the morning. Dad was a wreck, and I knew Becky would be crying into her pillow for months, and I lost it.

"I dragged her out on the porch and told her I'd stop Dad's check if she tried to leave. Told her if she had any decency, she'd stay with her daughter and her husband. She laughed—angry and kind of hysterical, and she said that was just it—Rick Vance wasn't her husband because she'd still been married when they met. She'd gotten tired of her husband and left him—didn't even tell him, much less get a divorce. She came out here for something *different.* But she'd never divorced her first husband and that made Becky a bastard—she said that. If I wanted her to tell Dad and Becky, she'd be only too happy to—and if I stopped the check she'd tell them no matter what. Only time in my life I had to fight like hell to keep from hitting a woman."

Under her hand his muscles had tensed to rock.

"I said the check would clear, but she had to leave right then, no more pretending, no more of her lying. And she was not coming back. Ever. She packed up and left. None of them knew why."

Remembering Gran's concern for Thomas over the turkey, Judi wasn't so sure, but he continued, "She didn't even say goodbye to Dad and Becky. They came in expecting dinner and her. And I...I..."

"Couldn't stand to have them eat food prepared by that lying witch."

He twisted around at her words, as if to see if she was as angry as she'd sounded. She was.

No wonder his feelings about Maureen were so strong— she not only threatened the ranch, but also threatened his family.

"I don't blame you a bit for throwing out the meal she'd fixed. You probably should have fumigated the place. How she could do that to Becky, to your Dad—to all of you… I'd like to get my hands on her—"

He threw his head back and laughed.

"What?" She supposed she should be glad she'd broken his grim mood, but really, justice for a woman like that would be a good—

"You're a fierce one." He kissed her, gentle and long. Justice for Maureen was long forgotten when he said, "I'd rather have you get your hands on me."

"Ow! Why are we doing this again? Am I being punished for something?"

She and Becky were picking strawberries from plants nestled against the gooseberry bushes at the back of the garden. At least Judi was picking berries. From the amount and volume of complaining from Becky, she was mostly fighting the prickly bushes.

"Because these strawberries make great pies, and Gran says Thomas loves her strawberry pie recipe."

Becky muttered something that combined a less than flattering adjective with her brother's name.

"Are you feeling like you should be punished for something?"

"No. Thomas just treats me like a criminal even though I haven't done anything."

"Why do you think he does that?"

"He never lets me go out, and when he does, he practically locks and bars the door if I come home five minutes late—"

Ignoring the illogic between *he never* and *when he does,* Judi interrupted. "I mean *why* as in what is his motive for doing that?"

"I dunno."

Judi nearly clucked her tongue. But Becky would have to find out on her own that sullen rarely sounded like innocent—even when the speaker truly was innocent.

Becky's head was down, her bottom lip caught between her teeth, and her shoulders hunched. She looked miserable and...*guilty?* Maybe that hadn't been sullen she'd heard in Becky's response. Maybe it had been guilty. But what could the girl have to feel guilty about?

"Oh, I think you do know..." The soft voice and gentle intonation were straight out of her own teen years—when she'd been on the receiving end. Good Lord, there she went channeling her mother again.

Becky raised her head in a blaze of anger.

"He hates me because of my mother, all right?"

"Why would he hate you because of her? She's not even here."

"That's the point. She left and she ruined everything—for the ranch, for Thomas, for everybody." Becky squirmed as if poked by thorns, only Judi suspected these pricks were inside. "I'm her kid. She's not here to hate, so he hates me."

"Becky, I don't think—"

"Dad said he wanted her to have a share of the ranch so she knew he'd meant it when he'd said this would always be her home. He'd pledged to give her a home when they got married, and her leaving didn't change that. Dad was such a...so—"

"In love," Judi supplied.

"Not with Maureen." Becky's bald reply made Judi blink.

"But—"

"Dad always loved Thomas's mom—Denise."

"But the will— And Thomas—"

She stopped herself just in time from saying that Thomas thought his father had been heartbroken at Maureen's departure. He and Becky had to talk to each other, not through her.

"I heard him—Dad—talking to Maureen on the phone about six months before he died. He'd tracked her down, reminding her to call the next day because it was my birthday. I knew he did that—birthdays, Christmas, Thanksgiving. Sometimes he found her and got her to call, sometimes he didn't. I—" Becky looked up at her through her eyelashes, as if checking for her reaction "—didn't like to be surprised. I'd listen in on the day-before calls, so I'd know if she was going to call.

"He told her he was sorry he hadn't made her feel loved. He said he cared about her, but so much of his heart would always be with Denise that maybe there hadn't been enough left to make her want to stay and make this her home."

Judi kept her eyes open, afraid if she blinked tears would flow over.

Thomas believed his father had been betrayed by love. But it had been guilt that had pushed Rick Vance to try to make things right with his second wife—guilt that he'd loved his first wife so much that he had short-changed Maureen.

"But she got the last laugh. As soon as she could, she set it up for her share of the ranch to be sold. Thomas thinks I don't know, but I'm not an idiot."

Becky clearly saw Judi's impending tears. She thought the girl might give way to tears, too, but Becky stiffened her chin, and a harsher emotion took hold.

"Don't feel sorry for her," Becky ordered. "She never cared that much. She makes a good show of it. Called and said she wanted me to understand. Had this long explanation about selling her share. She said it was for me— the money for her share of the ranch. Though, of course, she'd keep some, just for a nest egg." Becky's imitation made Judi wince. "She said she was going to make sure I had money for when I want to leave—college or whenever. I told her I don't want to leave—not like that, just for college. I told her I don't want the ranch carved up. She wouldn't listen. She said someday I'd come to my senses and want to get out.''

A car horn blared from around the front of the house. Who would—?

But Becky was going on. "I just wish—what I should've asked her is if she thought it was horrible here, how could she have left me? I'm not saying I wish she'd taken me—I *don't!* But how could she leave her kid in what she thought was the worst place on earth?''

"Maybe she thought you'd be better taken care of here, better than if she took you with her," Judi said.

Becky raised her head, and Judi saw in the girl's eyes both sorrow and acceptance. Becky didn't believe that any more than she did. It seemed the teenager took a giant, painful stride toward maturity in that silent moment.

"If she cared about me, she'd leave the ranch in one piece and things could go back the way they were, and Thomas wouldn't have to work so hard, all because…''

Becky's voice faded, but Judi mentally filled in the end. All because of a self-centered woman who didn't understand what she'd been offered by her ex-husband—a way to reclaim her home and daughter.

The car horn sounded again.

"I know it's hard, Becky, but…'' Judi put an arm around the girl's shoulders and leaned down to look at her. "Wait a minute… You don't—you can't— You think it's your fault? You do… You think it's your fault Thomas is working so hard, and you think *he* thinks it's your fault. And that's what's making you so prickly around him.''

"She said it was for me,'' Becky muttered.

"I don't care if that was one-hundred percent swear-on-the-Bible truth. It still wouldn't be your fault. And Thomas still wouldn't blame you.''

"I…but it's because of me…''

"Baloney. It's not your doing. It's Maureen's. You didn't ask her to—?"

"No! Of course not."

"Then see—how could it be your fault? Just because—"

"Missy!" Gandy's shout came from the front of the house.

"You might think that, but Thomas—"

"Missy! Somebody sayin' they gotta talk to you." Gandy had come around the corner of the house, and called to them across the garden.

"Who is it?"

"Don't know 'em. Mighty impatient fella. And he parked where any fool could see he's blocking the ranch truck from getting out if need be."

"Probably the man I called about the used car. Tell him I'll be right there."

A frown pursed Gandy's mouth into a dot inside the whiskers, but he headed back. "Not tellin' that one anythin'. Tellin' anybody, it'll be Thomas."

She didn't want Thomas involved. The chance to tell him that she was going ahead with her car search hadn't presented itself—and she hadn't sought it out. But more important than intercepting Thomas right now was making this point to Becky.

"Listen to me. Your brother does not hold you accountable for his having to work so hard to keep this ranch in one piece. You've got to believe that. But even more important than believing me, you've got to talk to him about it."

"I can't!"

Judi took her shoulders and gave them a little shake. "You have to. You—"

The car horn sounded again. Long and annoying.

"After I get rid of this guy—whose car I will not buy even if it's a brand-new Lexus for three figures!—we're going to work out how and when." She backed away from

Becky, keeping eye contact as long as possible to drive home her point. "But for now I'm just saying tell Thomas. You have to tell him. I'll be right back."

At the corner of the house, she turned and sprinted. First she would blister this bozo's ears, then get back to Becky before she'd reconstructed her walls. She would make the girl get this straight with Thomas. If she could do that, then maybe she wouldn't feel guilty about staying here under false pretenses. Maybe she and Thomas—

The thought died in the time it took for her brain to register the scene before her eyes.

Sterling Carroll stood beside an obviously rented Cadillac parked so it partially blocked both the ranch truck and the barn door. He had his arm in the open driver's window preparing for another assault on the horn. When he saw her, he crossed both arms across his chest, looking supremely irritated.

But what turned the scene into a complete nightmare was Thomas striding in from the direction of the pasture, closing fast.

She hurried toward Sterling, hoping against hope to steer him away before it was too late.

"My God, Judi, what are you doing in a place like this?" he said in a voice that carried even more in the clear Wyoming air than it used to in crowded Chicago restaurants. "Look at you—you look like you belong on *Dukes of Hazard*. I could hardly believe it when that idiot P.I.—after all these weeks of demanding to be paid while he reported failure after failure—finally said he'd tracked you down to some two-bit ranch in Wyoming, for God's sake."

"Sterling, what are you doing here? No, I don't care—just go away."

"You wouldn't believe the place I had to fly into. And the rental cars— My God, you'd think they'd never heard of a BMW, much less a Land Rover."

From the corner of her eye she saw Thomas hesitate. If he left this to her, she still might…

Sterling stepped forward, as if to put a hand on her arm. She avoided the touch. Thomas picked up his pace again and moved between them. Calm, silent and threatening.

"Who the hell are you?" Sterling's demand sounded querulous.

"I'm the owner of some two-bit ranch. Who the hell are you?"

"I'm Sterling Carroll, Judi's fiancé."

Chapter Nine

"Fiancé."

Thomas's emotionless repetition of the word, along with the way he drew back from her without even moving, brought her out of her trance.

"Not anymore. I left him at the altar—no, I didn't even make it to the altar. I was halfway down the aisle before I turned around and…"

She saw where that led too late. Saw it in the tensing of his jaw and the chilling of his eyes.

"What? You turned and ran? You ran away? Looking for something different?"

Sterling tried to step between them. "Judi, that's what I'm here to talk to you about. Let's get out of here and—"

"It's not like you think, Thomas. It's not like Maureen."

"No?"

"I want to talk to you in private. Judi—"

"Thomas—"

"Sounds like you've got talking to do with your fiancé."

"I told you, he's not—"

"I don't know who this guy is, but he's right. We can talk this out, Judi. There's no reason we can't. The engagement was never called off—"

She turned to Sterling. "I ran out on our wedding, if that doesn't break an engagement, I don't know what does."

It was a mistake, because the instant she addressed Sterling, Thomas pulled back—translating the growing distance she saw in his eyes into physical space.

"Thomas—"

"I've got no standing in this." He turned and strode toward the barn.

Sterling grabbed her arm. "Let him go—he's nothing to us. This is between you and me. Believe me, we can put this back together."

Judi didn't follow Thomas, but her reasons had nothing to do with Sterling's words or his hold, and everything to do with the chill in Thomas's eyes and voice.

"I understand, baby. You got scared. Cold feet—that can happen to anybody. And running off and finding this guy—it doesn't matter. I can get past that. I forgive you. There, it's all forgotten."

Her heart felt like every foot of space between her and Thomas was a ton of weight pressing down on it. But her mind was finally starting to work.

"I don't need to be forgiven, and I don't want it forgotten. I made my decision—my final decision—when I left that church, Sterling."

"Now, Judi, think about what I can give you." He'd slipped from magnanimous to desperate. "What we have together is special. You don't want to throw that away."

Sterling had paid someone to track her down, had come here himself, was practically begging her to still marry him. It wasn't out of love. She knew that now. Because she'd seen the glimmer of the real thing in Thomas's eyes. In comparison the extravagant compliments, lavish dates and elaborate promises she'd received from Sterling revealed itself as so much rubbish.

Sterling's reason for being here had to be something that benefited him. The scheme Geoff's ersatz girlfriend had alluded to was the best bet.

"Think of everything you'd lose," he said. "I'll transfer assets to your name on the very day we marry. Lots of assets. You'd be rich in your own right. As soon as you become Mrs. Sterling Carroll."

"I don't want your assets. I don't want to be rich."

He showed no sign of hearing her. "I don't have to go back to Illinois until Sunday. That's plenty of time to go to Vegas, get married, have a few days. I'll get the presidential suite. Then I'll fly to Chicago on—"

"Sterling, listen carefully. I am not going to marry you. Not in Vegas. Not in Lake Forest."

"Judi—"

She backed away from his hand and shook her head. "Nowhere. Ever. Not going to happen."

"If this has to do with some roll in the hay with this cowboy—" His lips stretched tight over his teeth. "Hey, I'm no prude. If I'd known you wanted action, I could have supplied that— I thought you'd go for that wait-for-the-wedding crap."

"That's just it, Sterling. I was perfectly happy not having any *action* with you. That should have told us both something."

"You—" He reeled off terms that would have made the ladies of Larraine Carroll's bridge club faint.

Judi refused to be goaded into losing her temper—and the upper hand. "Since that's what you think, you're well rid of me, Sterling. You go your way and I'll go mine and we can both hope that never the twain shall meet."

"Not so fast. You've got something that belongs to me."

"You're right. But we can take care of that."

She walked over to the wreck of the junker she'd driven here. Wondering if Thomas was watching from the barn, she flipped open the door that protected the gas cap, pulled away packing tape, and unwound a heavy-duty plastic freezer bag she'd formed into a lumpy coil to wrap around the cap.

When she opened it, the contents fell to the bottom, mixing driver's license with credit cards, ID, family snapshots, prepaid calling card. She fished around until she found the hefty engagement ring Sterling had bestowed upon her.

"Here you go, Sterling." She put the ring in his hand. "May you wear it in good health."

Her humor did not go over big with her former fiancé. He shoved the ring in his pants pocket then stuck his now-empty palm under her nose.

"Hand over the rest of it. I want all of it. Everything I gave you. Everything!"

"There's nothing else—"

He snatched the bag, yanking it free when she reflexively tightened her hold.

What was he looking for? The earrings he gave her? Or the narrow gold chains for her throat? They were nice but nowhere near as expensive as the ring, and it wasn't like they were family heirlooms. The only other item of any value he'd given her was that detested charm bracelet she'd given to Becky.

Sterling shoved his hand in the bag, stirring the contents like a mixer gone wild. Swearing, he dumped everything onto the hard-packed ground, then dropped to his knees and shoved her few belongings around.

Still swearing, he got up, not bothering to dust off his Armani slacks.

"You think you're going to hide it from me?"

"I've given you the ring. Anything else you gave me was a gift, and there's no reason I should give it back."

She was pretty sure Miss Manners, Emily Post and Ann Landers would agree with her on this one—not that it mattered. The earrings and chains were in the house and the bracelet was in Becky's possession. With the way Sterling was acting she didn't want him anywhere near the house, Gran or the teenager.

Sterling stepped toward her, drawing his arm back as if to slap her. Judi saw the motion, but disbelief threatened to paralyze her. She had to move. Had to—

Sterling abruptly spun away from her, his expression of mingled fury and astonishment almost comical.

Thomas had grabbed his arm—his would-be slapping arm—to pull him around, then landed a blow to Sterling's jaw that continued the rotation, and sent her former fiancé sprawling in the dirt, facedown.

"Oh, my God. If you hadn't… Is he all right?"

Without bending, Thomas looked him over. "He's breathing."

That was about all Sterling deserved at this point. She gave a nod and stepped around her one-time fiancé.

"Thomas, this isn't what you think."

"Yeah? What do I think?"

"You've got your suspicious mind going a hundred miles a minute and it's all adding up to me being guilty of every sin in the book."

"Like lying? Did you ever lose your memory?"

"No. I heard something and I needed a place to hide out for a while—"

He stiffened, his face taut with anger. But he nodded as if everything was clear now. "Someplace to escape to and get away from a mess you'd made in real life. And we looked like likely patsies."

"It wasn't like that. I was just following roads, and I saw the roofs and I was hungry, so I turned in and there you were, on Dickens. And then Becky was saying I must be Helga and have amnesia, and you needed somebody to care for Gran and the house. I thought I could—"

"Lie to us, and run away again when it suited you."

How often she'd thought that the atmosphere changed when the two of them came together, creating thunder and lightning. Now the storm had turned into a tornado. Dark and menacing and unpredictable.

"I was going to tell you as soon as... I didn't want to drag you into it. If it's what she said it was—well, sort of said—"

"You can't even remember which lie to tell." He picked her driver's license and a credit card out of the dirt. "Judith Marie Monroe of Lake Forest, Illinois. I'd like to say it's a pleasure to meet you, but that would be a lie. I'll give you this much—you're just engaged, not married. You must have gotten a real laugh out of my little story the other night."

The winds of the funnel cloud whirled tighter and faster.

"I wanted to tell—"

"You better quit while you're behind." He extended the cards to her. "Besides, your fiancé's stirring."

She glanced around at Sterling, who groaned, but didn't move.

"You can stay out of sight until your fiancé—"

"He's not my—"

"—leaves. Then you can borrow a truck to get out of here, and go back to Lake Forest. On one condition—don't you be the one to bring the truck back, because I don't want you around here ever again."

"Thomas, you knew I didn't have amnesia. You knew I was somebody other than Helga. I know you did—*you* know you did. There were a hundred times I tripped up, and you caught every one of them. And it wasn't that hard, because I'm a lousy liar. I always have been."

"You lied just fine. You said you'd never hurt my family."

She sucked in a breath at the pain of that, but she didn't give up. "I deserve that. But I'll come back when I can explain, Thomas. And if you would trust me a little longer—''

''I'd like to oblige a lady,'' he said in a cutting voice. ''Even one who thinks she's played me for a fool. But I can't trust you a little longer, because I've never trusted you at all.''

Thomas had his doubts that a bucket of water over the head could rouse a man from unconsciousness. But pouring it over Sterling Carroll's head gave him a small measure of satisfaction.

It might have been a larger measure of satisfaction if it had been over Hel—no, Judi's head.

But the sooner he got rid of the frustrated groom, the sooner the bride could come out of hiding in the bunkhouse, pack up and get the hell off the Diamond V.

Swearing and spluttering against the mud in his mouth, Sterling Carroll scrambled ungracefully to his feet. He sure didn't look as pretty as when he'd arrived.

''You!''

''Yup. Owner of this two-bit ranch, remember?''

''Where is she? You can't hide her from me. She has something that belongs to me.''

''You won't find whatever it is you're after here, because she's gone. While you were sleeping in the dirt, she left with everything she came with.''

''She's gone?''

''Yeah. And you have five minutes to be gone, too.''

''Where'd she go? How long ago? You have to know where she was headed. I'll make it worth your while. Fifty bucks.''

''Four minutes.''

''Two hundred bucks. At least which direction.''

''Three minutes.''

''That bitch has the bracelet and I got to have it. It's gold. A charm bracelet—you know things hanging off it, like a…a…'' He swore. ''The only one I care about is the

heart. A gold heart hanging off that damned bracelet I gave
Judi.''

''Then you better go after her. One minute.''

''Listen—''

''Forty seconds.''

Muttering about the charm bracelet and a key, the man
wasted no more time in leaving. Scuff marks in the dirt
and the trail of dust pluming behind the rental car were
all that proved this hadn't been a dream.

But it was true all right.

What had been a dream was the rest of it. Letting her
fool him into thinking she was something she'd never
been—the woman for him.

Becky rushed into the kitchen. ''I can't find Thomas
anywhere.''

Judi's eyes welled again, so she had to stop writing the
note of instructions, updates, warnings and schedules for
the people of the Diamond V.

She'd hoped—a desperate hope she'd known even as
she nurtured it—that he might give her a chance to explain
before she left.

From the bunkhouse, she'd heard Sterling's car peel out.
By the time she'd reached the barn, there'd been no sign
of Thomas. While Becky had searched for her brother,
Judi had packed. The bags she'd arrived with were now
in the truck Gandy had filled up at Thomas's orders before
he rode off on Dickens. Thomas, no doubt, would have
liked it if she'd cleared out without leaving any evidence
that she'd ever been here. Defiantly, she'd left the silk robe
on Becky's bed with a note, and she'd left a lacy bra on
the inside handle of the bathroom she'd shared with
Thomas. She'd packed the jeans—as if memories of the
Diamond V weren't going to go with her no matter what.

''He doesn't want to be found.'' A tear fell on the paper

under her hand. She blinked hard to hold the rest back. "I wanted to say…goodbye."

"He'll come around." But Gran didn't sound certain. "He's hardheaded, but he's not an unfair man."

"If you just stayed…Thomas would have to—I mean, you made me see he might be a pain, but when he really cares about somebody… If you just stayed, he'd have to—"

"I can't." Even if she hadn't worried that Sterling might come back and somehow bring his trouble down on the people here, she couldn't have stayed. Not with the way Thomas felt about her.

She finished the note, not signing it, because what would she sign? *Helga* was a lie, and *Judi* was a stranger to them.

"I can't explain it all now. But if that man comes back, you tell him the truth—that I never told you who I am, and now I've left and you don't know where I went. Be angry at me, don't defend me to him. Don't let him think you're on my side. Understand? Becky?"

The girl nodded, then burst out. "Oh, God, I think it's my fault! I told Yvonne about you not being Helga, and we were trying to figure out what you could be running from. And she told Mary Beth. And Mary Beth heard this guy asking around at the motel over by the Interstate, and she thinks she let something slip. And—"

"It's okay—"

"—she told Yvonne and she told me, and if that's how—"

"Becky, it doesn't matter. I'm not angry. I would have gone back in a few days anyway." Although she'd hoped that would be temporary. "I just don't want my mess to cause problems for you all—"

"Don't you worry about us. We'll take care of that skunk if he comes back. As for Thomas—"

"No, no, don't say anything to Thomas. He has reason to be angry at me. To…" She couldn't bring herself to say *hate me.* "He needs you both. He doesn't say it, but he does need you. Please, don't let him down. Please. And I'll write when this is all over and explain it. I promise."

"You do what you need to do. We trust you to do right."

She bent to hug Gran, her throat clogged with thanks and tears. Then she opened her arms and Becky came into them, the girl's hold fierce around her. She stroked the blond hair and reluctantly backed away.

"Take good care of Gran. Be good to yourselves. And—" she looked from one now loved face to the other "—take good care of Thomas."

She turned and pushed out the door, barely able to see.

And there were Gandy, Keith and Steve lined up by the truck. Their hats came off in unison, as compelling as a twenty-one gun salute.

"I…I don't know what to say."

"We just wanted to tell you thanks for all you done," Gandy said gruffly.

Steve murmured thanks. Keith added, "You made the Diamond V a better place."

Gandy held the truck door for her. "God's speed, Missy."

The old-fashioned farewell nearly undid her. She fumbled blindly through fastening her seat belt, fighting back the tears.

She stopped where the drive met the back road, where she'd first caught a glimpse of a lone ranger and took a chunk out of a tree. She looked back once.

Thomas was nowhere to be seen.

She made the turn, and drove away from the Diamond V ranch, and all that it held.

The truck was easy to spot as it came along the back road. From Dickens's back atop the ridge, he watched it make the turn onto the highway. She was off Vance land now, heading back to a life of presidential suites and pampered hands, of jet-setting and huge diamond rings.

But she ran away from the kind of life that man offered.

He shook his head at himself. Her fiancé had said it, she'd gotten cold feet. Ended up on a ranch for some little fling. She would have gone back to her real life soon enough.

It was like those executives who loved leaving their cushy offices to spend a couple weeks "vacation" at the hard labor of surviving in a wilderness. But ask them if they wanted to stay in the wilderness with a packet of matches and a pocketknife for the rest of their lives, and they'd laugh their heads off.

As for his feelings… He would kill them soon enough. Because he'd be damned if he'd turn into his father, mooning after some woman who'd played him for a fool. Searching for her all over the country.

Lake Forest, Illinois. Hell, he didn't even know where that was.

Except that it was out of his life. For good.

He turned Dickens and gave him the signal to go.

He'd returned long after all the lights were out in the house.

He'd fallen into bed, hoping the hours in the saddle would let him sleep. Instead, he'd watched the first creep of dawn the same way he'd watched the stars—from under a forearm across his forehead.

In the bathroom, he'd splashed cold water on his face. Reaching for a towel, he'd spotted her bra dangling from the doorknob.

A scrap of airy white lace hanging there so innocently.

The taste and scent and feel of the flesh meant to fill that scrap of material exploded into his memory, practically doubling him over with its force.

He never knew how he got out of there. On automatic pilot, he saddled Klute and rode out. He was still on automatic pilot when hunger drove him back to the house in early afternoon.

He'd wolfed down chicken and a couple pieces of bread before he heard Gran coming down the hall on her crutches. Becky was right behind her. He kept eating over the sink, not turning even when Gran spoke.

"You got what you wanted, Thomas. She's gone. So there was no reason for you to stay away all night."

"Didn't. Got in late, left early. I got behind and have to make it up."

"You're going to keep on getting behind with her gone. Did you see the note she left? Did you see all the things she does for all of us? Not a woman in a million could take to running this place the way she did. Are you going to pretend you don't care that she's gone?"

"I care— I'm glad."

"Thomas. If she hadn't made us promise to be kind to you, I'd tell you what I really think of your behavior. I'd tell you—"

"*My* behavior? You know she's been lying to us? Used us every step of the way. She only stayed here because it was an escape from something she was running from. You know she's no more Helga Helgerson than I am."

The quantity and quality of the silence behind him finally penetrated. He spun around. One look at them and all he could think was *Damn! Damn, damn and damn.*

"You knew. Both of you. You *knew.*"

Neither of them denied it.

"When? From the start? All that hogwash about amnesia? That was just playing me? How did she rope you into it? How'd she get you to—''

''Judi didn't get us to do anything,'' Becky said. ''She didn't tell us, we…uh, figured it out.''

''Great. You figured it out. And you never thought to mention to me, 'Hey, Thomas, by the way, we no longer believe the woman living under our roof, cooking our meals and taking care of our grandmother is who she said she was. And we have no idea who in the hell she is or what she wants or why she's lying'? But you managed to tell each other, didn't you? Anybody else? Steve? Or—''

''Of course not!'' Becky said hotly. But there was something about the way she said it…

''Did you mention it to… No.'' He shook his head. ''Tell me you didn't talk to her about this. You didn't tell me, but you talked to *her!*''

''Not for a long time. Not until—'' Becky compressed her lips into a thin line.

''Until what?'' he demanded of his grandmother.

''Until,'' she answered as calmly as she might have told him the time, ''the real Helga Helgerson showed up ready to start work.''

''*What?!*''

''Don't shout, Thomas.''

''This is damned well worth shouting about. You knew she was a fake! You had the proof of it, and you didn't tell me? You knew she'd gotten rid of the real Helga—''

''She didn't do that. We did.''

He dropped back against the counter, pressing his fingers against his throbbing forehead. ''Why in the hell did you do that?''

''Because we wanted Hel—our Helga—Judi to stay.'' Becky made it sound like an explanation a two-year-old should understand.

He thought his head might explode. ''When?''

"Last Thursday—a week ago yesterday."

The day they'd ridden out to Six-Mile Creek. The day they'd made love for the first time. If they'd told him then, he would never have made love to her. Would that have made the past day any easier? Or harder?

"The other Helga—"

He interrupted Becky. "The *real* Helga."

"—showed up and said she was ready to work."

"A month late." Gran harrumphed. "I'd nearly healed by the time she got herself here. Said she'd been delayed at another job and the agency never got in touch with her about not coming here."

"Why would...? Oh, God, you called the agency."

Gran said, "As a matter of fact, the agency called us. To explain the delay. Fat lot of good that would've done if we hadn't had Hel—Judi. We—you—would have been out of luck if we'd relied on the agency. We told them to forget it and we told Helga Helgerson we didn't need her when she showed up, because we had Judi. We would have told you if we'd thought you'd be reasonable about it."

"Reasonable? *Reasonable!* I'm not the one who's been lying all along. It was damned reasonable to tell her to get out after all the lies—"

"*You* told her to get out?" Becky demanded. "She said she had to leave because of some trouble involving that snake she was engaged to. She didn't say you *made* her. How could you? You're horrible, awful—"

"Right! I'm the monster. I'm the one who lied. I'm the one who made up stories. I'm the one who brought some ass—"

"You're the one who's shouting," Gran said.

He clamped his lips shut. The snap should have been audible halfway across the country. At least as far as Illinois.

"I can't believe you—"

"You, too, Becky. Be quiet. That's better. I'm sure Judi is very sorry that she hurt you, Thomas. That's the last thing she wanted to do. But she had reasons. And now she's gone off alone to deal with those reasons. And you're standing there shouting at each other. That doesn't strike me as a good solution at all. In fact, it's a waste of time. Thomas, what you need to do—"

He dropped his arms against his sides. "You're right. It's a waste of time. All of it. It was from the start, and it sure as hell is now. She's gone. That's the end of it. That's the way it should be. What I need to do is get back to work and try to hold onto this ranch."

Chapter Ten

Dickens let the spotted calf get past him and back into the herd a third time.

"Damn it."

Dickens's ears flickered around.

Thomas concentrated on keeping his commands soft and reasonable as he brought Dickens to the section of fence farthest from the herd. He dismounted, tied up the horse, then walked a dozen yards along the fence, hands on hips, head down.

Becky nearly rode him down before reining in Xena and jumping off the horse.

"I want to talk to you—"

"This isn't the time, Becky."

"You told her to get out—"

"Damn right I did."

"Because she was on my side. Because she understood me, and—"

"This has nothing to do with you, Becky."

"Right. Just like Maureen selling off a quarter of the ranch has nothing to do with me. Just like your having to practically work yourself to death has nothing to do with me. Just—"

"Did she tell you Maureen's selling? What else did she tell you? Helga—Judi—whatever the hell—"

"No! I told her."

"*You* told— How did you—?"

"You think I'm stupid? You think I don't know what my mother's been up to? You think I don't know that if it weren't for me she wouldn't have an excuse to be selling? You think I don't know that if I could just get through to her—"

He took his sister by the shoulders and made her look at him. Things were falling into place so fast and so hard he could feel them reverberating.

"Are you thinking it's your fault? No way—"

"She's my mother."

"So? Are you blaming yourself for what she's doing? Are you thinking *I'm* blaming you? Is that what's been going on?"

Her face gave the answer. Good God, how could he have missed this? Why the hell hadn't he suspected this before? The flare-ups over his work, the sullenness and the talk about leaving the ranch. Not because she hated the ranch, not because she wanted to leave home. But because she'd feared she might lose her home through the actions of her mother.

And how much worse could it have gotten if it hadn't come out now?

She dropped her head, her shoulders still stiff under his hands. "If it weren't for me…"

"You're nuts, Rebecca Jane Vance. If it weren't for you, and all the work you've done this past year, we'd have no shot in hell of buying back Maureen's share. That's what you're responsible for—the work you've done. You're not responsible for your mother. You're not

Maureen. Just like I'm not Dad. This is *their* doing. Not ours. We just got left cleaning up the mess. Is this why you've been working so hard, because you thought I blamed—''

''No! I want to keep the Diamond V together as much as you do.'' She looked up at him. ''But she said the money was to send me to college.''

He started to fob her off by excusing her mother. But maybe it was time for a different approach. *You need to be treating her more like an adult, so she'll become one.*

''I don't think you're ever going to see any of that money. Do you? Besides, we don't need money to send you to college. That money's been set aside.''

Becky gave a kind of shudder, and he thought he felt a weight coming off the shoulders he still held.

''That's what Judi said. She said you didn't blame me and I had to tell you.''

So he had *her* to thank for finally getting this out in the open between him and Becky. It figured. It was just like something she'd do. Not just pushing them to talk, and pushing him to treat Becky like an adult, but putting him in her debt again.

''She made me promise to tell you right before... Oh, Thomas, you can't really let her go like this.''

That has nothing to do with you. It's none of your business. It's complicated. All true. And all answers that could start him down the same path with Becky as the one they'd just left.

''Right now what I have to do is take care of Dickens. Anything else...'' He shrugged.

''But Thomas—''

''I'll think about it. All right?''

Becky's expression said she wanted to argue. But she didn't. She really was growing up—why did that make him both sad and proud?

He watched her ride out the gate, then headed toward Dickens.

"Fifty-seven days worth of work!" Gandy shouted as he rode past.

As he talked quietly to Dickens, Thomas didn't need an explanation for the phrase. The fifty-seven days of work he'd put in on Dickens would be down the drain if he let loose now. He could forget the training fee, much less the bonus, because he'd be turning over a horse who'd had his confidence chewed to shreds by an idiot rider—him.

He swung up into the saddle.

He had ridden Dickens hard yesterday. He never should have started working him on cutting today. But he couldn't let the horse quit now, not with his last effort such a failure. He had to give Dickens a success, so when they called it quits, that's what was left in the horse's mind.

He patted the proud neck and murmured, "C'mon, devil horse. Put her out of your mind. Just for these few minutes. We can do this. You and me. She might've tied us in knots, but we haven't lost every last one of our brains. Let's give you a finish you can remember in peace."

Focusing all his will on the horse beneath him, he positioned Dickens in front of the same spotted calf. The horse shifted as if to step away. Thomas applied gentle pressure to keep him in place, then a nudge to move him forward.

Dickens made the moves to cut the calf out of the herd, but without the crispness of three days ago. As they tacked across the pen toward the chute, pushing the calf erratically in front of them, Thomas kept the angles wider than in their previous session, leaving the calf more latitude, but also making it harder for him to skirt around and rejoin the herd. Moving the calf was tedious, but with each pass Dickens's movements seemed to regain a sliver of certainty.

At last the calf stepped into the chute. Gandy leaned over to close the gate after him. "Well, that's more like it. You might make it after all with that renegade."

But Thomas barely heard.

Pushing down his anger to maneuver Dickens had opened a gate inside him, and now echoes of words and sights and thoughts hammered in his head.

He owed her. ...She said she had to leave because of some trouble involving that snake she was engaged to... She had reasons. And now she's gone off alone to deal with those reasons... That asshole getting ready to hit her.

He started giving orders as he dismounted.

"Give me Maddox and you baby Dickens in. Give him a couple days rest, then have Keith work him easy on cutting."

Gandy immediately swung out of the saddle, but as Thomas adjusted the stirrups on Maddox for his longer legs, he asked, "Where will you be the next couple days that I'm going to have Keith working Dickens?"

"Where do you think?"

"Three days left to turning Dickens over to Upton for that bonus. You'll miss the deadline and you won't have the money for Maureen." But he was grinning.

"We'll deal with that when it happens."

"Yeah, we will. You find that girl and bring her home."

He didn't tell Gandy that he intended to do the first half come hell or high water, but the second half was not going to happen.

He had the practicalities worked out in his head by the time he rode in. He took the stairs to his room two at a time, not caring about the racket. He heard Becky and Gran call out from Gran's room, but didn't answer. He grabbed a duffle and had clean underwear, a pair of jeans and two shirts in it before another thought hit him.

"Becky! Rebecca Jane!"

"What?" She must have been on her way upstairs to have arrived at the open doorway that fast.

"Get me that bracelet Judi gave you."

"Why?"

"Because it's part of whatever mess she's in. It's what that jerk kept yapping about."

His sister stared at him another twenty seconds. "You're going after her. You're going to help her. You're gong to—"

"I'm going to make sure this mess she's in gets wrapped up and make sure she doesn't get hurt. I don't want her on my conscience and I don't want you and Gran hounding me."

"But—"

"Get the damned bracelet so I can get out of here, Becky."

She hesitated another half minute, then turned and pounded down the stairs.

Downstairs, he found Gran leaning on her crutches at the counter, packing sandwiches. He stood still until she turned toward him, so she would see this wasn't any romantic chase across the country. He was going so he could live with himself. Not in some wild hope of living with Judi.

Gran studied him then sighed. "Well, at least you'll have some food. The sandwiches are turkey." She shoved the bag toward him. "Don't try to drive all that way without sleep."

"I won't."

"I found it!" Becky came around the corner at full tilt. "Here—"

"Thanks." He opened the wad of tissue paper and held up the bracelet. Yup, a gold heart about two inches long hanging from a chain with other gold trinkets. He closed the paper and put the lumpy package in his duffle.

"How do you think that's going to help Judi?"

"I don't know. I just know it's what that ass was bellowing about. If she gives it to him, maybe she'll be free of him." He swung the duffle over one shoulder and grabbed the bag of food. "Take care and I'll be back in a few days."

"A few days, but—" Becky bit her lower lip.

It didn't need to be spoken. The time for turning over

Dickens would have passed before he could drive to Illinois and back.

"I'll take care of everything when I get back."

"We'll be fine." Gran's certainty spread well beyond the days he would be away. She was saying that whatever happened with the money, with failing to preserve the ranch, maybe even with losing the ranch entirely, the three of them—the family—would be okay. "You be careful. And give Judi our love."

He pushed out the door, hoping he'd hidden a wince at her final words.

"Thomas!" Gran called.

He turned at the bottom of the steps.

"How are you going to find her?"

For the first time in more than a day, his mouth lifted in something resembling a smile. He'd memorized an address in Lake Forest, Illinois, but he had another idea to try first. "I'm going to look for a Hot Dog Inn—since that's one thing she admitted remembering from the start."

The knock on the door of Room 4 brought Judi out of the bathroom where she'd been hanging washed-out underwear. She stood in the middle of the room, maybe the person would go away. Maybe they hadn't seen the Do Not Disturb sign on the handle. Maybe—

A second knock. This one louder and less patient.

"Who is it?"

"Open the damned door."

Joy came first, then surprise. They were both still at high tide when she pulled the door open.

He stood there, holding the strap of a duffle bag over one shoulder, two days worth of beard, and probably the only man to look right wearing a cowboy hat within a hundred-mile radius of Chicago. She couldn't think of a single thing to say to him.

"So, your name's not Helga."

"No."

"That's one relief."

"I'm sure there are a lot of fine, upstanding women named Helga."

"I'm sure there are. It just never fit you."

Because she wasn't a fine, upstanding woman. She swung the door closed, almost to where it would click shut. Almost didn't cut it with Thomas. He pushed it open and brushed past her into the room, would have brushed against her if she hadn't stepped back.

"Tell me what this is about."

"Thomas—"

"You owe me that much." He let that settle, then added, "And I owe you—Becky and I talked. About the ranch, about Maureen, about the past year."

A proud man calling in one debt, and determined to pay off another. That's why he'd come. To pay off a debt so he'd have no qualms later about cutting her out of his life. She probably should have told him tough luck, live with the guilt. She couldn't. If peace of mind was all he would let her give him, she couldn't deny him that.

Sitting on the edge of the bed while he sat in the only chair, she told him. From running into Sterling that day on the street through the courtship to the moments at the back of the church. Her confusion. Her father's question. Her sprint out of the church. The journey that had taken her to the Diamond V.

By the end, Thomas's frown had become a scowl. He'd interrupted only once—with a muttered curse when she repeated what the undercover woman had said.

"How'd he find you? You didn't—?"

"No! I left that one message on my own answering machine for my family, and that was it. Apparently Sterling hired a private investigator, and…" She shrugged. "I guess there was some talk in town about the stranger at the Diamond V."

"As far as anyone in town knew, we had a health aide

named Helga. How would anyone…? Becky. Becky and her friends…''

''But Becky knew me as Helga, too, so—''

''Give it up. I know about the real Helga coming—and going. Besides, you really aren't much of a liar now that I'm looking for it.''

His tone wasn't as harsh as the words—if she hadn't known better she'd have thought there was even a tinge of amusement in it. But she did know better.

He shifted then spoke again. ''So you figure this woman you overheard at the church was an undercover agent of some kind.''

''Yes.''

''How're you planning on getting in touch with her?''

''I called my answering machine from the road and retrieved my messages. There was one from my mother.''

Actually, there'd been two-dozen messages from her parents with nearly as many from the rest of her family. But only this one particular message had to do with the situation Thomas's stiff-necked pride demanded he help her get through so he could forget her with a clear conscience.

''Mom said she'd received a call for me from the Church Lady, and to call a certain phone number. I knew Mom wasn't talking about the *Saturday Night Live* character, so it had to be a way to contact the undercover woman. I called and asked for the Church Lady. She's supposed to call me back. Sterling wouldn't have tracked me down if he didn't need something from me. He talked about putting assets in my name, so maybe he needs a signature or something. From what I overheard, Sterling's supposed to have this shipment arrive the day after tomorrow—''

The day after tomorrow. July 15. The deadline for returning Dickens to his owner to collect that crucial fee and bonus.

"Oh, God! Thomas, you can't stay. You have to get back and get Dickens to Upton. If you leave right now—"

"I wouldn't make it. Forget it."

"Forget it? How can I forget it? If you're not there on the fifteenth to turn him over, you won't get the bonus, and without the bonus… Oh, Thomas, you can't! Not because of me."

"You're not going up against that asshole alone."

"Maybe I won't see him at all. But if I do, the undercover woman…I'm sure I won't be alone."

"I'm sure you won't either."

He took off his hat and flicked his wrist, spinning the hat past her and onto the bed in a blatant declaration that he wasn't going anywhere anytime soon. She watched it land near the pillows, fighting a bone-deep longing that it was Thomas, instead of his hat, settling in on the bed.

She shook her head. Focus on what you can do something about.

"Thomas, there's no need for you to—"

"There's need. There's one thing Gran was right about—" Judi wondered what Gran had said that he *didn't* think she was right about. "We would have been hard-pressed getting by these past weeks without you. I owe you."

"You don't owe me, Thomas. I wrecked the car to avoid hitting you and Dickens, but you saved me when that creek bank…" She couldn't finish it—behind that memory too many others rushed in, each beautiful and painful. "Even without the early bonus, if you get back to turn Dickens over before Maureen's money is due… You can do it, Thomas. You can. I'll give you everything I have left from the salary you paid me, and—"

"I won't take money from you. It's time we got back to relying on ourselves, not looking to outsiders."

Outsiders. The pain of the word drove her to her feet. She walked blindly to stare at a painting of dachshund puppies above the television. He saw her as an outsider who threatened the Diamond V, and him. Someone who'd intruded on their lives, then streaked off leaving devastation behind, just like—

She spun around, moving so fast that he jerked his head up.

"You think you're ahead of schedule. You think I'm your dose of middle-aged crazy, like your Dad got about Maureen. You think I'm like her. But what if I'm your mom, Thomas."

"Pardon?"

She shook her head in frustration. "It's so clear in my head, and I'm saying it all wrong. I mean what if I'm in your life what your mom was in your dad's? I make you laugh. I help with the ranch. We think the same things are important. Those are all the things you said about your mom and dad."

"I'm not here to talk about my mom and dad, or any of the other things I might have said to Helga." He paused, letting that sink in like a dagger. "I'm here to make sure you get through this mess. Is that undercover person calling you back here?"

His eyes were as cold and hard as his face. He wasn't letting her in. Could she blame him?

Would he ever realize his father had not been a fool in love with a selfish woman, but an honorable man trying to live up to his obligation. The original lone ranger.

"No. I called from a pay phone, and left the number for another pay phone."

"Good." It was the first word he'd said without that edge to it. "What time?"

She glanced at her watch then reached for the keys. "I better go to make sure I'm there in time." Maybe alone she could think of another way to get through to him—or come to terms with the idea that she never would. "I didn't want anyone to know where I'm— Wait a minute! How did you find me?" She'd been so lost in emotions that had slipped right by her.

His mouth twitched and one corner lifted for an instant before he quelled it. "Are you kidding? You think I was going to forget the Hot Dog Inn? When I tracked one down off I-90 on the way into Chicago, I knew I'd find you here." He took the keys from her. "But we'll take the truck I drove in. It's in better shape and it doesn't have the ranch name on it."

"That's not neces—"

"I'm coming."

"You're just being stubborn."

He held the room door open. "Someone once said stubborn was what I do best."

"So, you put your IDs and valuables around the gas cap that night I saw you sneaking around your car."

"I wasn't sneaking. But, yes, I put them there that night."

"Why?"

"Because you didn't trust me."

"You bet I didn't trust you—you were lying."

"Yes, I was." She shifted to face his profile. "About my name, and not remembering who I was. You thought that all along. And I figured eventually you'd look through my belongings trying to get the answers that would satisfy you."

"I should have. Don't know how many times I told myself…"

Her heart sped up. He should have—which mean he hadn't. And the rest of his words meant he couldn't make himself do it. *Oh, Thomas… The honorable, brave lone ranger.*

Even with the door open, the old-fashioned phone booth was a snug fit. Too snug. He could smell her and feel her. But she'd suggested he stay in the truck, and there was no way he was going to leave her exposed in this glass box while he lolled around in the truck.

The phone rang. She jumped then drew in a deep breath that brushed her back against his arm. Her hand shook as she picked up the receiver.

She gave one-word answers at first, then a phrase he recognized from her account of what she'd overheard at the church—apparently the undercover woman was making sure she was really talking to Judi Monroe.

Judi looked over her shoulder toward him and said, "No, I'm not. A…a friend's here… I suggested that… No, I don't think he will." Another glance toward him that didn't quite reach his eyes. "Yes, I do."

The conversation seemed to shift, with uh-huhs from Judi indicating she'd followed what the other woman said. Then her expression changed, dismay spreading across her features. God, how had he ever fallen for her ridiculous lies—the woman's face showed everything.

"No, I don't have it. I left it in Wyoming. I never thought—"

He pulled the bracelet out of his pocket and reached over her. It clanked onto the metal shelf. "This?"

Judi's eyes widened. "Wait! Yes, I do have it. My friend brought it.… Yes.… Okay."

She picked up the bracelet, examining and dismissing trinkets until she came to the biggest one—the heart. Holding the receiver with her shoulder, she pried at it.

He reached over her again and took the bracelet, leaning farther into the phone booth, so they were closer than they'd been since— No. He couldn't afford those memories. He set the heart charm on the shelf, searched for the seam he'd found before and used the handle of his pocket knife to crash down on it.

"We're trying… Wait…"

Two blows and a sliver of space appeared. He flipped open the knife and used the tip to pry the sides apart. In a hollow inside rested a safe-deposit box key.

"Oh my God." Judi looked up and smiled at him.

He had to back out of that phone booth. Now.

He dragged in air that smelled like earth and grass and hot asphalt, picking up enough from Judi's side of the conversation to know the key was to a box that held the funds Carroll needed to pay for a smuggled delivery arriving the next night. Carroll had given her the key in the charm bracelet and had planned to transfer the box registration to her—a precaution in case something went wrong to make it look like Judi had been involved in the smuggling, not him.

In order for the authorities to charge him, he had to make the payment. In order for him to make the payment, Judi had to get him the key.

"She can't tell me details until after they arrest him. I'm to call Sterling and tell him I'll meet him tomorrow," Judi said after finishing the call with the undercover woman.

"We'll meet him tomorrow," he corrected.

She stopped feeding the coins they'd picked up ahead of time. "What? No. You're not coming with me. There's no—"

"I'm coming."

She stared at him another second, huffed out a breath, then kept feeding coins.

"Sterling? It's Judi. I… Don't—…Sterling, if you go on like this, I'm going to keep it all. A pawn shop might not give me much for the earrings and chains, and that charm bracelet's as ugly as sin, but… All right then. I don't want anything of yours, especially the way you've acted…. As soon as possible…. No, not today. Tomorrow. I'll meet you in Evanston—the parking lot at Northwestern's Ryan Field at one o'clock. East side parking lot…. Yes, you can get to it off Central Avenue." Thomas almost grinned at her irritation. Apparently Sterling required easy driving for his handoffs. "Because I've got errands to run and that's convenient." She glanced toward Thomas

as she listened, then turned her back. "Not exactly...
No—it's none of your business. I'll see you tomorrow at
two. Goodbye, Sterling."

She hung up, took a deep breath, then fed more coins
in.

The undercover woman must have answered on the first
ring.

"All set.... Yes, I know where that is.... Okay, nine
o'clock."

This time when she hung up, she sagged. He scooped
up the bracelet, key and remaining coins in one hand and
wrapped the other around her arm to guide her to the truck.

"I'm all right."

"I know you are. To make sure you stay all right, we're
going to get some food."

"That sounds good."

"And I'm going with you tomorrow."

"There's no reason for you to come."

Thomas rolled his eyes as he held the motel room door
open when they returned after burgers. "Are you going to
spend all night arguing?"

"Not if you agree there's no need for you to come with
me."

He grunted and turned his back, surveying the room.
"I'll sleep on the floor."

Did he know the tiniest sliver of a question slid into
that statement? No, or he'd have squashed it.

"You don't have to."

He looked at her. Over his shoulder first, then turning
all the way to face her.

"If I sleep in the bed, if *we* sleep in the bed..."

They would make love. But it wouldn't make a difference in the end. She understood he was telling her that up
front. Telling her that he still would see her as an outsider.
He still wouldn't trust her.

But she knew it was not only because she'd lied to him

about having amnesia and being Helga. Not only because she'd had a fiancé she'd run away from. Not only because she was a stranger who'd shown up unexpectedly and who had never experienced ranch life before. It was because he didn't trust that she could be anything else.

Because he wasn't willing to take the risk to find out.

"I know."

Never breaking eye contact, he closed the space between them, then stopped. Giving her a chance to back away. *Oh, Thomas.*

He slid one hand into her hair, his palm caressing her cheek. Without their bodies touching, his lips brushed hers. He lifted his head, looking into her eyes again. Then he kissed her for real. She opened her mouth to him, and closed the space between them, drawing him into her with her arms around his neck.

Maybe knowing there would be nothing beyond this time should have made her run. Should have made her protect herself by pulling back. She couldn't—no, she didn't want to. She wanted to give him everything, and take everything. To leave him with this, when he wouldn't let her give him anything else.

His shirt came off, her blouse and bra were opened. But they didn't slow to complete such niceties.

Together they peeled away her jeans and panties. Together, they discarded his jeans and briefs. Together they fit protection on him. Together they found the fast, desperate rhythm. Together they exploded.

He pulled out of her, but not away. She felt his weight on her like a blessing, and the deep, fast pulse of his breathing like her own heartbeat. They kept her from being alone now that they were no longer together.

Then he moved. Rolling off the bed in a fluid motion, and disappearing into the bathroom.

She should cover up. Pretend she was sleeping. Get dressed. Walk out.

She hadn't moved a muscle when he returned. He pulled

more packets from his duffle, dropped them on the night-stand and came back to the bed.

It had to be her imagination, but it seemed he found precisely the position he'd left, sprawled mostly over her. He pushed her blouse from her shoulder and kissed the skin over the bone.

"Guess we were in kind of a hurry." He pushed the blouse more, and she shifted to help him ease it off.

She gave a chuckle. "When haven't we been?"

She thought she felt a faint tremor in his touch as he slid the other sleeve off. She rolled on her side so she faced him.

"Hey, I've shown a lot of restraint."

He was pretending the indignation. Using it to ease the moment. If that's what he wanted, needed, she wouldn't deny him.

"Right. Lots of restraint."

He pulled her bra free and dropped it over the side of the bed, then he slid his fingertip across the tip of her breast. A pulse of renewed heat and need clutched her.

"If I'd known a knot and a few buttons were all that held that long skirt with the slit and that top on you, I would've had you out of them a hell of a lot faster."

"Oh, I think we did just fine that night in the truck."

"I don't mean that night." He slid his hand down her side over her hip, then around to the top of the backs of her thighs. "I mean weeks before that. And that skirt, the one with the blue flowers…that about drove me nuts."

She leaned back enough to see his face more clearly. "It did?"

"Oh, yeah. I kept wondering if you were wearing any-thing under it, and kept hoping you weren't."

"Nothing under that skirt? That would be—"

"Sure would be."

And he showed her just how it would be. Slow and drawn out, until she wanted to scream…until she had to scream, and he swallowed it into himself and held it, just as she held him inside.

He couldn't stop his hands from moving over her, stroking her arms and back. She stirred, murmuring his name. He touched his lips to her forehead. "Go back to sleep, Judi."

Judi…

Funny how it had taken him no time to get used to calling her that. *Helga* had never felt right.

Right. None of it should have felt right. It was built on lies, and his making a fool of himself.

You think I'm your dose of middle-aged crazy, like your Dad got about Maureen.

When that slick ass had said he was her fiancé, and she hadn't denied it, he couldn't say his first reaction had been seeing the similarities to Maureen—that came later. First, had been a gut-deep pain that the other man—any other man—had a claim on her. Too deep a pain to listen when she'd tried to tell him the situation was something more than a spat between bride and groom.

For that failure he deserved this period in purgatory—being with her while knowing every minute together brought them closer to being apart for good.

He would see her through this, make sure she didn't get caught in Carroll's underhanded dealings, wipe out the bitter taste from the day she'd left the Diamond V.

A finish he could remember in peace. That's all he could ask for.

Chapter Eleven

The next morning they met up with Katherine—the undercover woman finally had a name—in another motel room twenty minutes from the rendezvous with Sterling.

"We'll have people stationed around. Here's the east parking lot." Katherine pointed to a diagram propped against the headboard. At the desk, a man soldered the heart charm closed with the key inside. "We'll have people here, using the archways under the stadium for cover. And in this equipment building—it looks like a garage— and here on the street to the south. But stay on your toes, Judi."

"I'm going with her."

"Thomas, you heard Katherine—people will be all over—"

"Not close enough to stop you from getting hit."

"Sterling won't hit—"

"Right."

"I know he would have slapped me if you hadn't stopped him, but—"

"Not slap. Slug. He had his hand in a fist."

"Oh. But…" Her eyes widened then slitted in anger. "You're right. He's more of a jerk than I thought. He was going to punch me!"

He almost smiled at her indignation. Almost.

"But even so, he won't hit me this time, because he thinks he's getting his way. He'll be all charm and smiles."

The way he must have been when he'd courted her. Probably bought her expensive jewelry instead of jeans four sizes too big. Fed her fancy meals instead of making her cook. Took her to nightclubs with loud music and neon lights instead of a starlit field with the sounds—and smells—of cattle.

"Charm and smiles," she repeated. She grimaced, and something eased in him.

"Maybe so, but I'm going to be there anyhow."

Judi turned to Katherine as if to say, *You're the professional, you do something.*

"You'll need a cover story."

Judi huffed in exasperation, turning her back on both of them.

"I figure we'll tell him we're getting married—Judi and me." She spun around and stared at him, but he kept his eyes aimed at Katherine. His peripheral vision wasn't as easy to command. "I'm the jealous type, and don't want her to have anything of her former fiancé's. I'm there to make sure she gives all the presents back, and there're no ties left between them."

"He should buy that—especially since you've already decked him once."

They'd started this meeting with an account of Carroll's visit to the Diamond V, and Katherine had admitted she'd longed a few times to deck Sterling—and Geoff.

"He hasn't told anyone about this snafu with the key,"

she said. "If the big guys have figured out he's a screwup they'll protect their investment by making damned sure he can get the money out of the safe deposit box. You don't want to mess with those guys. So if somebody else is with him, get the hell out of there."

Sterling's car was already there, and he was the only person visible.

"Wait until he gets out."

Judi understood the unspoken message. As long as Sterling stayed in his car they couldn't know if he was armed or if he might try to use the car as a weapon. After a few seconds, though, Sterling climbed out and started forward.

Thomas circled behind the truck and opened her door. "Let him come most of the way."

Sterling had stopped midway between their vehicles. Thomas halted her progress a couple yards beyond the truck. After a momentary standoff, Sterling grumbled a foul oath and started toward them again.

Ignoring her, he demanded of Thomas, "So she got you to lie for her and say she was gone, to send me on a wild-goose chase. But what the hell are you doing here? Are you really that desperate to get laid?"

"I'm here making sure you don't try to treat Judi the way no real man treats a woman."

He'd put a touch of emphasis on *try* and *real* in case Sterling missed the point.

"Yeah?" Sterling brought out his best sneer. "Looks like you're thinking it's not just *a* woman but *your* woman. I suppose that explains how she got you to lie. Caught you by the short hairs. Feeding you all that crap about not screwing without marriage and how you're so important to her."

Judi opened her mouth to point out those had been *his* lines, but the pressure of Thomas's left hand on her back advised silence. Just as well. If she'd gotten wound up, she might have said too much. And it wouldn't do Sterling's mood any good.

"I'm here to make sure you get all your trinkets back and to make sure you know there's no reason for either of us to ever see your face again."

"Fine by me."

But when Sterling turned to her, Judi knew that wasn't entirely true. He might have wooed her and planned to wed her to use her name as an insurance policy against any legal fallout from his smuggling, but his pride had been stung by her flight from the church.

Suddenly, all the precautions seemed wise and necessary.

Her hand trembled as she handed over a pair of earrings, two thin gold necklaces and the bracelet. She'd bundled them together so it wouldn't look as if she gave the bracelet any special significance. "I'm sorry, Sterling."

"I bet you are. You know, cowboy, at the rate she's going, first with me and then with you, she'll fall in bed with the next guy in another fifteen minutes. Better enjoy your fifteen minutes, cowboy."

Without taking a step, Thomas shifted his weight forward. Sterling backed up a step.

"You got your things. Turn around and leave, Carroll."

For six painful beats of her heart, Judi thought Thomas had pushed Sterling too hard.

Then his fine-cut lips spread in a smirk, and his posture relaxed.

"You're right. I got what counts. And it's sure not some Lake Forest bitch. Have a great time down on the farm, Judi." And then he laughed.

As soon as he turned away, Thomas's hand at her back held her still.

"Don't turn your back on him."

Sterling had pulled out before they returned to the truck.

She directed Thomas to Green Bay Road, then they drove in silence to the rendezvous. In an underground garage, Katherine got out of a sedan. Behind that was another, larger car with dark-tinted windows.

"All set?" Katherine asked, looking closely at Judi.

"All set."

She nodded, then looked to Thomas. "We'll put your truck somewhere where nobody will see it. You'll get it back when we've got Carroll and the others secured. In the meantime, you'll be staying at the Monroes like I promised. I filled your family in this morning and they're waiting for you. And you'll stay there until I come and tell you otherwise—inside. Understood?"

"Is that necessary? If Thomas and I were really a couple, it would be natural for us to be at my parents'. Sterling would expect it."

"Maybe. But we're not going to take any risks with Carroll getting a case of the jealous ex-fiancé and messing this operation up now."

The car with the tinted-glass windows swept past the impressive front lawn, bypassed the circular part of the drive that would have deposited them at the massive front door and pulled all the way to the back of the Monroe's driveway, where the house, landscaping and distance hid it from view of any passersby on the street. Also "just in case," Katherine unobtrusively hustled Judi into the back door, with Thomas right behind them.

Once inside, no one could get much beyond the entryway, because the kitchen was clogged with greeters.

Judi's mother folded her into a hug before she was all the way into the room. She returned the embrace full measure, saying, "I'm okay, Mom. I'm okay."

Nancy Monroe loosened her hold enough to look over her daughter, checking the accuracy of her statement, Judi knew.

That allowed Judi to see her father reach out a hand to Thomas.

"You must be Thomas Vance. I'm Judi's father. Katherine here has told us a little of what's happened and where Judi's been. Her mother and I—all of us—thank you for taking such good care of our girl.''

Thomas met the handshake, but said, ''She took care of us. That's the way it really was.''

He looked toward her, and their eyes met. In that instant it was like she'd heard happened to someone drowning. This was not entire lives passing before their eyes, but the past six weeks, from that first instant of meeting Thomas's eyes before she wrecked the car to now.

Each moment with Thomas flashed between them, because they both knew it was over now. He'd paid his debt. He would go back to the ranch, where she no longer had a place because he didn't believe enough in her to see past the lie she'd told to the truth beneath it.

The surge of introductions and greetings and talk broke the connection.

Tears welled in Judi's eyes. Everyone watching her would take them as tears of relief and joy at being home.

Katherine extricated herself, ducking thanks aimed at her and promising that she would deliver the all-clear as soon as possible.

Thomas looked up at the portrait of the distinguished gentleman who seemed to be staring at him, then around the dining room.

There'd been no shortage of food. Mrs. Monroe had served a beef roast, baked potatoes, salad, fresh rolls and peas, with apple pie for dessert. While the adults ate in the formal dining room, the kids had the same menu in the breakfast room, with college-aged April Gareaux volunteering to look after the Dickinsons' twin toddlers. ''There're just too many of us to fit around one table,'' Mrs. Monroe had said with regret.

''That's okay, Aunt Nancy,'' Tris Donlin Dickinson had said, ''the kids love being out from under our thumbs.''

There'd also been no shortage of conversation as everyone around the table contributed, though Judi, sitting across from him, had talked in fits and starts at best. The only time she'd become animated was when she talked about Gran, Becky and the Diamond V.

From the others, he'd learned that the Diamond V had not been Judi's first exposure to Wyoming—she'd spent a summer waitressing at Yellowstone Park. "And all she could talk about was how much she loved Wyoming," her mother said. "And hated waitressing," her brother Paul added, drawing laughter all around.

He'd learned she had a degree from Northwestern University, had quit a good job at a medical supply company before she was supposed to get married, and had an apartment in Chicago. Her family obviously adored her. She spent a lot of time with them, including her nieces and nephews, biological or otherwise.

She had a full life here in Illinois. A happy life, now that Carroll was out of it.

She'd had good reason for showing up at the Diamond V, even for lying. But understanding that didn't change the fact that she didn't belong at the Diamond V.

A woman raised in a house like this—twice as big as his barn, sitting on the shores of Lake Michigan, and with most of what was in it either new and valuable, or old and even more valuable—wasn't equipped for life on a ranch, not permanently. In every material way, she was better off here.

The best thing the Diamond V could offer her had nothing to do with the material, because it was the warmth and laughter and caring of the people. But she had warmth and laughter and caring here, too. Along with everything else.

His eyes returned to the portrait. The distinguished gentleman's stare had turned to disapproval. Probably never expected a small-time rancher to slip his boots under this table.

"His name is Walter Mulholland," Bette Monroe said quietly from beside him. She tipped her head toward the portrait. "He's Nancy Monroe's father, Paul and Judi's grandfather. Not the jolly type from everything I've heard. He built this house."

"It's a hell of a house." The setting alone, with the big lawn in front, and the even bigger lawn in back leading to Lake Michigan, was a jaw-dropper. Then add in the house with God-knew how many rooms.

"Yes, it is. But it wasn't until Mom and Dad Monroe moved in that it became a home. Just remember to look at the people, not the house. And don't fall for Walter's bull."

"What?"

But Bette had already turned to Michael Dickinson on her other side.

In another minute, everyone was rising to clear their dishes, and clean up in the kitchen. Everyone helped, he noticed. Even in such a large kitchen, the crowd would have been overwhelming if everyone hadn't known the routine. But they moved with the ease of people who knew each other well, who belonged together.

For once in his life, Thomas wished he smoked.

It would have been a good excuse to get out of the house, now that it was dark. But he didn't smoke. So he simply stepped out the French doors between the kitchen and the breakfast room without telling anybody.

He crossed dew-covered grass toward the lake, spotting a wooden deck jutting out over the water. In the distance to his right, light spread up into the sky and out across the water—must be from Chicago. Straight ahead, the dark lake met the dark sky in an invisible horizon.

He heard the gentle lapping against the deck's piers, as inexorable as sunrise and sunset.

Voices came to him, then shut off. He saw by the lights from inside the house that two men had come out the French doors from what he guessed was a den, followed after a moment by a third, who caught up with the first two before they reached him.

"Nice night, isn't it?" Michael said while he and Paul and Grady were still several strides away. He was the one Judi had said was so nice to her. Also the one she'd said let her flirt with him. Thomas was holding off judgment.

"Yeah. Nice night."

"We haven't heard much about this ranch of yours, why don't you tell us about it," Paul said.

Some invitation, Thomas thought. Like the judges at the Salem Witch Trials saying, "Tell us about your last chat with Satan."

"We run a cow-calf operation, along with raising horses for ranch work. I train horses on the side. Mostly working cow ponies, a few rodeo horses."

"I know folks with a place in Wyoming," Grady said. "The Herbertsons."

"Right. A place in Wyoming, another couple in Montana, and Colorado. I don't exactly move in the same circles." Thomas turned to Michael. "What about you? What do you want to know?"

He raised his hands in mock surrender. "Hey, I'm the voice of reason here. Tris sent me after these two to even up the odds a little."

"You saying you're on my side?"

"I wouldn't go that far. I'm on Judi's side. She seems to think you're on her side, and I'm giving you the benefit of the doubt based on that—unless I see evidence to tell me otherwise."

"Fair enough." He tipped his head to the other two men, their frowns apparent even in the dim moonlight. "And these two?"

Michael chuckled dryly. "I'd say doubt, and no benefit. You'll have to forgive them. They've both known Judi since she was born. She might be frozen in pigtails and braces in my mind, but that's a giant step up from diapers."

"Are you done, Michael?" Paul didn't sound amused,

but neither did he sound angry. He sounded like a man determined to check out a threat to his family.

Thomas could understand that. He turned to Judi's brother and said evenly, "Why don't you say what you've got to say?"

"Okay, I will. Judi says you treated her right and helped her, but she isn't always the most practical judge of—"

"Don't sell her short." Thomas damped down his anger, keeping his voice cool. "Nobody should question that she's got a good head on her shoulders."

"Stalemate," Michael said. "I think you should try a different move, Paul."

Judi's brother scowled at his long-time friend, but took his advice. "Our parents seem to have accepted that you saved Judi."

"She was doing fine on her own."

"Nice block, Thomas," Michael murmured.

"I meant—"

"I know what you meant," Thomas interrupted Paul. "You're not prepared to treat me like her savior. Hell, you're not even prepared to trust that I did right by her in any way, shape or form. The thing is, there's no way for you to know that. Because even if you knew everything that happened between Judi and me—and I wouldn't tell you because it's between her and me—it wouldn't matter. Because it's like Michael said—it's how Judi sees it that matters."

"So you're saying—"

"I'm saying," he looked at each of them, "that it's none of your damned business unless Judi chooses to make it your business."

He had more to say, but he didn't rush it. If they wanted to take issue with what he'd said so far, he wouldn't stop them.

"That's what Leslie and Bette said," Grady admitted, a sheepish grin tugging at his mouth.

Thomas addressed his next words to Paul, who hadn't backed down an inch.

"I'll tell you this, Judi thinks you three and her father are the best men she's ever known. And she thinks you're the finest brother that ever walked this earth."

"She said that?"

Thomas grinned. "No. Are you kidding?"

For the first time Paul relaxed a little. The other two men laughed.

Thomas continued, "I've got a little sister, too. Fifteen. I'm her guardian."

"Fifteen," Grady repeated, with what sounded like sympathy.

"Yeah, and every time I turned around, Judi was telling me how I was doing things wrong with her. And how I could do them right—if I'd be more like her brother Paul. How I could end up being friends with her when she's all done growing up, if I play my cards right—the way you played yours."

The only sound was someone clearing his throat—he thought it was Grady.

"And the last thing I'll tell you is if somebody arrived at the Diamond V ranch with Becky after a situation like this—and I wouldn't care if she was twenty-nine years old and independent—I'd feel the way you do, and want to boot the guy out on his butt."

In the silence, tension still emanated from Paul. Thomas kept his hands unfisted but his weight on the balls of his feet.

Then Grady laughed.

Even before Paul turned away, Thomas knew the first phase had passed.

"What are you laughing at?" Paul demanded of his friend.

"You. You know how your mom always said when we were kids and she'd get exasperated with us that she hoped someday we'd have kids just like ourselves, who would drive us nuts? Well, it sounds like Judi brought home a guy just like Big Brother—and now it's driving you nuts.''

When Michael joined the laughter, Paul turned back to Thomas.

"You shoot pool?''

"Yeah.''

"Let's leave these two hyenas and shoot a few.''

"Sure.'' Thomas didn't fool himself that the examination was over, but it had de-escalated.

It wasn't until an hour later—an hour of being observed very closely—that Paul returned to the earlier topic.

"You know when I asked if Judi had said that about me being the finest brother around?''

"Yeah?''

"If you'd said yes I would have said either you were a damn liar, or aliens had captured my sister and I would've turned the pod person who'd taken her place over to the CIA.''

"If you think of anything you need—''

"Nancy, you've told the boy that twice. Let him sleep.'' James Monroe stood beside his wife on the stairs, urging her step by step toward the second floor.

"I'll be fine, thank you, Mrs. Monroe.''

Thomas stood next to the bottom of the back stairs. Behind him, the couch in the den had been made up for him. Even the large Monroe house was stretched by the number of guests tonight.

She would have her old room to herself. Paul and Bette had Paul's old room. Leslie and Grady were in one of the guest rooms. April Gareaux and Sandy Roberts had another guest room. Anne Elizabeth and Cassie Monroe were in the third one. Their middle brother Nick, Jake Roberts and Brian Dickinson were bunked down dormitory style in the basement rec room. Tris and Michael were in the room over the garage with the twins.

They had all gone to their separate quarters, although whispering could be heard from the basement.

"Do call me Nancy or Mrs. M, like the other boys do."

From the bottom of the steps, Judi watched her father put his arm around her mother's waist. "Say good-night to the young people, Nancy."

"Night, Mom. Night, Dad."

Their quiet good-nights floated back as they disappeared around the corner at the top of the stairs.

She went up two steps, needing that advantage before she stopped and said, "Guess I'll say good-night, too."

He looked up at her, then placed his hand over hers where it rested on the wide wooden banister.

"You didn't have to work so hard." He took her hand from the banister, turning it over between his two.

"I wanted to earn my keep."

He slid his hand under her palm, stepped in close and brought her hand to his lips.

Looking down on his thick hair she felt the warmth and tenderness of his mouth as it brushed and caressed her skin. And in feeling the touches now she relived the other touches—of his mouth, of his hands, of his body.

She glanced toward the top of the stairs. No one was in sight. Just her and Thomas, no surveillance, no watchdogs, no family, no friends. For the first time since nine o'clock this morning they were alone.

She backed down a step. The longing that flooded through her was deeper and wider than the blade of desire.

"I could—"

He shook his head. "Not here. Not now."

He reached up and laid his palm against her cheek. The gesture made her want to weep.

"Get some sleep." He didn't need to say she hadn't gotten much rest the night before. The memory of it was there in his eyes, and in her blood. "I'll see you in the morning."

"You'll be here?"

Oh, God, why had she asked that? She wasn't going to ask him for a commitment. She wasn't going to ask him to do what he could not—or would not. And yet she'd said words edging toward it.

"I'll be here in the morning."

She heard the qualifier like a booming warning bell reverberating through her bones. But she wouldn't—she wouldn't cry, or beg, or bargain.

"Good night, then."

"Good night, Judi."

She made it to the top of the stairs before her eyes filled. She made it to her bedroom before any spilled. But in the sanctuary of her room, she cried tears she would cry nowhere else. And she admitted truths she would admit nowhere else.

She loved Thomas Vance. And soon he would leave her.

Thomas wove his fingers together and put them behind his head.

Thomas, you knew I didn't have amnesia. You knew I was somebody other than Helga. I know you did—you know you did. There were a hundred times I tripped up, and you caught every one of them.

She was right. At some level he had known. And he'd gone along with it, because it let him keep her around. He'd even trusted her despite it.

If he hadn't trusted her, he wouldn't have left her to care for Gran.

If he hadn't trusted her, he would have searched her room.

If he hadn't trusted her, he wouldn't have fallen for her.

He couldn't lie to himself about that. And he couldn't put all the blame for the lies and secrets on her. That day at Six-Mile Creek, before they'd made love, he'd known he could get the truth. Ask one more question, just one, and she would have told him. He'd bargained away the truth to be with her.

God, all these years he'd thought his father was so damned weak falling for a woman any fool could see didn't belong on the ranch, and here he was just like him—falling for the wrong woman, even bargaining away a piece of himself to have the chance to be with her.

But at least he had the sense to leave Judi where she belonged.

Chapter Twelve

"Sterling Carroll is in custody, along with several of his associates," Katherine Powers told those assembled the next morning in the Monroe kitchen. Her professional demeanor slipped for a second as she gave Judi a slight grin. "Including Geoff. The operation went smoothly, and all the charges should stick."

"And Judi?" Thomas asked. "Will she be dragged into this any more?"

Judi was aware of looks flickering around the room, but didn't focus on them. She was too busy dividing her attention between Thomas and Katherine.

"She shouldn't have to testify, at least not from our end. What the defense does…" She shrugged. "We'll keep you up-to-date."

"So what was the man smuggling?" Leslie asked. "Drugs? Gold? Cuban cigars?"

"T-shirts."

"T-shirts!"

Katherine smiled at the chorus of exclamations. "T-shirts this time. Other times he and his organization have brought in jeans, jogging suits, ties—about any kind of clothing that could have a designer label. His group has the clothes made in sweatshops in South America and Southeast Asia for pennies, puts false labels on them, smuggles them in, feeds them into the retail system through a few crooked distributors and—voilà—huge profits."

Questions came at her from all sides, but she warded them off with a laugh. "Sorry! Even if I could tell you more at this stage, I couldn't take the time. Gotta go now. Judi? Would you mind walking me out?"

Thomas was to the door ahead of them, holding it open. Nearby, the kids were playing on the swingset her parents had installed for their grandchildren.

Katherine gave Thomas a resigned look when he followed them out. "Fine. It's nothing you can't hear anyway." She turned to Judi. "If things play out the way we hope, we won't need your testimony. But if you're going to take any more extended trips, let us know where you'll be."

Judi took the business card the other woman held out, then they shook hands.

"Thank you, Katherine. It's been...uh..."

"If you say a pleasure I won't believe you. Let's settle for *educational*. You two take care. Hey, and feel free to keep the toaster from Geoff and me!"

With that, she disappeared into another tinted-glass car.

Judi turned to go back in, but Thomas stayed where he was. "They brought my truck back at first light. I've got my things in it."

It was here already. "Don't want to burn daylight?"

"Right. Well..."

"Thomas, I have something I want to say." Her rush of words ended abruptly. She dragged in a breath. "I owe you an apology. I did a lot of thinking on the drive back from Wyoming, and I know I gave you grief about thinking money was so important—that wasn't fair.'' She couldn't sustain the intensity of his green gaze without tears starting, so she focused on her hands. ''I think it was Sterling's relationship with money that I was reacting to, but I took it out on you. I'm sorry.''

''No problem.''

But the bigger problem of lies and secrets remained. The problem she couldn't undo. The problem that meant he would return to Wyoming and she would stay here.

She looked down. ''Thank you for seeing this through with me, Thomas. I'm sorry it's cost you so much. The ranch, I mean. I wish you would reconsider...''

But there was a shortage of wishes coming true these days. And that one clearly wasn't going to be fulfilled

''I thank you for what you did for us. Taking care of Gran—''

''Just doing my job. Helga's job, actually.'' She tried to smile. Her lips trembled.

''Looking out for Becky. Helping get me and Becky straight. And what you said about keeping the ranch but maybe losing the people. I'll...'' He hesitated, then said the final word with deliberateness. ''Remember.''

He bent his head and his lips brushed her cheek.

Numbed with loss, she watched him swing into the truck with his usual grace. He'd turned over the engine and twisted to look through the open driver's window to back out before she half ran to the truck.

''Thomas.''

She touched his forearm where it rested across the door. He stilled. She waited until his eyes came to her face. She needed him to know the truth of this.

''I'll never forget you. Never.''

''Where's Thomas?''

''He's gone.''

''He'll be back for breakfast, won't he?'' Her mother

waved a spatula toward a pan where more bacon was cooking.

"No." Every face turned to her at that word. Might as well get it out now. "He won't be back. He's gone home."

Looks ricocheted around the room faster than Judi could have kept up with on her best day. This was not her best day.

"What are you going to do about that?" Bette asked the question that Judi could see mirrored in all their faces.

"He went home. It's where he lives and works. I couldn't very well hog-tie him in the garage. He's going back to his life, where he's happy."

"Yeah, he looked real happy this morning," muttered Michael.

"Maybe time apart is the best thing for you both," her father said. "You've gone through an intense situation, and you need time to put it in perspective."

"Well, I think you should go after him." Tris had addressed Judi, but as she crossed her arms at her waist, she looked around, challenging all comers to disagree.

Leslie nodded. "I agree."

"Hey! She's not running after some guy," Paul objected. "Absolutely not…" The rest was lost among the rising tide of voices.

Leslie hushed everyone else to let Judi be heard.

"I know you're all concerned, and I appreciate that, but this isn't something… I mean, I'm the only one who can decide whether or not to…"

"In other words," said Michael, "we should all butt out."

"We're family," Paul said. "Butting in is what family does."

"What are you going to do, Judi?" asked Bette.

"I don't know. I feel… But I jump into things. Sterling and… What if I'm jumping again?"

Bette studied her face for a long moment. "There are two points about that."

"Uh-huh," Paul said. "A list." While the others chuckled, his wife pretended to scowl.

"First, Sterling. Granted he was trying to rush you off your feet. But you usually don't let yourself be railroaded. Why do you think you did this time?"

One part of Judi wished this conversation could be in private. But what shred of pride she had left was nowhere near as important as the possibility that Bette might help her find answers. Besides, what good was pride with the people who not only knew all your foibles but loved you anyhow?

"Because I wanted what you all have."

"What we have?" Grady sounded perplexed.

"The single among all the couples," Leslie murmured.

Judi glanced at her, thankful she'd said it. "Yes. Finding love, settling down, having kids, homes of your own. Lives."

Bette nodded. "And you very reasonably thought Sterling could help you find all that—you grew up together, your families knew each other, as far as you knew they liked each other—"

"*As far as I knew?*" Judi looked around at her parents. "You don't like them?"

"No," her father said.

"Larraine Carroll cheats at bridge. I refuse to play with the woman anymore." Nancy Monroe's defiant stance melted into concern. "I knew I should have told you."

"And," Bette picked up seamlessly, "Sterling was knocking himself out trying to persuade you that he would be exactly what you thought you wanted."

"But I fell for it! I shouldn't be allowed loose on the streets much less..."

"Falling for someone else," Tris filled in.

"Give yourself credit, Judi," Bette said. "You got out."

"Yeah, after I was hit over the head with it."

Bette was shaking her head. "You had doubts or you

never would have listened. If someone—a stranger—had said to you that Thomas was doing something illegal—no proof, just said it—would you have believed them?''

"No, but he would never—"

"That's the second point. Who Thomas is, and even more important, how you feel about him."

"I love him." The words sounded solemn and grand, yet they floated through her like bright balloons. Then reality popped the brightest balloon. "I love him, but he—"

"Is head over heels for you," declared her mother with a small smile.

"I deceived him, and there are other issues—"

"No issue trumps love, Judi." Her father had his arm around her mother's shoulders and squeezed. She'd never questioned that her parents loved each other but these past few years her father had become more openly affectionate.

"I have two words to say, Judi," Grady announced.

"What?" The word came from a throat tight with love, gratitude and, yes, fear. If she couldn't persuade Thomas to give her another chance, if he didn't see how good they were together... But if she never tried, the result would be the same.

Grady looked from face to face, a smile growing. "Road trip!"

"What?!" Judi's horrified squawk didn't get a single glance of sympathy. "But I'm not... I can't..."

Paul slung his arm around her shoulders. "If you're going to run after this guy, you're not going alone. Gotta make sure he treats my sister right."

"Anybody know if they do any bull-riding on this ranch?" Grady asked.

Leslie patted her husband's arm. "*They* might, dear, but you won't."

Dust clogged the truck's windshield, so it was like looking through gauze. Thomas had run out of wiper fluid somewhere right after his last fill-up. Any other station would have had a supply. But he hadn't wanted to stop for it.

He'd barely stopped for anything but an empty gas tank, necessary food and a few hours of sleep when his body and his compassion for the other souls sharing the highway with him demanded it. He'd wanted as many miles between him and Judi as possible. The theory was it would cut the temptation to turn around and go back.

Theory and truth weren't always the same.

In theory he'd been glad to see the kids out in the yard when he'd left. He'd figured it would keep him from touching her. The truth was he couldn't deny himself that one last contact.

And then the touch of her soft cheek against his lips. The scent of her... He would have been perfectly happy to have those kids disappear.

Another truth was, the farther away he got, the more he wanted to go back. Stopping was one step closer to turning around, so any stop was dangerous.

Besides, he didn't need to see well now. He was on the road that bordered the Diamond V on the east, so he'd only see the stretch Maureen would soon be selling.

Maybe he could take on more horses to train to ease the pinch of the lost land. He sure as hell couldn't afford to add anybody to the payroll, but Keith could help him. Judi would like that.

He would have smiled at that if he hadn't been so tired. Lord, he couldn't remember ever being this tired.

It was loss.

The quarter of the Diamond V, sure. But he was too tired to lie to himself. Judi had been right—big surprise, there—the ranch was important as a way to support and keep together the people he cared about. And now she was no longer in his life.

Just in his head and his heart.

Yeah, he was just like his father. But she was nothing like Maureen.

What if I'm in your life what your mom was in your dad's…

Going slow, he turned into the back road to the main house, taking the corner where Judi had driven her car into a tree rather than hit him and Dickens.

What if Judi was right—again—and he was wrong? If he went back, what would she say? Would she give him a chance…?

He spotted activity around the corral first, without recognizing who was there or what it meant. He turned off the truck engine and let it coast to a stop behind the lineup of unfamiliar vehicles.

What the hell was going on?

The first clench of his gut was that buyers were looking at the acreage. But they couldn't be, not this soon. And why would they be at the corral?

He got out of the truck slow, partly because he was stiff from the long hours, partly to give his exhausted brain more time to figure out what was going on.

A voice came to him—clear and persuasive.

"As you can see, Dickens has perfectly good manners. But it's even more important that the rider knows what he's doing than Dickens does, so I'm glad you've agreed to the horsemanship program, Warren."

Warren? Warren Upton, Dickens's owner was here? Why—?

It didn't matter, because what he'd heard finally sank in—not the words, but the voice.

Judi. No, it couldn't be. It had to be the effects of two days of driving. But his pace picked up.

Looking between people he didn't even bother to identify, he spotted her. Alone in the center of the ring, astride Dickens, with pride and pleasure beaming from her face.

Two days of driving be damned—she was here. Back at the Diamond V. Not like Maureen had always come, looking for what she could get. But looking at what she could give.

"Ah, Thomas!" Upton shouted, spotting him. "C'mon over here."

Judi's head whipped around, and he saw an acre's worth of other emotions cloud her pride and pleasure; so many, and each with so many possible meanings. It was the infinite variety that was Judi, but at this moment, he could have done with a shade more simplicity. Like joy at seeing him. Or love. Either one would give him something to build his life on.

"Thomas!" Upton hollered again.

Judi blinked at the noise, and that loosened their connection enough that he got his feet moving toward the client, though his attention remained with Judi. He passed Grady and Leslie Roberts, and Tris and Michael Dickinson. Paul and Bette Monroe, along with Becky and Keith, were on the far side of Upton. He knew all that—*what the hell were they doing here?*—he just didn't have attention to spare for them.

"I, uh, better get Dickens cooled down, and ready for the trip home." Becky opened the corral gate.

"I'll help you," Keith said.

Thomas started to follow them through the gate, to where Judi had dismounted. But Upton blocked him.

The man had rested his checkbook against the rail and was dashing off his signature. He tore out a check with a flourish, planting his hand and the check on Thomas's chest.

"Here you go—and after watching what you can do with horseflesh, I'll be sending more business your way."

Thomas automatically looked at the check before folding it to put in his pocket while he watched Becky take the reins from Judi, who stood apparently frozen in the center of the corral. Midmotion, Thomas stopped, brought the check to in front of his eyes and opened it.

"There's been a mistake. This includes the bonus."

"No mistake. It's money well spent." Upton tracked his horse's progress, pride of ownership stark in his face.

Only when Becky, Keith and Dickens disappeared into the shadow of the open barn door, did he turn back to Thomas. "Why to see first your hand, then your little sister, then somebody who doesn't ranch horses hardly at all working Dickens, was more than I ever expected."

"But the deadline's past."

"We rescheduled it."

"We?"

"Becky and me. That sister of yours called and asked if having the best-trained horse possible was worth waiting a few extra days." He laughed. "Drives a hard bargain, that one. Then she called last night and said to come on over today."

"But..."

Tris stepped smoothly into his speechlessness. "You know, Warren, now that the business is over, I think it's time we go in the house and get more of that cake Becky made and a cup of coffee."

"You don't have to ask me twice. You've got quite a gal there, Vance. Praised you to the skies."

"Becky?"

He laughed "Two great gals, then. Becky and Judi. But Judi was the one doing the praising. Can't expect that of a sister, now can you? Though they both talked me into this new horsemanship program you're offering."

The Dickinsons and Robertses flanked Upton as they headed to the house.

Paul seemed inclined to say something as he came even with Thomas, but Bette hooked his arm and murmured, "You're not the one he needs to talk to."

That left Thomas on the outside of the corral, and Judi on the inside, appearing as frozen as a Popsicle at the Arctic Circle. Becky or Keith, or both, had left the corral gate open. Closing a gate was drilled into ranch folk from the time they could understand words. He'd swear neither of them had done it before in their lives.

But there was an exception to every rule, and this time

he thought he got the symbolism—the gate was open if he was willing to step through.

His own muscles felt unfamiliar, and as stiff as if they might have a touch of frostbite. Maybe it was the driving. More likely it was what walking through that gate, closing it behind him and walking up to Judi meant. Could mean.

"Judi."

"I didn't ask them all to come." She spoke to his left shoulder. "It wasn't my idea. Actually, I couldn't have stopped them. But I'm glad they've been here. And don't think Gran was neglected while we were out here. Mom and Dad stayed inside with her along with the little kids. Oh, the older kids are out with Gandy in the truck changing irrigation pipe and—"

"Judi." He wanted to laugh—he could have predicted that it would be her mouth that thawed first. Otherwise she was still standing stiff and wide-eyed. He didn't dare laugh. Not yet. If he was wrong... Maybe if he worked up to what he really wanted to know, he'd have a better gauge. "How'd you get here?"

"Grady flew us all in his company's jet. I called before we came—we didn't just show up—and Gran said of course everyone should stay here. We juggled rooms around, with the older kids and Becky in the bunkhouse, and—"

"I don't care about the sleeping arrangements." At least not yet. He hoped he would soon, but there was always the pickup.

"No. Oh, of course, you're wondering about Dickens. Well, that was mostly Becky. Like Warren said, she'd called him and arranged for the deadline to be extended. She was going to wait until you came back, but we didn't know when you'd get here and with Maureen not budging—Becky called her, too, which I think was very grown-up of her. I wish I could say the same for her mother."

He wanted so badly to kiss that indignant face. But she was already going on.

"Becky, Keith and I put our heads together and figured we could show Upton what Dickens could do. Uh, maybe you're wondering about that horsemanship program he mentioned. That was your idea."

"My idea?"

She nodded emphatically. "Remember telling me how it didn't matter how well you trained a horse, if he went back to a rider who didn't know how to handle him the bad habits would be right back? I was telling them about that last night, and how even though we'd get the money, it was sad Dickens was going to someone who didn't know horsemanship. Leslie said that sounded like a business opportunity to her, and Tris—no, maybe it was Mom—anyway, someone said we should draw up a program. And you won't have to be involved much if you don't want to—Becky and Keith can handle most of it. Especially since you'll be hiring more people again after you pay Maureen. Bette and Grady helped us draft a business plan. And then Michael pointed out we had a customer already waiting, so we tried it out on Upton to see if he liked it and..." She had clearly run out of steam, and words. "He did."

"Judi," he said again, liking the saying of it. She flicked a look from his shoulder to his face, and he concentrated on holding it. "You came back."

It was a statement riddled with questions, and he knew she'd heard every one of them.

She swallowed once then straightened her spine, her eyes never leaving his.

"I told you I'd come back the day I left. But you didn't believe me. I don't lie, Thomas—well, except about being Helga and amnesia, but not usually. That was an exception, and you'll figure that out after a while. Because I'm back to stay. Remember what you said about ranching and—"

"You're going to throw my own words up at me again?"

She barely slowed down for the "Yes," then kept on going. "And how you have to be good at everything and not zero in on one specialty? Well, that's me—that's always been me. I've been miserable in my other jobs because they kept trying to make me do just one thing. So I realized ranching's perfect for me. I was so happy here. But I let you leave me in Lake Forest without a fight, and I shouldn't have. So, I'm also here to show you I won't be left so easily. I'll pull my weight and help you around the ranch. Now that you can buy that share from Maureen, you can start thinking about the Diamond V's future, instead of worrying so much. And I'll be here to help you any way I can, to remind you to lighten up, and to prove you can trust me and trust what I feel for you—I'm going to stick around, whether you like it or not. I'm not Maureen and—"

"I know that."

She drew in a sharp breath. "You do?"

He took another step closer to her. "Yeah. I had this idea—had a lot of time to think on the drive back, you know—and maybe you had it wrong all along. Maybe you're not the Maureen in my life. Maybe you're like my mom was for my dad."

"*I* had it wrong! You—"

"Yeah, I'm not blaming you—easy mistake to make, what with you being a stranger and the way you arrived and everything." He stood close enough that she had to tilt her head back to keep eye contact. "But now I see things clearer."

She let out a sort of shuddering breath, and the faintest smile lifted her lips.

He wrapped his arms around her and brought her to him, and she wasn't the least bit like a Popsicle at the Arctic Circle. She was Judi, warm and soft and welcoming. He took her mouth, and knew he'd truly come home.

"Judi…I have one question."

"Just one?" She sounded breathless, and he liked that.

"Seems like you've been interrogating me from the minute I regained consciousness."

"One question to start, anyway. What you said about showing me how you feel about me, how about telling me first?"

She leaned back in his arms, trying to plant her hands on her hips like she was angry, which wasn't the least bit convincing because her lips were pink and swollen from his kiss. Not to mention the look in her eyes.

"You're going to make me say this first, aren't you?"

"Yup."

"Chicken." The teasing scold evaporated from her tone when she continued. "I love you, Thomas."

He kissed her again, making this one hard and fast.

"I love you, Judi. And as for your sticking around whether I like it or not, I like it fine. More than fine." His voice dropped. "I've got another important question for you."

"Yes?" Her eyes held a new sheen.

"Can we name our first daughter Helga?"

"What!" But he'd dropped a kiss on her mouth, so her combined outrage and laughter both fueled and were consumed by the desire that flamed between them.

Only lack of oxygen and a vague memory of being within sight of the house stopped the kiss from becoming more.

He rested his forehead against hers. "Will you meet me down the road tonight, Judi? I'll fix up the truck, and we can watch the stars—"

"Yes. Oh, yes, Thomas."

"And will you marry me? Will you walk all the way down the aisle to me?"

She wound her arms around his neck, sliding her fingers into his hair.

"With you waiting at the end of that aisle? You bet."

Epilogue

Everything was ready. Becky and Bette had gone down the short aisle between folded chairs in the living room ahead of her. Paul and Gandy were beside Thomas, who stood in front of the minister by the fireplace.

In the kitchen the wedding dinner was in the oven— roast turkey, with all the trimmings.

It had been another whirlwind of preparations for a wedding. But this was entirely different. No wedding planner, no Caribbean honeymoon.

Thomas had said he'd be happy to be married in Wyoming or Illinois or anywhere in between…then he'd pointed out that there was no waiting period for getting married at the Diamond V.

That had decided that.

With everyone they cared about here, they were getting married.

Bette's friend and business partner, Darla, had gone to Judi's apartment in Chicago, found the ivory silk sheath dress and shipped it overnight, along with a few other items. The pearls Bette had worn at her wedding. The garter Tris had worn at hers—which Grady had caught, leading to his first dance with Leslie, who'd caught the bouquet. The antique earrings Leslie had worn at her wedding.

This morning another package had arrived—perfect blue puff-ball blossoms from the hydrangea bush that Nancy Monroe had planted in their backyard the summer they'd moved in. Leslie and Tris had bound the stalks together with ribbon and lace to make her bouquet.

"Ready, baby?" James Monroe extended his arm.

Judi smiled at him. "I'm ready."

His eyes glistened with tears as he smiled back. "I believe you are."

"Of course, she is," said her mother from her other side.

Walking between her parents, she turned the corner to the living room and saw only Thomas. She knew the chairs were there because she had helped set them up. She knew the guests were there because most of them hadn't left in the four days since Thomas had returned home. A few others had arrived within the past hour, and from her bedroom, she'd heard them calling out.

But none of that mattered as she walked toward Thomas.

Judi's parents released her, clasping hands and moving aside.

For a moment she and Thomas just looked at each other. Then he extended his hand, and she put hers in it.

"Are you sure?" he asked in a low voice.

"As sure as you are."

He smiled as he drew her the final step to his side. "Then you're about to become a bride."

* * * * *

▼ SILHOUETTE®
SPECIAL EDITION™

AVAILABLE FROM 20TH JUNE 2003

BUT NOT FOR ME Annette Broadrick

Rachel Wood had never confessed her love to her boss, millionaire Brad Phillips. So why, when she was in danger, did he insist on whisking her to safety—as his convenient wife?

TWO LITTLE SECRETS Linda Randall Wisdom

After a fortnight in the arms of gorgeous Zachary Stone, Ginna Walker sensed that he had a secret he wasn't ready to share. She was sure that she could handle it…but she didn't know that he had *two* little secrets…

MONTANA LAWMAN Allison Leigh

Montana

Librarian Molly Brewster had a new identity…and Deputy Sheriff Holt Tanner had a case to solve. Would his search for the truth force her into hiding—or would his love set her free and make her his?

NICK ALL NIGHT Cheryl St. John

Shock became passion when sexy single dad Nick Sinclair mistook former neighbour Ryanne Whitaker for an intruder! Could his kisses persuade her to swap city life for the warm glow of hearth and home…forever?

MILLIONAIRE IN DISGUISE Jean Brashear

Tycoon Dominic Santorini introduced himself to Lexie only as Nikos—but after an unplanned explosion of desire he couldn't help wondering if she was really a corporate spy. Could he trust the truth he felt in her every touch?

THE PREGNANT BRIDE Crystal Green

Kane's Crossing

Brooding tycoon Nick Cassidy married beautiful Meg Thornton when he learned she was carrying his enemy's baby. The perfect plan for revenge soon turned into love—but would Meg discover the truth?

FREE
4 BOOKS
AND A SURPRISE GIFT!

We would like to take this opportunity to thank you for reading this Silhouette® book by offering you the chance to take FOUR more specially selected titles from the Special Edition™ series absolutely FREE! We're also making this offer to introduce you to the benefits of the Reader Service™—

- ★ FREE home delivery
- ★ FREE monthly Newsletter
- ★ FREE gifts and competitions
- ★ Exclusive Reader Service discount
- ★ Books available before they're in the shops

Accepting these FREE books and gift places you under no obligation to buy; you may cancel at any time, even after receiving your free shipment. Simply complete your details below and return the entire page to the address below. **You don't even need a stamp!**

YES! Please send me 4 free Special Edition books and a surprise gift. I understand that unless you hear from me, I will receive 6 superb new titles every month for just £2.90 each, postage and packing free. I am under no obligation to purchase any books and may cancel my subscription at any time. The free books and gift will be mine to keep in any case.

E3ZED

Ms/Mrs/Miss/Mr ....Initials..

BLOCK CAPITALS PLEASE

Surname...

Address...

....

....Postcode ....

Send this whole page to:
UK: FREEPOST CN81, Croydon, CR9 3WZ
EIRE: PO Box 4546, Kilcock, County Kildare (stamp required)